the
Isolation
Door

Anish
Majumdar

First trade paperback and ebook editions: February 2014

Ravana
PRESS

Publisher's Cataloging-In-Publication Data
(Prepared by The Donohue Group, Inc.)

Majumdar, Anish.
The isolation door : a novel / Anish Majumdar. -- 1st trade paperback ed.
276 p. ; cm.

Issued also in Kindle and ePub formats.
ISBN: 978-0-9899081-0-8 (pbk.)

1. Children of mentally ill mothers--Family relationships--Fiction.   2. Students--Fiction. 3. Schizophrenics--Family relationships--Fiction. 4. Social isolation--Fiction.
5. Friendship--Fiction. 6. Domestic fiction. I. Title.

PS3613.A486 I86 2014
813/.6   2013919445

Cover & Interior Design by David A. Gee
Author Photo by Erin Cummings

Manufactured in the United States of America

10 9 8 7 6 5 4 3 2 1

Majumdar, Anish.
The isolation door : a novel /

The Isolation Door

for Erin, with love and amazement

You need not comfort me
by lightening my load
I ask for strength
to carry my burden

-TAGORE

THE FIRST MEMORY I HAVE OF MY MOTHER *is her straddling an open window, pink sari bunched about her waist like a protective cushion, shouting she'd jump. Her arms were out like wings and every few seconds one would dip for effect. Dad stood a few feet away trying to shame her down. Large theatrical gestures, combined with the full beard he wore in those days, gave him the look of a rogue preacher. Our apartment was two stories above ground, giving passersby ample opportunity to take in the proceedings.*

Dad pulled out his wallet. It was a brown, weather-beaten thing, one of the few items he'd brought over from West Bengal.

"Is this what you want?" he asked, holding it out toward her.

"Don't come any closer!" she warned, lifting the leg that tethered her to the bedroom floor. Each toenail was perfectly painted maroon. One of my weekly chores was holding her foot up while she painted. I didn't mind. I was six and enjoyed the sharp smell of the polish.

He tossed the wallet at her feet.

Mom looked at it suspiciously, a frown creasing her oval face. A breeze blew strands of hair across her eyes, hazel that darkened or lightened in accordance with her moods.

"You think I don't know your tricks?" she asked. "Moment I reach down to grab it you'll pull me in."

Dad cursed under his breath, went over to the bed, and sat down. It was secondhand furniture and the springs wailed. Aside from the twenty-two-inch Trinitron in the dining room, our one real luxury, the apartment felt transient, covered by grime that did not disappear no matter how often my mother cleaned it.

"I look like a beggar," she said, face flushed with exertion. When Dad didn't answer she leaned her head out the window and said, "He treats me like a servant! He wooed my parents with big promises and see?"

She would have gone on, but her English was limited and she'd learned quickly that nothing alienated the other wives of the graduate students who lived in our building, black and brown and yellow skin covered by slacks and formless sweaters, quite like a woman who lapsed into her native tongue. Her sole act of rebellion was continuing to wear her saris and jewelry.

Dad noticed me standing in the doorway. The expression on his face didn't change but I felt sick to my stomach.

"Tell Niladri," he said to her, very quietly.

She lowered her foot to the ground. Its intricate webwork of veins bulged as she retrieved the wallet. "Two pairs of shoes. A handbag."

She gave me a wide, false smile as Dad calculated the expense.

"The MasterCard," he said finally. "Two hundred dollars and no extra treats at the grocery Friday."

She wriggled her body indoors and extracted the card from his wallet. Someone outside clapped. The bracelets on my mother's wrists jangled, making a sound like entering a curio shop.

She was cautious approaching the bed, laying the wallet down close to Dad. He grabbed her wrist and yanked her to him. A sigh escaped her lips. Dad raised his right hand, palm out flat. Mom flinched. Their bodies shook with tension.

He let go and she stumbled. Recovering, she fixed her sari and rubbed at where he'd held her. Then she came to usher me out of the room, but I wasn't budging, my mind fixed on what had just happened.

When my mother's foot had lifted off the ground I'd seen—not imagined but actually SEEN—a sentient force yank the rest of her body out the window, leaving behind only a snaking contrail of pink that had disappeared a second later. My toes curled on the floor as I tried to reconcile the specter that stood in front of me with the absence that felt so much more real.

She squatted down so our faces were level. When our eyes met she winked and slipped the credit card into her blouse.

August 21 – December 8

1

I took a makeup pad heavy with granules of brown powder and began spreading it across Mom's face, reducing the appearance of the deep-set lines around her mouth. Her jittery eyes scanned the wall behind me, unable to find a point of focus among the pictures of gurus with red paste daubed over their black-and-white foreheads. On the nightstand lay notebooks filled with the overflow of voices that grew unbearable after dark. Bottles of cheap perfume littered the vanity table next to where she sat, reluctantly allowing me to do what her hands no longer could. Though she reeked of them, the perfumes could not disguise the gangrenous smell coming off her in waves.

What had once been a guest room had been transformed, first gradually and then not, into the place she retreated to when the smell became impossible to hide.

"Not too thick," she said. "I'm not looking grainy on camera."

I worked the blemish scars on her forehead. Down her temples in long strokes to swollen cheeks. She'd lost most of the defining features of her face, and it was only in kneading with the pad that I was able to make out a bit of jaw or cheekbone. She'd always had the look of a girl with mischief on her mind, but the schizophrenia had changed it to something mournful.

I pressed too hard and she jerked her head back. Two fingers went to her forehead. She inspected the residue and held it out accusingly. The fingers trembled.

"Idiot," stressing the last syllable in her crisp Bengali accent. "Do you know what you're doing?"

I started to mutter an apology but there was an obscene quality to her anger. Her back was ramrod straight, belly bulging out against orange sari silk. Her lips were primly pursed. Black whiskers above them like cilia sensed the air for threats.

I held the compact out to her. "Go on, show me how it's done."

She hesitated before taking it. Energy was building inside of her as steadily as thunderclouds. "Little makeup. Directors like me best that way."

She picked up the makeup pad. Her fingernails were chewed down to the quick. She raised it partway to her face before the tremors reasserted themselves. The pad slipped from her grasp. I retrieved it and the compact and continued.

"I can't play ingénues anymore," voice dropping half an octave. "I'm realistic." Traitorous hands kneaded the flesh of her thighs.

When she was a teenager growing up in a well-to-do Calcutta suburb, Mom had been approached to do on-camera work. Extra roles mostly, along with a few walk-ons in forgettable Bollywood weepies which had served to make her classmates jealous and add a little spice to the negotiating table when it came time for her to be married off. Five years ago, when I was eighteen and Mom thirty-six, her illness had gone from being a leech on our family's happiness to an altogether different monster. Mom got arrested for shoplifting and racking up over a thousand dollars in unpaid parking tickets. Friends of my parents stopped attending their *nemontons* because Mom would start shrieking about a perceived slight one of the guests had made twenty-odd years ago. Worst of all was that to her, all of this became somehow acceptable, as extra roles and walk-ons had become genuine Bollywood stardom. Through some form of sorcery my father had robbed her of all that, stolen the life she was meant to lead, and everything else was simply the fallout from his deception.

"But mothers!" she now exclaimed. "I know how to play that. I can do a mother role, no problem."

I placed the compact on the vanity table. "It's just a five-minute interview."

"But that's how it starts," she said, eyes half-closing with pleasure. "My fans, they haven't forgotten."

I picked up a lipstick and she puckered her lips. When I began applying it she said, "You don't understand. What it feels like, to be loved like that."

"It was a long time ago."

"Your father hides the mail they send. Why do you think he never lets me get it?"

"Let you? You haven't left this room in weeks."

The words just slipped out, and my punishment was seeing the momentary doubt cross her face, changing it to that of a girl lost in the dark. Her eyes increased their restless scanning. Her hands kneaded faster, crushing the prim folds of her sari. When her gaze settled on a point beyond my shoulder I knew the voices had regained dominion.

I gave her a tissue to blot.

"You don't understand how it is in India. A few more interviews and the offers will come pouring in. I won't say yes at first, mustn't give in too easily, but the right role..."

A car horn blared outside.

I took the tissue from her. "I'll check," I said, and went over to the window.

An unmarked ambulance stood in the driveway. Dad's car was easing to a stop by the curb. The driver's side door of the ambulance opened and a tall black paramedic got out.

"Is it them?" Mom asked.

"Yes."

She gave me her hands and I pulled her up, her sari making a chafing noise against the chair. Her entire body was shaking but I don't think she was aware of it. The chorus of voices, their conflicting demands and suspicions and insults, was so powerful it left little room for anything else.

Yet she thanked me. And when I muttered acknowledgment her gaze softened, becoming both diffused and generous. Her hand went to the unkempt locks atop my head, found a knot, and pulled gently to loosen it.

"When will you let me cut this?" she asked and it was really her, she'd resurfaced, if only for a moment, and all I had to do was meet her gaze, let her know there was still someone waiting for her, before the next wave dragged her back down and the undertow sheared away another part forever.

But I couldn't do it. "When you get back," I said.

Two doors slammed outside in quick succession.

I retrieved her shawl from the bed. As she busied herself with putting it on I brought out the folded sheet of paper and pen I'd carried around in my pocket all day. "One more thing—you need to sign this."

She pulled the shawl in close about her. Her forehead glistened with sweat.

I pushed aside perfume bottles and jars of skin cream and laid the paper flat on the vanity table. There was a bank logo in the upper left-hand corner in the form of a lion's head. "It releases the tuition money for my school. You sign and Dad signs." I held the pen out to her.

She frowned. "My hands hurt."

"I just need a signature."

"I'll give it to you later."

"Mom—"

"Not now!" she shouted, and started fanning her face to keep it from getting unduly flushed. "I need to concentrate."

She strode over to the door, hesitated, then pulled it open and went out into the hall.

I glanced at what remained of the vanity mirror: scraps of silver peeking out amidst a collage of Mom's old pictures. There were hundreds of them, hastily Scotch-taped over one another until it had blocked the troublesome sight of what she'd become in place of what she'd been. And she had been beautiful. Skin the color of heavily creamed coffee, shrieking as Dad splashed her at the beach. Hair grown long like a gypsy, winking saucily at the camera as her hands cupped a pregnant belly. The photos blended together until you didn't know what you were looking at, only that you'd been thwarted somehow and your fingers itched to tear away the covering to see what festered beneath.

I grabbed the paper and pen and followed her out.

She struggled on the upper steps. Her knees had grown weak,

unable to support the excess weight. She took my arm without it being offered, grunting with exertion.

"I'll tell them what an adventure it's been, raising my boy in the States. But he's grown up now, doesn't listen to me, and I want to work again." A lower stair creaked like a gunshot. On the wall, Tagore prints of a patrician face, a sparrow, observed our progress. "I've missed my fans, my friends, hundreds, thousands of them."

When we reached the ground floor she bent over, taking quick, shallow breaths. Hair fell off her neck, revealing an ugly reddish rash.

Footsteps sounded beyond the front door.

"Now all you have to do," thrusting the paper in front of her face, "is sign at the bottom."

The screen door creaked open. The doorknob jiggled and went still. Low voices like the scratching of mice inside a wall. Precious few moments were left before my father would unlock it for them.

I put the pen in Mom's hand and she let it drop to the floor. She straightened up, carefully pushing her hair back into place. The skin of her face looked like melting wax. She stared at the front door.

"Why are you doing this?" she whispered.

I didn't know what to say. I could only hold the paper out to her.

She went to the foyer, adjusting the bracelets on her wrist. "You'll have to help me down the front steps as well," louder as if fending off warning voices. "I won't have studio men do it. It wouldn't be appropriate."

"When did you make your last movie? Do you even remember?"

She spun around with surprising litheness. "I sign that and you and your father go on living like kings while I rot." She wagged a finger at me. "Out of sight, out of mind upstairs. You think I don't know?"

The doorknob jiggled again. And this time there was the scrape of a key entering the lock, and tumblers falling into place.

"I tried to get you out of that room," I began.

"You didn't want me out," she answered with something like triumph. "Easier to pretend I wasn't here."

The door began to open.

"Now hush," she said, turning toward it, adjusting her shawl with openly shaking hands, "I need to..."

Two paramedics, the black man I'd seen earlier and a partner, stood in sharp relief against the late afternoon light. Thick leather boots and belts, heavy metal flashlights, and low-slung key chains jutted from plain uniforms. We spent several moments taking each other in, perhaps as a courtesy to my mother, who was silent in that particular way that accompanies the worst blows. Then the spell broke and they tramped in, staining the foyer tiles with grime, fanning out to either side of her.

Mom involuntarily took a step back, hands out behind her meeting nothing.

The black paramedic moved like a snake charmer and wore a jocular expression on his face that instantly made me dislike him. His partner lingered by the door, harsh Eastern European planes betraying little. When Mom said, "You're not from the studio," a question that came out as a statement, she directed it at him.

The black paramedic thrust his hands out, pinkish palms crusted with moisturizer. "Easy, miss. We're here to help."

Dad followed in their wake like a whipped dog, thick glasses on crooked. He held a briefcase in front of him like a talisman. "Don't fight, Priya," he said in Bengali.

Mom backed up to the basement stairs and stilled, the animal part within gauging whether she could make it down the stairs before the black paramedic was on her. He was less than six feet away and closing the distance, all split turnip of a nose and wet lips. She turned to me, reappearing again in crisis.

"This has happened before."

I nodded dumbly, wanting to move to her but afraid to.

The black paramedic stopped less than a foot away. The Eastern European man took a step forward. In his hand were cloth restraints.

"She doesn't need those," Dad said.

"Stay back, sir," the black attendant said.

Mom stared at me. A smile as broken as a child's toy in an empty house came over her face.

"How many times?"

The black paramedic grasped her wrists. She resisted, but did not look away from me.

I raised three fingers. Three forced committals over the worst five years of my life. Always more or less the same, wiped clean by Mom's selective memory upon release.

The Eastern European man looped the restraints over her wrists. Her bracelets jangled.

"Wait, please," she said.

"We'll bring your things," Dad said. "Don't worry." They began dragging her toward the front door.

"I won't hide," she begged my father. Her feet slid along the floor. "Raja, I've been hiding, I'll stop…"

Dad swallowed. They passed within inches of one another.

"Niladri," she called out, trying to turn around to see me. And then they were gone.

Dad went to the living room window to watch her get loaded

into the ambulance. He muttered instructions to the paramedics under his breath, be gentle, you don't need to treat her like that. His breath fogged up the glass.

I slipped the paper and pen into my pocket. I went into the kitchen, opened the cupboard beneath the sink, and started taking out the bucket, sprays, and paper towels placed there to clean up messes. My ears were buzzing angrily, warped echoes of the paramedics' and my parents' voices, but what I was doing had been done three times before and did not require thought.

"Brutes," Dad said, washing his hands at the sink. "They should go back to jail where they belong."

I didn't answer. I didn't like the way his voice echoed in the new emptiness.

He shut the sink off abruptly, causing trapped water to shake the pipes. "They didn't have to twist her arms."

I tore some garbage bags off a thick roll and threw them into the bucket.

"Just leave it." He picked up everything and started up the stairs. His suit jacket was wrinkled.

"You're in enough trouble with the hospital," I said, following him to her room.

Dad struggled to get the window open. I sprayed the vanity mirror a few times, relishing how it ate into the photo paper.

"Don't do that," Dad said.

"What?"

He fixed his glasses, looking over the photos like a teller settling accounts. "Those are the only copies."

Dad opened her closet and was greeted by a landslide of jeans and moth-eaten turtlenecks. Mom held onto things like they were about to be confiscated.

He sputtered, then waded deeper inside, pulling out faded floral dresses and undergarments. The smell of mothballs permeated the air.

"How many times have I told her: clean room, clean mind. Does she listen?" He whistled. "Holy macro, what is this?"

He came out brandishing an empty Pringles canister and a Chips Ahoy package. "Skipping dinner because she wants to lose weight. 'I'm exercising while you teach.' Right."

"You're up here every night to give her medicine," I said. "You never saw that?"

He seemed startled. "I can't watch her all the time, Niladri."

He began poking through her drawers.

I flattened the paper out on the vanity table and traced Mom's signature in the air a few inches above the dotted line. By the fourth or sixth time my fingers remembered the absence slips I'd forged in high school, the looping whorl of the P in Priya.

Dad banged a drawer closed. "Where's that bag of hers? You know, the red one?"

I touched pen to paper, making my thumb and index finger go nearly limp.

"What are you doing?" Dad asked, a moment after I'd signed. I presented him with the document.

He looked it over dubiously. Grunted. "Not bad." He laid it on the nightstand. "We have to pack quickly, they're admitting her in less than an hour."

I knelt down beside the bed and peered into the foot of space between the frame and floor. I spotted the familiar looping handles and pulled the bag out. Blew on it to remove some of the collected dust. Opened it to reveal neatly packed clothes and toiletries, untouched since she'd returned home six months ago.

Dad stood over me. "Oh."

"Dad, I need the money. First semester starts tomorrow."

"I'm aware of when it starts."

I got to my feet, holding the red bag. A lawnmower started up in a neighboring yard. "I tried," I said. "I asked her."

"Well?"

I nodded to where the paper lay.

"What world do you live in? I can't go to the Public Trustee with a forged signature."

"They won't know the difference."

He fiddled with a button on his jacket, looking uncomfortable.

"Her signature changes all the time anyway. What does it matter?"

"It matters," sighing like I was a particularly dense student. "You know what dogs they are. They have fifty/fifty control of her finances now. Something like this and they'll push for all of it."

"Fine, so get the money somewhere else."

He laughed, a forced sound. "Where? The overdrawn bank account? Or the retirement fund that went to pay for hospital costs? We're in debt, Niladri."

"But you said yes when I got the acceptance letter. Gave me the form, told me to get her to sign—"

"And you didn't."

"You said—"

"I know what I said." He took the bag out of my hands and zipped it up. The cuffs of his shirt were ringed with dried sweat. "Theater school," he said, shaking his head. "You had years after high school to try classes, work a few odd jobs, fine. I held my tongue. There was only the two of us through most of it, and you could have done with some softness." The paper seemed impossibly

27

far away, like a relic of a time that had already passed. "I may be a hard learner. Maybe...I can't see what she's become. But to follow in her footsteps..."

"Shut up."

"Out of some stupid sense of obligation." The buzzing in my ears flared.

Dad kept shaking his head like a swami. "I won't do it." He went to the door and paused, waiting for me to follow.

"You never thought she'd sign, did you?" I asked, not really caring anymore.

His grip tightened on the bag. "I'll start the car."

"Fuck you."

"Fine." He left.

My gaze fell on the mirror. The photographs blended together nauseatingly and I was standing in front of them. I grasped the corner of one and pulled it off. The glue-streaked portion of mirror underneath reflected my crooked nose, thin lips. I scratched at the others, tearing off strips, ceding to the blood rush in my ears until bits were all that remained and the table was littered with ruined pictures. I breathed quickly through my mouth.

The mirror stared at me, daring me to look into it. To prove that I possessed more courage than the woman who had imprisoned it these past months.

But I couldn't. Not in bathrooms or passing storefronts or car windows, and not now.

I waited for the sound of Dad's car starting before moving. When I did, my foot brushed up against a small, hard object.

A plastic pill bottle had rolled out from beneath the bed. I picked it up. It was full, the seal unbroken.

I reached beneath the bed and pulled out bottle after bottle, lining them up on the floor like toy soldiers. At first most of what I found were empties, and I thought the full one was just a fluke. But then bottles started holding pills along the bottom, then more and more, until there were several other full ones alongside my first discovery.

I sat cross-legged with my back up against the bed, inspecting labels.

Most of the empties were dated from March through June, a golden period following her release where the medication the nurses had pumped into her system still flowed freely. She was absurdly agreeable, taking strolls along the college campus that surrounded our home hand-in-hand with my father like new lovers. She cooked, made an effort to re-connect with friends, rarely raised her voice, and if sometimes I'd catch my father's eye and realize he was thinking the same thing, that the medication had gone too far, smoothing out the flinty edges we missed most dearly...what of it? We had become pragmatists in her absence, willing to compromise any number of intangibles in exchange for her presence.

July was where the bottles started holding unadministered pills. It was the month the switchover had occurred. She slept in later and later. When she did get up it was to prepare moori with onions and retreat to the basement to watch Hindi movies and talk to herself. The way she ate changed, open-mouthed and smacking. When Dad came home she'd lie to his face about chores done and plans made. I didn't call her on any of it. Dad stayed at school later and later. I stayed out. It's hard to have a living reminder of your failure to come home to.

By mid-July every bottle was full. Which meant that for over a month Dad had given her nothing, essentially speeding up her relapse. My mind fought understanding.

I opened a bottle and poured the contents into my hand. Little yellow-jacketed capsules, three to be taken nightly with a glass of water. And supervision. The directions were explicit on that point. When you were dealing with a schizophrenic who didn't accept the fact of her illness, there was no such thing as trust.

How many times had Dad shirked his duties before? What role had he played in her previous committals?

The whine of the lawnmower outside stopped, thrusting the room into silence.

I gathered up the bottles and went to my room. I stashed all but one in the bottom of a dresser drawer. I went downstairs on feet that grazed the floor, out the door into the sun's angry flush as it crept below the horizon line.

I stopped at the edge of the driveway where broken pavement met the uneven cobblestones of Albert Street. The sprawling commons of Raleigh College spread out before me, the red brick buildings, the planetarium's dome of black glass, the bell tower to the east where you could hear birds roosting. I didn't really see any of it, any more than I saw the students who walked along the paths or sprawled on the lawn like extras on a movie set. Streetlights made to look like gas lamps were coming to life. Before they'd reached full brightness I'd pulled out my cell phone and called Auntie.

"Well?" she asked. When I didn't answer she sighed. "It's what we expected."

I went north along Albert Street, cradling the phone to my ear. I could hear her breathing softly on the other end.

"Are you upset?" she asked.

"No, it's great."

"I'm sorry, *janu*."

"For what? You were right. About Dad backing out, all of it. I'm the stupid one."

"Don't talk like that."

"Funny thing is, if it was just money I'd understand. But the excuse he used, like my studying acting was out of some debt to her... he's lost it, Auntie."

The smell of overripe vegetation reached my nostrils. I crossed the street. The lawn sloped downward at the edge of campus to a pond choked with thistles. The hanging boughs of trees, bark coated in grime from the exhaust of the parking lot it bordered, bequeathed fragile white flowers onto the water's surface. I started making my way around it, stepping over discarded beer cans and candy bar wrappers.

"Don't be so hard on him. A man like your father will do just about anything rather than say he can't provide for his family. He wouldn't be much of a man otherwise."

"What can I do?" I was nearly at the first row of parked cars. Identical windshields. Identical doused lights. "I don't know where to go, or..."

The headlights of a car came on in a row further back. Wide grille tapering to tensed metallic haunches. It didn't start; it purred.

"Can you see me?" she asked. I nodded.

"Then come."

2

Auntie didn't say anything when I brought out the pill bottle and laid it on the table. We'd just finished dinner on the back porch of her sprawling home, the white tablecloth cluttered with plates holding the remains of beef and rice pilaf. She instantly recognized it for what it was. After a moment she reached forward, and, with long fingers, turned it to the flickering candle at the table's center. The shadows accentuated her masculine jawline and the hollows beneath her eyes.

"Where did you get this?" she asked.

"It's been over a month with no medication. Medication he's supposed to give to her." She looked at me. Her eyes held none of the diffused quality of her little sister's; they were still and possessed an unnerving intensity.

"I have others," I said.

Arjun, Auntie's part-time housekeeper, came out and began gathering up plates. Auntie slipped the pill bottle out of sight. When his hands were full, they exchanged the quick, knowing look only those who'd lived in each other's orbit for many years possess. Torso hunched like a question mark, he disappeared through the French doors, dishrag hanging out of a back pocket.

A breeze crinkled the tarp covering an in-ground swimming pool. Two basketball hoops lacking nets at either end of a blacktop court creaked intermittently. Moonlight illuminated the backyard and made it seem like an abandoned dreamscape. I'd spent so much of my childhood in this place, and yet sometimes it felt as if I didn't really know it at all.

"What kind of person does that?" I asked. "Lets a sick person call the shots? You know what she's like when it comes to the pills."

Auntie nodded. Her skin, several shades darker than my mother's, looked ashy in the gloom beyond the candle.

"She'll give any excuse. 'It hurts my back.' 'I can't think.' 'It's making me fat.' But he's supposed to be stronger…"

"He's been doing it for almost twenty years," Auntie said gently.

"And?"

She pulled out a sterling silver cigarette case and lit a smoke. She blew out a thin stream toward the backyard. We watched it spread out.

"People get tired, *janu*."

"How can you defend him?" I scratched the underside of my wrists. "He as well cut you out of Mom's life…"

"Was that a punishment?" she asked, observing the dim glow of traffic in the far distance. "Not having to see *Dee Dee* go in and out of the hospital these past few years? Not having to sit beside that… thing that looks like her, pretending she doesn't make me sick to my stomach?" She breathed out deliberately, trying to calm herself. "Your father never saw her that way."

"No," I agreed.

"Your *Dadu* was like that. No matter how much trouble us girls got into, he still saw us as the babies he'd held in his arms. We couldn't pierce that even if we'd wanted to. Of course that meant our mother had to be the bad one." She remembered me and smiled. It was like droplets of rain pattering on desert sands. "Being the bad one was my job for a time in your family. And then it wasn't."

I mock-scrutinized her. "What is this, the wisdom of age?"

She crushed the cigarette out beneath the heel of her shoe. A new silence came over the table.

She slipped an envelope to me across the table.

My fingers touched it before I'd asked what it was. "There'll be another next semester."

"Oh..."

"Don't embarrass me," she said, smiling again.

I took it.

"Nothing else matters, you know. Whether you become a movie star or no, whether you kill time with girls, travel, don't travel... just get away. There's no life for you in that house."

I clasped my hands tightly beneath the table. "As long as she's in that house I'll never be free," realizing it was true as I said it. "Dad will keep trying and failing. It'll just go on and on."

"You don't know that," Auntie said, but there was little force behind the words.

"He loves her. He can't live with feeding her pills that hurt her. He never will. Which means trying will either break him, or I'll have to do it. And I won't." A strong breeze nearly snuffed out the candle.

I'm no son, I thought.

"You loved to swim out there," Auntie said, nodding toward the pool.

"It was quiet."

The tarp crinkled and slowly undulated. The metal handrails glimmered.

"*Dee Dee* would be sitting where you are now, gossiping. She'd get carried away by something or other, forget all about you. I learned how to pretend-listen while keeping an eye on you. Worrying when you swam into the deep end."

She'd brought the pill bottle back out and was slowly turning it in her hands.

"I would think, 'that boy needs a guardian angel,' and think of some excuse to call you inside."

* * *

The paramedics bring her into the Admitting section of the hospital, a free-for-all of patients suffering from mild to severe mental illnesses. A nurse, not trusting her enough to give her forms to fill out, asks questions instead. Mom answers as best she can. She regrets her finery when she sees how the other patients react to it.

She is taken into what looks like an oversized gym locker room. It is steamy. Men and women are in various states of undress. Some have bruises and lesions. Some are babbling. Some crying. The nurses look on.

She is forced to shower. There is no privacy and she tries to cover herself with her hands. Afterwards her clothes are taken from her and she is given a beige hospital gown to wear. She can't reach behind to tie the two strings at the base of her neck, but is too afraid to ask for help.

She is led via an underground passageway to Baker Pavilion. Her footsteps echo off the walls. She knows she's been through this before but her mind will not connect to it fully. Her eyes are unfocused.

She is given ten minutes to spend with family before being admitted into the pavilion. There is no waiting room, just a few chairs by a nurse's station facing two steel doors. Dad sits in one of the chairs with the red bag on his lap.

She sits down next to him. When he speaks it's from a distance. She nods when she thinks she should. She allows him to take her hand. She notices how red his eyes are.

She notices I'm not there.

When a nurse comes out of the station things go wrong. Her legs won't move. Dad has to help her up. He has to physically wrap her fingers around the handles of the bag so it won't slip.

They move toward the steel door with a porthole window. Through it they can see patients milling about. They do not look at the other door, which is faceless.

An indescribable noise is coming from Mom's throat. She's not aware she's making it. The nurse has heard it so many times before that she doesn't hear it anymore. She unlocks the door.

Dad discovers the loose strings at the last moment and ties them. A part of him passes to her, the absence of which he'll feel upon leaving the hospital. They embrace awkwardly.

She doesn't know where I am. Her last moments before the door closes behind her are spent worrying.

3

Arjun drove me back to campus to begin my first day in theater school. One moment frothing whitecaps of the Oswego River filled the windshield as we crossed Truman Bridge separating city from suburb, the next college grounds filled with students—both seemed equally distant and threatening. My only claim to being in their midst was the flimsy check in my pocket. I kept fingering it to make sure it was real. I'd been too nervous to eat back at Auntie's and every time I passed a street vendor cart with its aroma of warm cheese and bread my stomach gurgled.

Most of the classes I'd be taking would be in Carruthers Hall, a gray stone building with a jutting, triangular facade that gave it the look of a gothic church. I'd only been there briefly for my audition back in May, and there was no sense of familiarity upon entering. The wood floor creaked. The ceiling was high, the roof beams layered with cobwebs. Artifacts of theatrical history were displayed in glass cases. They may have served as a point of interest for a student who hadn't learned all he knew about acting watching movies.

A woman sitting in what looked like a converted coat closet called me over and made me sign in. Her skin was impressively wrinkled and her short white hair was cut like a flapper's. Before I could get a question out she was motioning me toward the waiting room that stood a little ways down the corridor leading deeper into the building.

It must have been a church in a past life, I thought, seeing the stains of organ pipes against the back wall. Students were sitting all along it, smiling benignly and checking cell phones. The room was ill lit and the glow of LCD screens made their faces look washed out. Most looked two or three years younger than me, which didn't help. I took a seat next to a girl in black crunching Mentos, methodically popping a new piece into her mouth on the heels of swallowing the last. I counted twenty-eight people in the room, quickly averting my eyes upon making accidental contact.

There would be relearning involved. I'd acknowledged that on some superficial level, but being confronted with it so blatantly was depressing. What had I done since graduating from high school five years back except look for reasons to avoid connection? I'd had some friends—even a best friend, Simon—but I'd let them lapse. I'd worked shitty jobs making lattes and cleaning dishes at bars, never once taking the time to get to know the people I was working with. The jobs were beneath me, which meant they were beneath me and who cared anyway, they were all just stepping stones to better things. I'd never kept a job longer than eight weeks, and then it was back to where I'd started from, scrabbling blindly from a home base that felt like a sinkhole. The loneliness grew.

I forgot how to make conversation easily. I'd annoy store clerks by asking inane questions about how their day was going and what their favorite products were. I'd keep a tally of these interactions to convince myself I wasn't drifting ever further. When I walked down the street I'd grow certain there were stains on my clothes and bald patches in my hair.

When you start asking yourself why anyone ever liked you and you can't come up with a good answer you've reached a terminal stage. That's when you avoid mirrors and begin accepting the low-grade ache in your heart as a constant.

The woman who signed me in came to the center of the room and started reading names off a list. When she finished she told them they were Group A and instructed them to proceed to room 114. The rest of us watched them get up, gather up their things, and leave empty seats behind.

The woman left as suddenly as she'd arrived.

I could have exited then. No money had changed hands; it would have been easy. To this day I'm not entirely sure why I didn't, except that I knew what lay in store for me beyond that room and it was flat and leached of color. The few times I forgot myself were in the cool of the Palisades movie theater, which ran two films back-to-back for six dollars. Sometimes I was one of only three or four people in the entire theater, watching Roman Polanski and Terrance Malick films while Libby, the longtime owner of the place, knitted in the back row. Afterwards I'd prolong the experience by wandering for hours along the college grounds, playing fast and loose with the dialogue to recapture a bit of the tingle at the base of my spine. Every actor onscreen had escaped themselves. I wanted to learn such magic. I wanted to believe such alchemy was possible.

A girl, blonde and a little fragile looking, was staring at me from across the room. When our eyes met she gave me a crooked smile, like she knew what I'd been thinking and commiserated. She had freckles and wore a man's blue chambray shirt. Her eyes were sharp but furtive, making the gaze meaningful because you felt it wasn't something she often did.

When the lady returned to read off students for Group B I already knew I wouldn't be called. Losers gain a kind of prescience. The girl was sitting next to a guy who looked like an Abercrombie & Fitch model, tousled hair and wide shoulders denoting his ownership of the blue shirt. Grinning at the lady like he was charming the bouncer at a nightclub. When neither he nor the girl were called, his face, boyish in a way that made subterfuge impossible, fell with cartoonish speed.

Again, the rising and gathering and leaving. The girl looked over at the eight of us who were left. I could see her trying not to form a judgment based on lack of looks or social awkwardness or the curdled feeling some people gave off when the shutters have been closed for too long. It was difficult to do, and ultimately pointless, because the only thing that bound us was not being good enough for either Group A or B.

The minutes stretched out. The lady did not return. The boyfriend leaned over frequently to whisper reassurances to his girl. She smiled a little, answered sometimes, but it always petered out. Finally she slid down in her seat and crossed her arms. The shirt was bulky against her bony frame. She'd withdrawn and wasn't really looking at anything anymore.

A half-hour, then forty-five minutes. Nothing. Cell phones were put away. Bags were held close. I wanted to confront the professors who'd seen me audition and filled my head with false hope. The nodders and note-takers with their chalky skin and musty clothes. I wanted to pinch myself hard for being such an idiot. My mother was the fantasist, avoiding dealing with what her life had become through silver screen lies. What had I done but follow suit?

I was twenty-three years old and had squandered all my options. Even Auntie's charity wouldn't be enough to stall the slide.

A buxom girl cursed beneath her breath and exited in the direction of the lobby, presumably to confront the woman. She wore a crinkly black dress that ended at full thighs the color of mottled cream. She came back less than a minute later, caught the eye of Chambray Shirt's boyfriend, and shook her head. A worried look came over his face. I could see them trying to figure out what to do next.

I fingered the check in my pocket. I didn't believe it could help me anymore.

The girlfriend was blushing deeply. Her spindly jean-clad legs rubbed against one another, causing a low friction. It stopped and she threw up onto her lap.

There was a moment where I was the only one who'd seen. Then she put a hand to her mouth and jerked to standing, causing the chair legs to squeal against the floor. Students turned to her and tried to make sense of what they saw—wet vomit trickling between her fingers, a shapeshifter's gray eyes caught in the corridor's light.

"Emily," the boyfriend began.

She ran out into the corridor and cut left toward the classrooms. The boyfriend and the buxom girl exchanged a panicked look. I followed her before either had gotten to their feet.

Her Keds squeaked on the floor as she passed door after door, seeking a bathroom. I was about ten feet behind, not knowing what I was doing or how to help. I vaguely noticed piano music coming from one doorway. A little ahead of the girl, a door opened and two guys came out chatting, heads turning in slow motion as she approached.

She slowed and tried tucking in a side of her shirt. The fringes of her jeans were ratty.

"You okay?" one of them asked, easy grin fading as he noted the distress on her face.

She stopped. Her torso wavered. Flaxen blonde hair absorbed the light of the overhead fluorescents.

A low, trapped animal noise was coming from her.

I spotted a sign for the ladies' room further down the hall.

"Can I help?" the guy asked, and went to take a step toward her.

I bridged the gap, grasped her elbow, and started leading her away. She resisted at first, then slackened. A dollop of vomit spattered onto the floor. She pulled away from me as soon as the bathroom door had closed behind us.

She bent low over the sink, fingers sliding across the slick countertop. Several of her nails were chipped.

I grabbed some paper towels from a dispenser and held them out to her. She wet them beneath the faucet and wiped her face. I kept my eyes lowered, sparing her further scrutiny.

Her skin was incredibly pale, almost translucent. When she had trouble cleaning her shirt I did it for her. I'd never acted this way with a stranger before but for some reason she didn't feel like a stranger to me.

The bathroom door flew open and the buxom girl entered, briefly assessing me before turning Emily by the shoulders to face her. There was a rough intimacy to the gesture that made me feel out of place.

"I'm fine, Quincy," she muttered. "I just got sick."

I shut off the faucet. The silence was enormous. Quincy stared at me through the mirror, coolly evaluating whether I was help or hindrance. The pupils were the artificial blue of contacts. Her hair was also blonde, but whereas Emily's thin hair was brown at the roots, every inch of hers was bleached.

"Tim's outside," Quincy said, speaking to her friend but keeping her eyes on me. "He got you some water."

Emily wiped her face with a wet towel. "That's nice."

"No one saw what happened. It was over too fast," Quincy said, checking first the countertop, then the worn aquamarine tiles beneath our feet. She gathered up spent paper towels and threw them into the trash. She smiled brightly at Emily.

"You and Tim should go on back. Really."

"I can still smell puke," Emily said.

Excessive foundation did Quincy's face no favors. It was crusted around her eyes and lips. "I don't smell anything."

There was a moment's pause before Emily's eyes moved to me. An astonishing shade of gray, like rain clouds coalescing toward storm. "Can you smell it?"

I could, a little. But her eyes were crudely rimmed with mascara, a child's roving hand preparing for her first day. It was the only bit of makeup she wore, and it could not mask how vulnerable she seemed.

"No," I said.

All the toilets flushed in automated synchronicity.

Emily nodded, not really believing me. But she shrugged and left the bathroom. When the door opened I caught a glimpse of Tim leaning against the far wall, dutifully holding a paper cup of water.

"She gets nervous," Quincy said.

I nodded, not knowing whether to stay or go.

She cocked her head and smiled, false and wide. She was a few inches shorter than me and the temptation to sneak a peek at her cleavage was strong. "We don't have to gossip about this, do we?"

"I wasn't going to."

She breathed deliberately through her mouth, chest rising and falling. Her dress was sheer, the body beneath full and fleshy. "It'd mean a lot."

"I won't."

* * *

When I came back to the waiting room, Quincy following a few steps behind, the remaining students had already been called. It took peeking in a few class windows to find out where they'd gone: a largely empty room with a cot and two chairs at center, students arranged loosely along three tiers of seating in back. An industrial spotlight was set up in their midst, so ancient I assumed it was for show. I saw Emily and Tim sitting in the front row. A man who looked like a boxer gone to seed hulked over a desk in one corner, writing like it didn't come easily. A small sign outside the door proclaimed he was Professor Gary Kilroy.

We went inside without knocking; that was the first mistake.

He didn't break off writing. His hair was gray and buzzed short. His nose, even from a distance, was a mess of broken blood vessels.

"What do you want?" he asked without looking up. I glanced at Quincy, who was frowning.

"I think this is our class," she said, clasping her hands together. A big sapphire ring on one finger.

He jerked his pen toward the students. "Why weren't you with them?"

"We were," Quincy said, an edge of annoyance creeping in beneath the supplication. "For the first hour."

He stopped writing. Raised his pulpy face to us, eyes flat like a rodent's. "Do you speak?" he asked me.

I cleared my throat and nodded.

Though less than thirty feet separated us from the other students, it seemed like an impassable stretch. As long as he held us in his gaze, we were stuck where we stood.

"Sit down, both of you," he said.

Quincy went toward where her friends sat.

"Not there," he said, and nodded to the two chairs in the empty playing area. They faced each other about three feet apart.

Once we were seated he told us to look at each other. The urge to smile or make some other kind of deflecting expression came over both of us, faded, and then we were just waiting out the clock.

"Tell me what you see," he said.

The chair felt cool against the back of my thighs. "You look pretty," I said.

She arched an eyebrow already plucked into an expression of surprise.

"Repeat it back if you can't think of something," Gary told her.

"I look pretty," she said, crossing a leg over. Her dress hiked up.

I scratched my neck. I itched.

"Continue," Gary said.

Her eyes stared at me with a marionette's blind expectation.

"If you can't think of something else, just repeat it."

"You look nervous," I said.

She made no reaction. "I look nervous," she answered.

I shifted in my seat. "You don't want to be here."

"I don't..." Her mouth twitched. "I want to be here."

"At last," Gary said. His chair creaked as he leaned forward. "Someone's home. I was beginning to wonder."

She tilted her head up. I could picture her practicing every single one of these motions in front of a mirror. "You're being a jerk," she said, eyes on me.

"I'm being a jerk."

"Are you?" Gary asked me. "Are you just saying these things to take the attention off you?"

I shook my head.

"Words, please," he said.

"All of it," gesturing toward her, "the clothes, the looks...I can't get past." The daring glint in her eyes disappeared.

"All of it..." she began repeating.

"Come on, really answer him," Gary said.

She exhaled slowly. "You don't know me."

"I know you."

Her mouth was prim.

"You're scared," I said.

She laughed a little. "Wow. Nice."

She pulled at her dress. I think she regretted wearing something so revealing. "Okay, what am I scared of?"

The wood slats composing the floor had been worn gray by thousands of feet. My eyes traveled upwards to her black peep-toe pumps, little black decorative flowers at the heels. "Of someone seeing you."

"Ask if she hates herself," Gary said. His voice was low, the tone almost off-handed. "Or if she's ever shown herself naked to a person."

She clutched the chair seat with both hands.

"She's insulting you." He rose to standing. "She doesn't respect you enough to show her true self so she hides behind this fantasy."

The air in the room had grown charged. The longer we students allowed the interaction to continue, the more we tacitly agreed to the tactics used, becoming participants in a conspiracy with unknowable ends.

"Look at me, son."

Quincy kept her eyes on me. Every word he said affected her beyond a level I could register. It was difficult looking away.

Gary stood less than a foot away, blocking a large portion of the audience with his frame. He took shallow breaths, mouth open to reveal a broken picket fence of teeth.

"Do you see what I do?"

I nodded, not sure of anything. Only that the ground felt less substantial, signposts slipping away as the first tremors rose from some place deep within, denied yet never forgotten.

"Then do something to make her stop. Because she's going to leave class and it'll just be the same thing over and over."

I couldn't say another thing.

* * *

When Gary ended the improvisation and called a fifteen-minute break there was a flurry of activity. Students chatted and got up to stretch their legs. Emily went up behind Quincy and gave her a hug. Both ignored me.

It was an effort to get up. No one looked at me. I dimly remembered the things I'd just said, and some of them were cruel, but I didn't understand what to do about it. I couldn't just stand there in the middle of the playing area and I couldn't sit down with the others like nothing had happened. I left the classroom and spotted a fire exit a few doors down.

Outside was better. I stood in the shadow of a few trees and gulped air. My chest felt like a creature was scrabbling to get out. Across University Street stood a bronze figure of a man I didn't know. He wore a pointed conquistador's hat and stared confidently ahead. His view encompassed more buildings and more students. I despised all of it, and wished I had whatever I was missing, and despised the missing of it too.

Tim came out, squinting against the sun's glare. He nodded briefly at me and pulled out a pack of cigarettes. After a few moments he offered me one.

"You gonna stick around?" he asked. The breeze ruffled his hair and made him look like a thwarted lover on the cover of a Harlequin romance novel.

I smiled weakly; it evaporated. "I don't know."

"Wanna hear a little theory?" His shirt was open at the chest, a few sparse brown hairs peeking through. "I think he made us wait in that room for an hour. A little test, to see which of us could hack it."

The cigarette was making me feel lightheaded. "Why would he do that?"

"You don't know about him?" He leaned in slightly. "Guy's been bouncing from college to college for the past ten years. Professors he came up through the ranks with, guys whose textbooks we shell out for, think he's gone off the rails. He used to be a proponent of the Method, then it was the Meisner technique. Now?" He shrugged. "I don't think there's a name for what that was."

The bell tower began to ring, its peals steadily building in force as they traveled up from the southeast part of campus.

"Will she be all right?" I asked. "Your girlfriend?"

"Nerves."

"Yeah."

He flicked the cigarette into the grass, where it smoked weakly.

"Quincy's saying all the right things to her. Calming her down. I don't even need to be there."

He watched the cigarette burn down to the filter. "It's true what Gary said. The block she has, keeping anyone from getting past a certain point. She's never needed to, as long as Emily was with her." He shrugged. "There are times I wish Em could take on a little of that shell, that hardness. Just so things like this morning don't rattle her. But..." He checked a chunky digital watch. "It's getting time."

I crushed out my smoke. "What's your name?" he asked.

"Neil," I answered.

We shook hands. His grip was unnecessarily firm. "Em and I are at Miller House. Do you know it?"

I nodded.

"Room four. Come over tonight if you want." He smiled.

"Okay."

* * *

Friends are more valuable than currency to a Bengali. Friends are currency when you'd packed up and moved halfway around the world to a place with too many locked doors. Dad took classes, taught a little, and tried to make inroads within the established school hierarchy. Mom struggled to learn English and mostly stayed at home with me, determined not to let the uncertainty felt every second of their lives trickle into their America-born son. Their only relief came when, at least once a week, one of the other Bengali families who lived in town would invite us over for a *nemonton*.

A *nemonton* is to a party what a debutante ball is to a high school dance. It's not about unwinding but spending a few hours living the way you wished to. Mom would spend hours getting ready. Dad would iron his shirt and put on a nice blazer for the occasion. Then they'd go to a crummy apartment or starter home that had been obsessively cleaned and smelled of incense, where their friends would be sitting ready to discuss Indian politics, or luxury cars, or new home developments in the suburbs, anything other than mundane details. I'd usually be in the basement or a guest room playing with fellow child-exiles, pausing when our parents' voices got too loud or their footfalls fell too heavily. Dad would passionately debate the merits of the Congress Party or particular standings of Bollywood royalty. Mom said little. But then she didn't need to.

Her skin would glow. Her smile, open and teasing, invited you in while making it clear you'd never get all the way there. She drank sparingly, helped serve the food, traded gossip with the other women—and none of it mattered. You didn't remember any of these things afterward. All you knew was that there had been this exceptional creature in your midst, a vessel for a fire so clean and pure it lessened you by comparison. Dad and I were merely specks of ash floating about her.

At home she talked too much and left the kitchen a mess. Her clothes would be tossed everywhere and she had a predilection for sweet wines. She was a hard taskmaster when it came to my schoolwork and rebellious when it came to marital traditions, kissing Dad in front of me or plopping down onto his lap while he pretended to disapprove.

Who she really was existed somewhere between these two poles. It was a mystery my father and I sought to solve, pinning down a point in constant flux. And when her mind and body began to warp and the light in her eyes turned inwards we still stupidly sought it, as if the discovery might serve as a bulwark against an attack which had already succeeded.

4

The ambulance had left an oil stain behind on the driveway. I rubbed at it with my shoe but it wasn't coming off. There was a thin stretch of grass beside the driveway leading to the backyard. We shared this stretch with our neighbor Eddie, a professor of African-American studies. By the clear line cut down the center of the grass I surmised he must have been the one working the lawnmower yesterday. Poor Eddie, who had the misfortune of living next door to a family requiring periodic ambulance visits.

Inside, the house was frozen in tableau. The shoe mat in the foyer was folded over itself, a victim of Mom's struggling. Boot tracks had turned the area into a public thoroughfare. The odor of one of the men lingered like sour milk.

The phone in the living room rang as I was scrubbing the floor. I made to get up before remembering that good news rarely came from answering it. It rang four times and went to the answering machine:

"Sir," Dr. Thibodeau began, nasal voice coated in a thick French-Canadian accent, "what you're doing is not acceptable. We've had this conversation a hundred times before, yet here we are again. You cannot linger in the corridors outside of visiting hours. You cannot pester the nurses for updates. And you cannot spend the night in your car in the parking lot." There was the sound of air sipped between lips. "I'm quite aware of your opinion of me, but the truth is I'm trying to help Mrs. Kapoor get her life back. She's in a...delicate state and doesn't need you adding to it." The answering machine speaker crackled with static.

A grimy rivulet of water seeped out of the sponge I held in my hand and ran into a gap between the tiles. I could picture the doctor sitting in his office, skin yellow in the glare of a desk lamp, chin like a dollop of wet clay.

"Leaving messages is tiresome," he said. "Next time I call the Public Trustee."

I rose after he'd hung up, wiping my hands on the back of my jeans. Nearing the answering machine I could see the red blinking message light.

I touched the "Erase" button lightly, feeling cool plastic. Pressed it and the message disappeared.

* * *

Dad sopped up the last bits of egg on his plate with a piece of toast and emitted a satisfied burp. The fading light coming in through the patio doors was merciful to the bags under his eyes, the increasingly haunted set to his face that was like a hole opening up in the pit of my stomach if I stared too long. He sat back in his chair and nodded at me across the table.

"Pretty good. Can't compare to what the chickens in Barakpur would lay, but still." He mimed holding an egg. "I'd pick them fresh every morning, can you imagine?"

Water dripped steadily from the kitchen faucet onto the pan I'd used to cook the omelets. Bags of trash were stacked in front of the refrigerator, bloated with the things I'd found hidden away in its inner recesses: blue-green pieces of fish in saran wrap, grayish goat parts swimming in grease, black broccoli heads and tomato halves. Mom, who used to measure in salt by the pinch, would eat these with relish, smacking her lips like animate flesh lacking higher functions. Every other facet of her personality had undergone a change: why should this be any different? No, the surprise came when she'd call us down to a dinner table laid out with these monstrosities...and watch as we tried to eat it.

Dad gave me a sly look. "You've never been to Barakpur, have you?"

I slowly turned a half-full glass of water. My plate was mostly untouched. "When I was six."

"Oh, that doesn't count!" His voice rang out in the quiet. "You have to experience it as a man; smoking *beedis* with the neighborhood *goondas*, eating hot *aloo kabli* on the street..."

"Sounds great," I muttered.

Imagine the almost furry sensation of moldering vegetable in your mouth. Imagine your throat seizing up because it perceived all too well there was no nutrition to be found here, just discomfort. Now imagine looking across the table to where your father sat gobbling it down, barely pausing to breathe until his plate was clean and he could praise her efforts.

"Ganguly Uncle used to be a *goonda*, you know," he said. "Very bad boy, stealing from the open-air markets, selling hashish..." He kept speaking but I tuned it out. The last of the light fell off the edge of the table.

I went around switching on lights.

"Easy!" he called out. "It's just the two of us, we don't need so many."

I remembered Mom taking me to college debates where I'd watch him passionately argue issues I didn't understand. I paid attention to the cigarette smoking between his fingers, the intensity in his eyes, the impatient, long-limbed pacing between thoughts. He could out-shout anyone, cow much older men into submission, then fling me over his shoulder and exit hand-in-hand with Mom like a warrior with his spoils. I'd emulate the pacing in my room. Waft an imagined cigarette in the air to underline key points.

When every light blazed I turned to observe him. He sat slumped in his chair, chest working overtime in preparation for another forced exchange. He leaned forward and stacked my plate atop his. A yellow checkered tie hung limply from his neck.

"You could go," he said. "I'd pay, for you to see it now."

What remained of his ideals was in those bags of trash. They had festered, been laid on a plate by my mother, cut into digestible chunks and swallowed down. The man who had fiercely argued for student rights and sneered at the petty excuses of administrators would not have recognized his doppelganger. He would have thrown Mom's meals back in her face, grasped her by the shoulders, and shook until she realized how far she'd sunk.

"Anyway, just think about it," he said, bringing the plates over to the sink. "But if you decide to go, we should book the flight soon."

"You said there was no money. For school."

He scraped my plate into the trash bin beneath the sink. "This is different."

"How?" When he didn't answer, "How is this different?"

He used the rinse attachment on the plates. His shoulders were permanently hunched with tension. "I know you don't want to be here. It's depressing."

"Did I say that?"

"I don't blame you. At least this way you get a chance to travel, see your roots and figure out what you want to do."

"I know what I..." I trailed off.

He was nodding to himself. Water gurgled down the sink.

"Dad," I said slowly, "what happened to you?"

"I'm not going to watch you fritter away the rest of the year doing nothing. We tried it your way. Now we'll try it mine and I promise you'll..."

"Auntie paid tuition."

The words hung there. Dad shut the faucet off.

"I handed in the check this afternoon."

He gently lowered the dish he'd been holding into the sink.

"I'm sorry."

"You didn't do this."

"There was no one else..."

He came toward me suddenly and I flinched. I opened my eyes and his face was inches away from mine, slack with anguish.

"Is that what you think of me?" he asked. "Did I ever raise a hand to you? To your mother?"

He smelled of the car he'd spent the night in. Shaking his head, he started walking away.

"Maybe you should have hit her," I said. He stopped with his back to me. "Better than eating her shit with a smile on your face."

His shoulders twitched.

"Don't confuse me with your Auntie," he said. "She was the one who'd leave bruises."

* * *

A group of students played soccer evenings near the planetarium, lanky Indians and Asians executing long kicks and sweeps in a friendly display of showmanship. Players would often switch teams and run down each other's balls. Sometimes play petered out for a few minutes for a water break before lazily starting up again.

I sat by a copse of elm trees nearby, sipping from a hip flask filled with rum from the basement liquor cabinet. The moon was faintly outlined against a violet sky, a halo for an angel who had long since departed its post. I thought about my father and Auntie. They'd always had the slight formality of two who did not fundamentally understand one another, but that was put aside when Mom got sick. Auntie moved into the house for weeks on end, engaging Mom in conversation and cooking meals. She watched over her during the hours Dad was teaching, and in the evenings they'd present a united front, outlining plans for India vacations while Mom forced down pills with a glass of water. And for a time, things did get better. There were three people drawing her away from the voices and she was still present enough to try, if only for our sake.

But the nights were long and remained their dominion. Long after we had gone to sleep the voices would continue working, stroking her vanity and muttering innuendos, gaining credibility within a psyche that was losing its grip on reason. None of us could insert ourselves into that place, and ultimately, it was the only place that mattered.

She'd sit in stolid silence while Auntie and I chatted. She grew self-conscious about her bloated body and made excuses not to go outside. Talk of vacations was put on hold and replaced with mentions of treatment centers. Money wasn't an issue; Auntie had plenty of it and would have fronted it no question. She showed my father brochures of exclusive places in Phoenix and Miami, filled with pictures of pretty people swimming and sunning. Dad was courteous and noncommittal. Auntie wouldn't be put off so easily. She could see the glassy look in her sister's eyes. She could smell the dying-animal smell that was beginning to come off her.

Auntie berated her for not taking better care of herself. She'd enter the bathroom after Mom, lock the door, and forcibly clean her while Mom shouted to be let out. She placed a padlock on the refrigerator once and wouldn't allow Mom to eat anything except saltines for two days.

These shock tactics might have worked if Dad hadn't undermined them at every turn. Sneaking food into her room, lying that yes, she was still every bit the beauty he'd married, he still loved her no matter what, I'll have a talk with your sister, maybe it's time she moved on.

A chubby Asian chested the ball, let it roll down his tummy, and kneed it high up into the air. We all watched it ascend, slow, and hover amidst a thousand embers of starlight.

I slipped the check out of my pocket and stared at it. So flimsy. I didn't know why I hadn't handed it in, except that my fingers had felt numb whenever I'd thought to.

Another memory. Auntie and I out on the patio eating fruit salad. Mom taking a nap in the living room. Only the screen keeping out insects was pulled, enabling sound from inside the house to pass out.

Auntie was spearing a piece of melon when she heard it. A low humming from the living room. I started saying something to distract her and she grasped my wrist. Her eyes moved quickly side-to-side. The buzz of locusts in the backyard momentarily fell away and it was unmistakable: Mom placating an invisible person, whining in her eagerness to apologize for some slight.

Auntie let go of her fork and wiped her lips with a napkin. I stared at the angle with which the fork rested against the inside of the bowl as she entered the house.

Mom cried out just once. Then there was just the flat smack of flesh hitting flesh, followed by low weeping. The locusts rose and faded three more times before I got up and entered the house.

When Dad returned home he took one look at Mom's face and it was over with Auntie. This had been a little over five years ago. I wondered if Auntie had considered how things had deteriorated since then and felt vindicated.

I carefully refolded the check and slipped it back into my pocket. There was a pleasant whiteness behind my eyes. I rocked forward onto my knees and stood. Play was winding down and the streetlamps were building in intensity, turning the campus into a playground for shadows and disembodied whistles.

Dad never brought up the attack with me.

It was easier to believe the patio door had been closed.

* * *

I passed by Miller House three times before noticing the ivy-covered sign next to the driveway. Nestled amidst the sprawling gardens of the campus's east end stood a Victorian townhouse, chipped marble columns clotted with more ivy, panes of stained glass on the upper floors lending the specters therein the air of suffering characters in an Edgar Allan Poe story. The smell of hyacinths drifted from the overgrown front yard as a stuffed scarecrow with broken corn stalks for hair stood guard. I went up the steps to the front door, glancing back once at the bike path and street beyond. A few cars went past, headlights scanning the darkness like blind moles.

Inside, a foyer with vaulted ceilings opened out to a large living room at right and a smaller kitchen further down. A wide staircase stood at center leading up to the second floor. The wrought iron banister was wrapped with decorative lights but they were doused, perhaps in deference to the musty chandelier overhead casting shards of illumination that shivered with the breeze I'd brought in with me.

A burst of laughter came from the living room. I headed toward it, rubbing my palms on my jeans though they were dry.

Tim was sitting cross-legged on the carpet alongside several girls, playing poker with Hershey's Kisses for chips. They paid close attention when he worked his cards, capitalizing on the opportunity to take in his physique and slightly removed air of privilege at their leisure. A few wore fluffy slippers. One had her back up against the couch, black-dyed pixie cut, tight black jeans. She took periodic sips from a bottle of beer and openly stared at him. When Tim grew aware of it she shook the bottle flirtatiously, inviting him to take a sip.

He shook his head. "I'm good."

The better part of a case of Rolling Rock lay nearby. A black girl wearing pastel bangles on each arm was making a screwdriver using the vodka and juice laid out on the coffee table. Yet Tim was dry. He had sneakers on, white headphones spilling out the pocket of his track pants.

Tim had been corralled, and accepting alcohol would mean resigning himself to officially being a guest.

The black girl spotted me standing at the threshold.

"Can I help you?" she asked, the words tinged by a faint English accent.

"What's up, man," Tim said, hopping up and unceremoniously dumping his cards onto the carpet. A windfall of numbered hearts, a jack of spades peeking out of a far corner.

"Is he your friend?" Pixie Cut asked.

"Nice to meet you," I said, waving to the group. There was a nonresponsive quality to them, like a motor lacking a sparkplug. Pixie Cut seemed to be the only one aware of the lack, and wasn't afraid to let it be known.

Tim came up quickly, arm raised for a high-five. When our palms slapped he spun me around in a single motion toward the foyer.

"What's your name?" Pixie Cut asked.

"Don't," Tim muttered but I was already craning my neck around for a look. The group had already lost interest in me, back to shuffling cards, peeling away the tinfoil of a Hershey's Kiss, staring blankly ahead like a bathysphere exploring the ocean floor. Then we were past the threshold and out of sight.

He took the stairs two at a time, displaying the muscled legs of an athlete. His back tapered to slim, almost girlish hips and his arms hung low. The chandelier's light caressed his hair like a fond parent.

We entered one of what appeared to be five apartments on the second floor. The ceiling was much lower than downstairs but the room was long, broken up by a flat-screen television, coffee table, and couch at center to create a living room. Moving boxes dotted the landscape like sand dunes. A leaning Tower of Pisa composed entirely of newspaper-wrapped plates teetered in the kitchen sink.

I was a little dizzy from the climb. He closed the door behind me and breathed out slowly.

"Elvira was staring like she wanted to eat my genitals." He went over to an open sports bag and changed into a fresh T-shirt. "Wasn't sure if you were coming."

"I wasn't going to," I began, then trailed off. This was starting to feel like a bad idea, one I would have considered longer had I not been drinking.

Tim checked his phone and placed a call. A tinny voicemail recording emanated from the phone's speaker. His grip tightened on the phone.

"Neil's here," he said, the words coming out on the exhale. "If you and Quincy get tired of seeing the sights and just want to hang..." He hung up and slipped the phone into his pocket.

"Girls night out."

I nodded.

A dullness came into his eyes in tandem with a false smile. He shook his head and his expression cleared. The smile broadened and became genuine. "I'm glad you're here."

I spotted a rolled-up shag carpet leaning next to the bathroom door. "Do you need help with that?"

We carried it over to between the couch and television, unrolled and tamped it down. On it was an intricate design depicting two Muslim armies clashing upon its surface, long faces and slitted eyes tranquil as they plunged swords into each other's bodies.

"Want to do a shot?" he asked.

One of the kitchen cupboards had a thin metal chain and combination lock on it, a detail I hadn't noticed before. Tim spun the garish purple dial and opened it to reveal several bottles of hard liquor. He poured two shots of Johnnie Walker Black and held one out to me.

The chain dangled off the cupboard handle, nearly long enough to reach the countertop. Taking the offered shot, I was acutely aware of the chain's presence yet careful not to direct my gaze to it and force a response. To do so would mean establishing boundaries, whereas ignoring it would mean continuing to enjoy the strange intimacy created that morning when I'd helped Emily. I assumed the chain had something to do with her. We clinked glasses and drank. He poured another round. I unfolded a map of the college campus resting on the counter, snaking paths in bright red and orange like a nest of maggots burrowing into spoiled fruit.

"Near as I can tell, it's completely random," Tim said, glancing at it over my shoulder. "None of the paths have names, and there aren't many intersections or landmarks."

"I think it's supposed to represent brain pathways or something," I said. "A nightmare to navigate when you're drunk."

There was a momentary silence that told me I'd struck a nerve of some kind. We drank the new shots. My throat had a scraped-out feeling that offered a kind of ballast as intoxication crept in.

"I don't want her to get lost," he said.

"She won't."

"She takes pills. Anti-anxiety. They don't mix well with booze." He grabbed the bottle of Johnnie Walker by the neck and went for the couch.

There was a weed tin on the coffee table. I rolled a joint while Tim plugged a PS3 into the television. We played a racing game for a while. Formula 1 engines screamed like banshees. The track edges blurred when I took corners. I couldn't tell whether it was a visual effect of the game or my flattened consciousness. Music started up downstairs, salsa or merengue.

A silence rose up between us. Finally he paused the game.

"Don't go after her," I said.

"Quincy won't tell her to stop. She could be wandering around lost right now..."

"Has she called you back?"

He started playing again but it was half-hearted.

"If you want to search I'll help." I ran my tongue over my lips, picking up the charred taste of the scotch. "The longer you look the more convinced you'll be of how right what you're doing is. How good. That will last right up until the moment you find her, look in her eyes, and realize she never wanted to be found." A thin tendril of smoke rose up from the crushed joint roach in the ashtray. "Not by you."

He paused the game and laid the controller on the coffee table. He rubbed his face vigorously for a few seconds. Then he reached for the bottle of scotch and held it up to gauge how much remained.

"Did you ever have a sweetheart?" he asked. "In high school?"

"No. The closest was this one girl, Janelle. Totally unrequited."

"What happened?"

Months of secretly falling ever deeper in love with her body. The slight bounce to her step and how it made her breasts, full and perky, come to the fore. Her husky voice with the perfect enunciation of a reporter-in-training. Milk chocolate skin surrounding what I imagined to be a thatch of soft black pubic hair. She made my cock stiff in homeroom, reciting cafeteria specials and volunteer opportunities over the intercom.

"Got fingered by some guy who had a face I couldn't stand." I winked like it was a joke, but it had been painful at the time. Realizing the grand feelings were all in your head. That they wouldn't magically seep out into your life and transform it for the better.

He took several deep swigs from the bottle. He nearly started coughing but suppressed it. His eyes were watery.

"How about you?" I asked.

His gaze had settled on the unlocked cupboard. "Yes," he said quietly.

He fell asleep soon afterwards, breathing soft and even like a child's. My heart was hammering in my chest and my first thought was to sneak out of the apartment but there was nothing for me beyond its walls.

I went into the bathroom and gently closed the door behind me. Toothbrushes, floss, and mouthwash were laid out by the sink, a few green specks on its surface where Tim or Emily had spat out.

I splashed water on my face. Usually when I felt hollow and exhausted it helped but not this time. I ran wet fingers through my hair, pushing it off my forehead. I raised my eyes to the mirror.

Dark brown dilated pupils. A few small hairs coming out of my nostrils. Thin purple lips. A shaving rash on the underside of my chin.

After a few seconds I placed a hand on the mirror, blocking out my image.

When I looked at myself I saw my mother. And even when I couldn't see anymore, her gaze on me lingered.

I went back to the couch and watched TV until I was tired enough to fall asleep in a strange place.

* * *

She lies on a cot in a dormitory that reeks of too many bodies. Dried skin sloughed off and covering the floor like a film. Sweat dried to a paste on frames that have lost all sense of proportion. Fans whirl slowly overhead but the smell is immovable, a boulder.

And the noises.

A few beds over a man is crying. It starts soft and hopeless then gradually builds. Daddy please don't I'll be good I promise I'll be good don't don't DON'T it hurts Daddy it hurts it HURTS don't hurt FUCK YOU please YOU COCKSUCKER please. Then an anguished shriek and more weeping. She can feel those still awake listening to it. No nurses come to help the man.

Burping and farting are constant. Sometimes the trickle of piss onto the floor. The furtive sound of rubbing flesh that she doesn't want to think about.

Time stretches out. She focuses on a particular fan blade and before it completes its revolution she is lost in a memory. Niladri's Amnaprasan at six months, holding him in her lap and using her sari to cover his eyes from the glare of flashing cameras. Everyone they knew had shown up, she'd have cut them out if they'd refused, brown heads and hands gathered in close to inspect the new member of the family. People kept asking her to hold him up so they could get a better look but she didn't. The boy didn't cry, didn't even pull away from the ruckus, yet she could feel the steady thrumming from deep within his body. Though she smiled and tried to look proud, the thrumming frightened her in a way she couldn't put into words. It was as if her organs had been transplanted, and from now on every bead of sweat would be shared, every chill along her arms would be his. Sometimes her fears and the sheer volume of things she didn't understand became a kind of golem within her mind, taunting successes and failures alike, and she worried that this too would be transferred to her son. As she held him close and smiled for photographs, she vowed that no matter what the cost, her son would not fall victim to it. He would parse mysteries and stride across the world with a confidence she could only mimic.

Footfalls outside the dormitory door. The door opens, light from the *hallway splashing her body beneath tucked sheets. She shuts her eyes tight.*

A man comes up the rows of beds whistling softly. His heels clack on the floor. He stops in front of the one who'd been cursing.

"Your daddy isn't here," he says, the words warped by a French-Canadian accent. "Do you want to know a secret?" The floor creaks as he bends over him. "The man's been dead over ten years. You cut through his neck with gardening shears. What about that?"

The man whimpers.

"There, there," Doctor Thibodeau says.

She can hear the smile in his voice.

Her hands clench into fists. Air escapes out the sides of her lips and she wants to sneak a peek in the doctor's direction to see how close he is but doesn't dare. And then she hears his quick, eager footsteps and realizes she should have leapt up, run for the door shouting for a nurse, anyone...

"You're not sleeping," he says. His face comes over her, lips pulled apart to reveal two sets of ferret teeth. "It's either sleep or treatment. Those are the rules."

His face comes in closer. He smells of talcum powder. Her father had smelled of talcum powder but nothing had ever wriggled behind her father's eyes.

"Or do you think you're too good for the rules?"

NILADRI—

* * *

I reached out blindly and found my arms enmeshed in a blanket. I thrashed wildly to extricate myself, vision pulsing with panic. Then I recognized Emily standing before me caught in the glare of the television screen and stopped.

Her eyes were startled but distant, like they were taking in a fireworks show. Her hair was tousled and stuck out in places. She switched her weight between feet and I realized she was drunk.

"You looked cold," she said, nodding to the blanket. "Just wanted to cover you."

"Sorry," the word coming out slurred. "I thought..." But there was nothing I could say that wouldn't incite questions.

"I was trying to be quiet," she said, looking toward the closed bedroom door. She inhaled slowly through her mouth and let it out, eyes partially closing.

Tim had left the couch while I'd been sleeping. The cushion he'd been sitting on still carried his imprint. I felt exposed thinking of him listening to whatever may have come from my mouth in sleep.

She came forward, hands out for balance. She was like the scarecrow in the front yard, one strong gust away from toppling.

"Here," I said, getting up to help her.

"I'm fine," she said, stopping me. "You don't always have to..." She looked down at her feet, as if trying to recall how they worked.

The blanket was caught around my ankles. I pulled it out, folded it in half, and laid it on the couch.

"Why?" she asked, bending over with her hands on her hips. Her shoulders rose and fell as she tried to keep the alcohol at bay.

"Why what?"

She moved her feet in increments until they lined up. She lifted her face and gave me a pained look. "Why'd you help me?"

I smiled a little. She really did look comical. "I don't know."

She tossed an arm out in the direction of the bedroom. "I've got a team of helpers. Didn't you know that?"

"Oh."

She shut her eyes and nodded solemnly. "So you don't have to worry. Is what I'm saying."

She was slowly able to raise her torso up. Her eyes roamed the ceiling. Her freckles were especially thick around her eyes. "I'll never be able to ignore you again. I'll always have to stop and say hello."

"Sorry."

"You're always apologizing." She gave me a crooked smile. Her lips looked soft. "You don't have to."

"Did you have a good time?"

She shrugged. "You know."

And the funny thing was I did. Though she'd never introduce herself to someone new, she'd answer a stranger's questions politely. She'd dance, but shyly and at the outskirts of the group. Her drinks would vary but she'd never settle on one. Afterwards, those who'd come into contact with her would not be able to remember specific traits, only a wanting quality she'd left behind.

"Was he mad?" she asked, nodding to herself. "He was, wasn't he?"

I sat down on an arm of the sofa. "More worried."

I grabbed the remote and turned the television off, bathing the apartment in the inky blue of late night.

I could feel her watching me; a spinning top stilled. Her chest was flat like a pubescent girl.

"What were you dreaming about?" she asked.

I rubbed my eyes. "Someone was coming for me," but it wasn't me, it was Mom, the doctor had been coming for Mom. "I called out, but there was no one." My throat started to hurt and I couldn't say any more.

She made it to the bedroom door. Hand on the doorknob, "See you tomorrow."

"Goodnight, Emily."

5

Tim crisped bacon on the stove the next morning, turning them over at ten-second intervals while the heavy smell of pork filled the air. Emily sat at the dining table looking green. A cup of coffee stood untouched in front of her.

The kitchen cupboard containing alcohol had been locked up again.

"Help yourself," Tim said, tapping the coffee pot next to him.

I got up from the couch, padded over, and poured myself a cup. "Thanks for letting me crash," I said to him.

"No worries." He wore a white chef's apron flecked with grease spots. He turned off the stove and used tongs to drop the bacon onto a plate covered by a paper towel. He closed the paper towel, allowing the excess fat to soak through, then opened it, took two strips, and put them onto a plate holding a piece of buttered toast. He brought it over to Emily, pushing the coffee cup out of the way to lay it down directly in front of her.

"I'm not hungry," she muttered.

"You'll feel better."

She looked to me and smiled wanly. Lack of sleep made her face look gaunt, like an artist's sketch instead of flesh and blood. She still wore what she'd had on last night, a loose navy blue shift dress.

Tim undid his apron and draped it over a chair. All evidence of newspaper-wrapped plates and cutlery had been removed, and now the kitchen stood as a bastion of order against the mess beyond it.

"You have to eat something." More firmly, "Em."

"I heard you," Emily said, pushing her index finger into the table like she suspected it might pass through.

Tim glanced at me. "Help yourself," he said, motioning toward the refrigerator.

I took a sip of my coffee and moved to the sink. My back was to them and I heard Tim mutter, low and quick, "I'm not the one who looks sick this morning." Loud crunching. "See? It's good."

I took another sip and laid the cup down into the sink. A green plastic frog affixed to the faucet grinned at me, eyeballs bulging maniacally.

"Did you sleep okay?" Emily asked.

Assuming she had addressed me, I turned around and saw her looking grimly back. I nodded.

Tim picked up her plate and threw it into the sink. Emily worked not to flinch at the crash. The toast slowly slid down toward my toppled cup.

"If you're not going to eat, go take a shower," he said.

"Do you want to take a shower?" she asked me.

"Don't bring him into this."

"I'm okay. I should get going."

"Okay," Tim said, not taking his eyes off her.

The air was loaded with a familiar energy that made my teeth ache. A warning signal, telling me to take what I could and exit. But before I could, Tim spoke again.

"You child," he said, not bothering to lower his voice. "Do you think I want to be like this?"

Pretending not to hear, I left the kitchen.

Quincy waited just beyond the front door, shades on, hair pulled back in a ponytail. The banister supported her weight, allowing her to take slow, deliberate sips from a light blue coffee cup. She wore a white ruffled dress tightly cinched with a black belt, causing her stomach to jut out a little.

Her eyes took me in through tinted glass. She sighed.

"Let's meet them outside," she said. "I need some air."

I watched her pull it together on the stairs, dropping her shoulders enough so she could greet the other tenants on the ground floor with a modicum of composure. Once we were outside though, her posture dissipated and she sat down heavily on the front steps.

I pulled out a cigarette and she made a noise signaling she wanted one. I passed it over and lit it for her. She took a few puffs and nodded.

"What'd you guys drink?" I asked. "Beer? Liquor?"

She waved the cigarette around. "An assortment."

"Where?"

"Gilbert's."

"Dive."

"Totally. Seemed appropriate, after the day she had."

"He was worried," I said, not knowing why I was bringing Tim into it, or why I cared.

She sighed. "He's good at that."

A couple of girls came out dressed in bright colors and gabbing away. I recognized one of them from poker last night. There was a bubbly, knowingly artificial quality to their speech. They smoothly avoided us without pausing conversation, sunlight dappling hair and skin as they joined the steady trickle of students headed toward the center of campus.

"She was wild, Neil. Like there was something chasing after her she needed to get away from. She'd drink, argue, stay up 'til dawn like it was all new and she was doing it for the first time."

She forced herself to standing and slung a heavy arm about my shoulders. I grinned like it was a joke but stiffened to better support her. A small part of me was acutely aware of how unprecedented this all was, and I didn't want to mess up.

"Tim got so freaked by what happened. There was no warning, just a cloud that came over her one day and sucked the joy right out. And I get it, I do. But sometimes it's like that's all he sees, her lying in a dark bedroom with the blinds closed, when all Em wants is to get back to that place where she was free."

I tried to reconcile the girl who, though stone drunk, had been considerate enough to give a stranger sleeping on her couch a blanket with the girl Quincy described. I could see it intellectually, like the role of wild child was one she might have played in a past life, but couldn't really accept it.

Quincy handed me the end of her cigarette, the filter rimmed with lipstick. I took a puff and tossed it into the broken clay pot beside the steps that functioned as a makeshift receptacle.

"I know she's not the same," she said. "I know I should walk on eggshells around my best friend. But it's nice to pretend sometimes."

She'd botched her lipstick. I found some tissue paper in my pocket and swabbed away the excess at the corner of her mouth.

"Why aren't we walking?" she asked, looking at me with those strange blue contact lens eyes, shells behind which she evaluated like a mouse peeking from a hayloft.

"No reason."

But we stayed until they came out a few minutes later, Emily a few steps ahead counting cracks in the pavement, Tim texting on his phone. His hair was well shaped and glistened with product. I wondered if he spent a long time preparing it.

I knew what it was to flounder in the service of a loved one. To know you were doing the right thing even as every instinct for self-preservation claimed otherwise. I'd witnessed my father do it through most of my life. Far from discouraging or depressing me, I felt bolstered by the realization. Like a newborn dropped into a tub of water and finding himself able to paddle forward, the rhythms of this world were known to me.

I handed in the check that afternoon.

* * *

The first week passed, then most of a second. With a little distance, the urgency to do something about the situation at home waned. I quickly found myself deluged by schoolwork, staying up nights memorizing snippets of Elizabethan history and retaining odd facts like the Parisian nobility version of hot chocolate was actually melted bars of chocolate. Restlessness drove me forward, through movement classes in unfortunately tight tights and singing lessons where I was told I had a strong voice (though I couldn't bear listening to recordings of myself to decide whether this was truly so). I applied myself with an intensity I didn't think I possessed, spurred on by a sense of lost time and an acute awareness of what my attendance had cost.

When I had dinner at Auntie's home I took care to keep the conversation light, purposefully steering the conversation away from the pill bottles I'd found. She was only too happy to oblige. Feet up on a chair in the back deck, bourbon in her glass, and the face she knew like her own sharing the crickets' songs in the darkness, she wanted for little.

I hung out with Tim during smoke breaks. The four of us even got together for drinks a few times. But the intimacy of that first day did not expand beyond it. We were all so busy trying to adjust to the program that there was little opportunity for those confidences which hew us to new people. At times the language Tim used with Emily and Emily used with Quincy became the shorthand of old friends, oblique references to events I hadn't shared and people I hadn't met. While I felt every inch the interloper during those moments, I tried to take heart in what I'd accomplished so far. Somehow I'd managed to become friendly with them, and even if it hadn't extended quite to the level of friends, perhaps next time, with others, it would.

At home none of this mattered. Home was a pocket of stale air along the rushing current of time, in its midst yet unaffected. A closet handle would break off or the DVD player would skip and things would just continue on without. I didn't bring them up because it was like picking up a single item of clothing off the floor of Mom's closet: one would lead to another, then another, until the size of the chore made you want to crawl out of your skin. At any rate my father was occupied. When I left for school mornings he was on the phone haranguing nurses, or on the Internet researching alternative treatments and side effects of medications. I don't know how he was handling his teaching workload; I feared he'd stopped caring. The one ritual we maintained was sitting down for dinner around eight o'clock every night, working through simple dishes in silence, or worse, forced small talk. A few hours later he'd gather some things and creep out of the house. I knew where he went, of course. The nights were growing cooler. Sleeping in a warm bed would have felt as if he were lying on his wife's restrained body.

Years of shit had collected around us. It was all we could do to keep our heads above it. My dreams grew indistinct, shapes of emotions and unseen presences whose aftereffects bled over into my waking life.

It was hard to believe things would ever change.

* * *

Gary's gaze swept over the class, evaluating micro-expressions and minute crackles of discord. His face was slack yet his eyes caromed between students like a composer witnessing the birth of notes for a new symphony. During these moments he looked every inch the madman Tim thought him to be. But the dread that blossomed in my stomach when his gaze passed through me, a beam of light peering into what lay in shadow, claimed otherwise.

He called on Emily. We watched her remove a gray knitted cardigan and drape it over the chair back. Exposed in a worn Rolling Stones T-shirt and jeans, she stepped out onto the stage.

After making her lie down on a cot with her back to us, Gary leaned in and whispered a few words. He brought two hands to his gut and cupped it lovingly; she did the same. He showed her how to breathe, slow and deliberate. When she'd fallen into a rhythm he stepped away, went over to the spotlight, and flicked it on. There were a few tings and then Emily was blasted with white light—an apparition caught between worlds.

He noticed the way I was watching her and motioned me forward. I came down from the third tier of seating, face feeling warm.

"*Nosce te ipsum*," he muttered, a tired balm offered to all wary participants in his exercises. Know thyself.

Gary positioned me so I was spooning Emily on the bed. My arm was draped across her chest, rising and falling with her breathing. Her shirt was thin and I could feel the heat coming off her back.

"She's your wife and she's pregnant," Gary said. "You haven't got money for a hospital so this will have to do." There was no teasing in his voice, no set-up for a punch line only he knew. The private space before an improvisation began was sacrosanct.

"She's close. Can you feel it?"

I nodded automatically. The light was almost blinding. Shapes danced at the periphery.

"Show him," he said to Emily.

She paused in her breathing, took my hand, and brought it to her belly.

I closed my eyes and Gary fell away, the class's presence fell away, there was only the hard flesh of her stomach, slowly expanding and receding. Her hand was over mine and there was such heat coming from her stomach, our heat, a combination of the two.

Gary stepped away.

Her heart was pounding. It made our hands tremble. I pressed her tighter to me, willing calm to enfold and surround us. Small noises came from her throat. I knew that the past weeks had been difficult for her, that she'd done everything she could to maintain but it couldn't quell the emptiness inside, the knowledge (laughing, pointless) that you were one way and mimicking those of others only made the distance grow.

I exhaled onto her neck. Light made the little hairs on its surface glow. She slipped her fingers through mine and squeezed.

Three hard slams shook the door. Emily started to say something and I made a dissenting noise. I rolled off the bed. Going around the foot of it toward the door, I signaled for her to stay where she was. Her eyes followed me, gray flecks of stone catching noonday sun.

The door's window was covered with a square of cardboard from the outside. Two more slams, harder this time.

I clasped the doorknob with both hands. "Who is it?" I asked, voice reverberating in my ears.

I pressed my ear to the door, slowing my breath enough to make out sounds on the other end. There was only a slight rustling like shuffled papers.

Emily gasped. I saw her folded into herself, fingers digging into the flesh of her belly. She looked up and nodded: very soon.

And then I heard something on the other side of the door that caused a profound feeling of unreality to sweep over and temporarily paralyze me: giggling. Several voices together, low but just loud enough for me to hear. Wanting me to know how excited they were.

Emily attempted to get up onto her arms.

"Don't move," I whispered harshly and the doorknob began slipping out of my hands. I tightened belatedly but it was no use, there were too many of them on the other side. I could see the doorknob moving through my hand, abrading the flesh. The rustling grew louder; it was the sound of their clothes rubbing together, blindly seeking entry.

"Don't move!" I shouted and the doorknob stilled.

My hands dropped to my sides. I stared at the gleaming doorknob with a strange sense of déjà vu, as if I'd been preparing for this in dreamscapes my entire life. Reality felt flimsy, irrelevant in the face of the warning bitter taste on my tongue.

The door flew open and there they stood, lolling mouths and open sores, bleeding scalps caught in the spotlight's glare and the smell, always the smell of sweat dried to a paste and sweated over again. One of the patients reached forward and rather than pulling away, I allowed his bony fingers to touch my shirt and gather it in his hand. I felt, if only for a moment, my mother's revulsion at these walking dead. Then I barreled forward into the interloper's chest, scattering others, breathing through my mouth to keep the stench at bay. We fell out of the entryway into the hall. He made an aborted noise in his throat as we hit the far wall. His legs gave out. I fell on top of him. Shapes at the periphery began composing themselves but I ignored this. My hands went for his neck. Someone shouted a warning but it was a distant, radio hiss. My victim's eyes were frantic, out of focus. I felt tendons beneath skin and squeezed.

A massive arm wrapped about my chest and pulled back. I lifted off the ground, hands losing their purchase, and went down like a ragdoll. Gary's arm hair was curly and gray.

"It's over," he said and still I struggled, raw electrical impulses making my legs twitch, fingers stretched out to crush the ringleader's windpipe. "Say it back to me."

I made a frantic last effort to free myself and went slack. Objects in the hallway were looking depressingly clear. "It's over."

Jeremy Park, a Korean student with protruding ears and short black hair, lay crumpled against the far wall, massaging his throat. His eyes tracked my every movement.

"You saw what he did," he said to Gary. The hoarseness of his voice made my stomach lurch. His eyes flicked to the students who were exiting the classroom and surveying the damage. "They all saw."

Gary let me go and began ushering students back inside. I sat on the floor, trying to process events that were occurring too quickly.

"It wasn't him," I said, trying to reconcile Jeremy with the thing I'd seen in the doorway.

Jeremy took his hand off his neck and I saw ugly red welts rising to the surface of his pale skin. I would never be able to escape those marks, I knew that right away. They would fade in time but I'd never be able to not see them.

Gary finished with the last onlookers and closed the classroom door. The pits of his shirt were soaked through. His eyes constantly darted up and down the hallway for witnesses but it stood empty.

"You saw," Jeremy said again.

"I thought you were someone else," I said.

"Up, both of you," Gary said.

I moved to help Jeremy up and he recoiled. Once we were standing the distance remained.

"Good work," Gary said to him.

Jeremy frowned like it was a trick. His mouth opened, then closed. His skinny body trembled.

"Jeremy, can you go in first? I'd like to speak to Neil for a minute."

"What?" he asked, and broke out coughing. When he'd regained control, he said, "He...attacked me..."

"I told him to," Gary said, scratching the back of his head. He wore faded brown cowboy boots. The heel of one was attached to the body with masking tape. "If he went too far, I'm to blame. But I wouldn't have asked him if I didn't think you could handle it."

Jeremy wiped his nose. His eyes went from Gary to me and back again, like he couldn't quite determine who was lying.

"What do you want to do, son?" Gary asked, bestowing him with a rare, wintry smile.

Jeremy's eyes went to the floor. He took a step toward the classroom. Another. Gary opened the door for him.

"I'm not going up with him again," Jeremy said.

"All right," Gary said.

Once the door had closed I made to sit back down.

Gary reached out with a speed belying his body and took my elbow. "Stay up," he said. "Keep moving and breathing. Can you do that?"

I nodded. My chest ached. His eyes roved my face but the unnerving intensity was gone.

"What happened?"

I shook my head. "I don't…"

"Don't try that." His cheeks were rosy, like he'd been out for a brisk walk instead of aborting an attack.

"The door opened and…" I shook my head, "I didn't see Jeremy."

"What did you see?"

I kept shaking my head. "What did I do?"

"What did you see, Neil?"

I put a hand over my mouth. "A monster," I said.

He waited for me to elaborate. When I couldn't he went over to the door and pried the cardboard loose from the window. I saw my classmates through the glass, many standing up and engaged in furious conversation. Joining them felt as improbable as joining the actors projected onto the pockmarked screen of the Palisades theater, the place where I'd gotten the moronic idea to study acting to begin with.

"Listen to me," he said, drawing my gaze to him. "You got carried away by the scene. It happens. You don't say anything else about it. Understand?"

I nodded, wanting to tell him that I should leave. That it was dangerous for the others.

"I'll have Tim bring your things to the next class. Go on, take a walk." He checked the hallway again and I glimpsed the worry he'd managed to hide.

I walked off, hands clasped tightly in front of me. My ears were ringing, ghostly echoes of voices, whether from dreams or waking I couldn't tell.

"Neil?"

I turned around, walking backwards.

"Whatever it is...find a way of dealing with it. This can't happen again."

* * *

I sat at the base of a tree near the fire exit, head tilted to my shoulder with a cell phone in between. A cigarette in my left hand slowly burned down to the filter.

"Do you still have the bottle?" I asked.

Momentary quiet as the line almost cut out. "Yes."

"Can you bring it this afternoon? I can't go back home. I can't get the others."

"One is all they'll need."

Leaves shook overhead. I lifted my head to a chiaroscuro of light and shadow. A leaf helicoptered past. One of the tree's enormous roots was pressing up against my thigh.

"I can't put it off any longer," I said.

"I wasn't asking, *janu*. Three o'clock?"

The cigarette's heat was beginning to singe my finger. "Three o'clock."

I hung up and crushed the smoke out. Slipped the phone into my pocket. I got up to re-enter Carruthers Hall and saw Emily watching me not ten feet away.

She neared. Her face was inscrutable. The lower half of her T-shirt was wrinkled from our hands.

She put her arms around me. Hugging me.

"Thank you," she said, bending like a reed in a gale.

6

Auntie drove smoothly and fast. Inside the vacuum of the Jaguar's cabin I watched the campus give way to inner city, tenements and billboards clustered thickly along its border like white blood cells repelling an intruder. Bags of trash were stacked on the curb. I glimpsed Styrofoam packaging and fast food wrappers through tears where animals had been at work. A woman hung laundry on her windowsill. A man in a grimy camouflage jacket slept on a park bench, lined face split apart in a smile of perfect contentment. Auntie didn't comment on any of this, just shifted gears when necessary and outpaced traffic. Tinted windows leached the world of its color.

In my lap was the pill bottle I'd given her. A few of the pills within had broken, coating the insides with a fine dust. I fought the urge to read the labels again and make absolutely sure.

"I'll come in with you," Auntie said. A bright yellow scarf was wrapped around her neck, offsetting the gray streaks in her hair. "Shouldn't take long. Just tell the woman from the Public Trustee's office what you found."

We pulled into a strip mall near the highway on-ramp, a massive slab of concrete lifting and turning in midair to join the thick flow of vehicles exiting the city. The air was gray from their combined exhaust. Auntie parked in front of an office between a fried chicken joint and a bail bondsman. The sign above the door read simply "Professional Services."

"What did I find?" I asked, picking the bottle up. "Some bottles? Okay. Maybe there are others. Maybe he's been giving her other pills and these are just, I don't know, backups..." I broke off.

Auntie was looking at me in a way that made the skin around her eyes crinkle. I felt like a fool.

"If you want to cancel, just say the word," she said, turning the engine off. "I know a place close by that has the best *dosas* in town, crisp and light." She brought three fingers to her lips and kissed them. "I'm getting hungry just thinking about it."

I looked through the front window of the office for clues but they were sparse. Middle-aged people sitting at desks. Rickety cubicle dividers. Bars of fluorescent light attached to the ceiling. Just a normal-looking office.

"There's no going back, is there?" I asked.

The engine ticked over. A man came out of the restaurant carrying a plastic bag of food. He tied it to the handlebar of his bike and set off, dreadlocks shaking as he bounced over cracks and pebbles.

"Back to what?" Auntie asked. A vein pulsed at the side of her forehead. "You know what's waiting for you back home," she said.

"Is that anything to hold onto?" She sighed when I didn't answer. "I held my tongue watching *Dee Dee* and your father raise you. It wasn't my place. But they should have built you up, prepared you, so every time you went out it would be with head held high, instead of..." She let the thought hang there. "They never really saw you, Niladri. Not for what you truly are."

I smiled weakly. "What's that?"

She undid her seatbelt. Reached over and depressed the clasp for mine. It zipped up into its berth above my shoulder.

"You're the one who never asks for anything. Who looks around at the world like you know it and it's good. Who cares about others, too much."

She pecked my cheek. She had trouble with physical contact and I knew it cost her to do it.

"You're what I feel when I think of family," she said. "I'll always be there for you. But if you don't get out from under this, it will drag you under."

* * *

By the time we exited the building the last of the day's light was escaping like a stagecoach pursued by bandits. I stopped on the sidewalk and leaned my head back against the wall as Auntie looked on. I took large gulps of air, tasting bitter exhaust on my tongue, watching the street go from diffused orange to violet, trying to piece together what I'd said.

"You did well," Auntie began.

I put a hand up, stopping her. I loved her, but if she'd taken a step toward me I'd have pushed her away.

It had begun civilly enough, introductions all around, coffee.

A mousy woman wearing bifocals had placed a voice recorder on the table. I'd started out cognizant of the limits of what I'd say: The pills. The dates. No conclusions. Except that somewhere between the coffee and the pitying looks of encouragement a dam had broken. Poison, years of it, had spewn out. At one point Auntie had squeezed my thigh to get me to lower my voice.

A black SUV with silver accents pulled into the lot, xenon lights pinning me where I stood. I squinted, trying to make out the driver. The car crept into one of the spaces but the lights stayed on.

Auntie snapped her fingers in the driver's line of sight.

The engine revved and went still. The lights blinked off and I made out a black kid barely tall enough to peer over the dashboard. A crooked doo-rag on his head. He was attempting to scowl at us.

Auntie didn't laugh. She didn't turn to me and offer a wink. Her arm lowered but she kept staring at the kid, making him afraid to get out of the vehicle.

It wasn't enough that he'd doused the lights. It didn't matter that he was barely a teenager who didn't know any better. He'd made a mistake and he would pay and that was all.

The kid hit the locks and moved away from the driver's side window. Auntie moved forward and rapped on it.

"Leave it," I said.

"Didn't you see him?" she asked the kid, who looked plainly frightened. "Didn't you see him standing there?"

"I don't—"

"You don't what?" she asked. "You didn't think anything would happen?"

She put her forehead on the driver's side window. The kid saw those hard, exhilarated eyes. He pulled his knees up to his chest and wrapped his arms around them. He was maybe twelve.

"What if I called the police? Told them a boy's riding around in a stolen car?"

She hit the window with the base of her hand. The kid cried out.

"Sonia," I said, calling her by her name.

She looked over at me.

"Show me that restaurant. The *dosas*."

"You want to?"

I nodded. "Please."

* * *

My phone rang as we were finishing dinner. Tabla drums played from hidden speakers, papering over the silence Auntie had lapsed into ever since the altercation. I took it out to see who was calling: Unknown.

"Take it here, it's fine," Auntie said, swirling a piece of *dosa* crepe in a pool of yogurt sauce. Specks of floating cilantro broke apart and formed almost discernible shapes.

I raised the phone to my ear.

"Neil?"

"Quincy?"

Auntie's eyes were glassy. Some of the makeup on her forehead had been left behind on the SUV's window, betraying faint discolorations in the skin.

"Thank God you picked up."

"What's wrong?"

I heard whispering on the other end. Frantic negating noises. "Is that Emily?" I asked.

Auntie registered my tone and signaled a waiter for the check.

"They had a fight," Quincy said. "Tim ran out a mess, drunk. I don't know where, I don't know the city."

"Is she okay?"

She didn't answer.

"Quincy."

"Will you try to find him? You're from here."

"How's Emily?"

Sounds of moving on the other end. Then, in a lower voice, "Neil, I think...he may have hit her."

*   *   *

The 3 Points district a few blocks south of campus rose up in the windshield, students wandering amidst the neon come-ons of bars, pizza shops, and hookah lounges. A girl stumbled and thrust an arm out for a guy who was already several steps ahead. She hobbled to catch up, passing empties lining the curb, a busker strumming a guitar, a cut-rate Mardi Gras.

"Just let me off," I said, clutching the phone like a talisman.

"I can stay if you need help,"

"No."

She pulled over and I got out. The smell of incense wafted out of an open window. I briefly scanned the gaudier bar signs, along with the miniature throngs waiting to get in at each, before crossing the street to Gilbert's. Its entrance was off the main strip, in an alley facing a brick wall and several defunct newspaper dispensers. There was no one outside. I remembered how Tim had clucked and shaken his head at passersby when I'd shown him the place, suckers who couldn't see what was right in front of them.

Inside, a jukebox played Johnny Cash records. He and Merle

Haggard and Waylon Jennings were the only three artists available. There was a long wood bar where professors drank and read next to students knowing better than to announce themselves. A pressed tin ceiling and naked brick walls illuminated by soft, hanging light bulbs. The hiss of the water spritzer as Vily, the taciturn Filipino bartender, made himself a drink. He adjusted his denim vest before taking the first sip.

Tim wasn't there.

I ordered a shot of whiskey and drank it quickly, hoping for clarity. No such luck. I just kept hearing Quincy say "I think he may have hit her," and picturing Em's face bruised, her lip split open. I don't know why I'd agreed to look for him, except to maybe hit him for doing that to a girl who had so little protection to begin with. You touched her and felt it wasn't quite enough but that was what hooked you. I hadn't hit anyone since I was a little kid, but if I thought about it long enough, maybe I still could.

I left a nice tip and exited the bar. On the strip a woman who may have been a tranny strolled by wearing what looked like a bear-skin coat. A telephone line cut across the street, two sneakers hanging down, shaking with the rhythms of ground level.

A few days after my twentieth birthday Mom disappeared. This was a few months after she'd gone through her first committal and in retrospect, the pressure to recover must have been tremendous. True to form she never broached it, dutifully carrying out all the tasks that were expected of her, telling me she loved me more often than necessary, denying the fear until it took over. Afternoon turned to evening and late night without her returning, or even calling to let us know she was okay. Dad tried everyone we knew without luck. On the second day he informed the police and we began searching.

Thinking like her allowed me to find her, putting myself so

completely in her shoes that the world began to reconstitute itself in line with her perceptions. What my father and the police focused on were standard needs: hotels in the area, tracing ATM withdrawals. What occurred to me was that she wouldn't be able to sleep, not without the daily activities that kept the voices at bay or the family she still cared about enough to not want to disappoint. At three o'clock in the morning everything in town was closed except for a small café and bakery on Stuart Street, approximately half a mile east of the house next to Raleigh College's training hospital. Sure enough there she sat, dipping a cookie into a cup of hot chocolate, four days gone, blinking up at Dad and me like she recognized but couldn't quite place us.

If Tim wasn't at the bar then he wasn't winding down. He wasn't nursing a drink, despising himself for what he'd done and feeling out a way to mend it. He'd left their apartment and come here, attracted to the noise, the babble of voices. But he hadn't come for comfort.

He'd come to hate. Their blank, healthy faces. Their stupid plans. Their fat tits and expansive gestures that said they'd never felt the breathlessness of TOO MUCH TOO VERY MUCH rising up like a breaker, obliterating consciousness, leaving you shaken and trying to pick up the pieces afterwards. Once he'd had their ignorance, but that was over with. Emily had stolen it from him.

I walked down the street, seeing those who crossed my path as he did. My stomach felt tight. Two blocks down the bars thinned out. Square of rubble from a construction project that had stalled, bricks, strips of plywood.

A single red light by an unmarked doorway. Etched onto the sidewalk, a Siren with heaving breasts in the midst of an ocean, calling ships to dash themselves on the rocks surrounding her.

Inside, the walls were painted black and covered with glowing graffiti, meaningless phrases like "Sex Pot" and "Temptation." A disco ball scattered light on the faces of tired girls in bikinis serving drinks from within a giant oval bar. They tottered on heels and made conversation with men sitting on stools watching them with the intensity of lions staring out of a zoo cage. Dance music poured out of broken speakers, squeals and bass beats that made the floor shake.

One of the girls laughed shrilly and retrieved a proffered bill without touching the man's fingers. He leaned over and said something to a friend in a beige hunter's jacket, who nodded slowly. His hooded eyes were locked on her torso, emaciated to the point where her rib cage was visible. The song ended and there was a pocket of silence during which I scanned the faces of other patrons. Tim wasn't among them.

A small section at the back of the bar was lifted up. Girls went in, girls went out toward a cordoned-off section manned by a bouncer, a wiry guido in velvet blazer and wingtips who paired them with waiting men and raised the rope so they could enter. A black stripper wearing stars-and-stripes panties and pasties was left without. Guido pulled her off to the side. He took out a baggie of coke and dipped the end of a gold cross he had around his neck for a toot. He gave one to her. It made her eyes water.

The music started up again. I was maybe six feet away from the ropes. It was all mirrors, stalls, and black light inside.

Every time the stripper wiped her eyes Guido gave her a look a hair's-breadth away from a sneer, never stopping his rapid patter about the benefits of a multi-core processor and discrete graphics, discrete not integrated, if it wasn't discrete it would just suck speed from your laptop and then where would you be? She nodded, eyes locked on the baggie. Her bare legs were riddled with goose bumps.

"Know what you can do with a discrete graphics card?" he asked, doing another bump. "Well, you wouldn't know, we're talking about computers, you know those magic machines that go on the Internet, but seriously do you know?"

I was at the ropes. The stall doors within had a gap at the bottom. I could make out women's legs stepping in half-hearted time to the beat.

The bouncer's back was mostly to me but I was in full view of the stripper. He scooped up more coke but didn't hold it out to her. She leaned in, head dropping to his chest, and snorted it. It was an ugly, unrestrained sound, like hacking a loogie.

"You can game on it. Gotta have a ton of memory and a solid-state drive, though. I'm not shelling out for a rig just to play on low settings." He made to scoop up some more, noticed her tracking eyes, and chuckled.

"You a gamer? Do you game a lot?"

The stripper's eyes betrayed a flash of irritation. "No."

"Stop crowding me, what's the matter with you?"

I stepped over the ropes.

The stripper stared right at me. Just for a second, then back to Guido. She smiled an old woman's smile and pulled back from him a little.

"Whoops," she said, pastie strings shaking.

The first stall was locked, rough guttural sounds. The floor was sticky. The second stall was partway open, a man in a trucker hat with his legs spread apart as a stripper ground down on his crotch. Third stall locked. Fourth stall locked and I paused, because I could hear through it a girl singing low in Russian, a crutch to distract herself from what she was doing. Then I heard a man sigh and knew it was Tim.

I knocked on the door.

"Go away," he said.

Rage narrowed my vision down to the latch holding the door in place. I lifted a leg and kicked it, making the entire row of stalls rock back on its foundations. The girl screamed. Assorted exclamations and movements further down. I kicked again. The lock splintered and the door flew inwards, hitting an unformed brunette teen in the ass.

Tim sat there, rubbing a flaccid cock through his pants with an aggrieved expression on his face. He didn't seem to register what had happened.

The girl, who looked all of sixteen, started gibbering in Russian. The lipstick around her mouth was smeared.

Tim looked up at me, squinting to focus. "Hey, what time is it?"

The girl pushed me out of the way and ran out into the corridor shouting for Lino. Her pipe cleaner arms flailed about like Olive Oyl in a Popeye cartoon.

I hauled him to his feet without looking at him. I was afraid of what I'd do if I did.

"I don't," he began, trailed off. "I tried..."

"Quiet." Arm around his shoulder, leading him out to the corridor. He smelled of her skin cream.

The music stopped. Overhead lights sparked on.

Loud voices came from the entrance and then Guido stood blocking it, the Russian girl peeking from behind one of his sloped shoulders. We stopped a few feet away. Tim's head rocked forward and back like a pendulum.

"What the fuck is this?" he asked, looking from me to Tim and back. "We had to cut a song."

"Oh noooo," Tim muttered.

I shook him and he giggled. His lower lip glistened with spit.

Guido/Lino fastened the center button of his blazer. In his mind he was finally playing out a scene from The Godfather in waking life. "Get Reggie," he said to the Russian girl. "Tell him to block off the back."

She went off. There was no room for us to get past him. Onlookers clustered by the ropes watching with dull, expectant expressions.

Guido stepped closer, pencil-thin goatee visible beneath the harsh lights. His eyes were jittery, undermining the calm menace he sought. "Stopping a song's three hundred dollars. Cash, not campus credits or whatever else you faggots use."

Tim laughed. Really laughed. And Guido laughed too, stealing the last bit of air from the room. "Funny, huh?" he said, holding his palms out, an age-old bit of misdirection while his accomplice snuck around back.

BACK. He said to tell Reggie to block the BACK.

Guido stilled. My skin felt stretched too tight. The lights went off. The music started up again and he lunged for us. I pulled us back, missing his long sculpted fingernails by inches. Tim's breath caught in his throat. I spun us around and dashed blindly toward the back of the room—just black wall.

"Stop!" Guido shouted.

Nothing but black wall, Tim's legs spasming trying to connect brain to muscle, we were going to slam into the wall, crumple against the wall, and then I saw a long steel emergency exit bar painted black like the rest and turned my shoulder in. It opened and we tumbled out into a side street, cool air on my face.

The door slammed shut behind us.

Tim pushed me away, frantically seeking the right direction. I ran one way and he followed, our shadows playing tag with overflowing trash bins and back entrances to buildings clogged with wet newspaper and flyers. Distantly I heard the door reopen and there was only cold fire in my lungs and weak pools of light from streetlamps until we shot out into the relative safety of the main stretch, Collingwood Street. Students were milling about, gathering energy for the trek back to dorms. We went up close to them and bent over, sucking in air and swallowing back the metallic taste in our mouths.

Tim put a hand on my shoulder. I knocked it away.

"Neil, please..."

I glanced back toward the side street, certain I'd see Guido there. Nothing. My legs trembled on the verge of collapse. A cop car cruised slowly past, somehow more sinister with its flashers off.

Tim broke out coughing. A few students backed away.

"Find your own way back," I said, straightening up. "Don't follow me, don't even..." I took off walking.

Very quietly, he said, "I don't know."

"What?" I shouted, whirling. He stood hunched over, too weak to raise himself. "What don't you know?" Hating how close the tears were.

Tim's mouth was turned downwards, pleading. Sweat matted his hair.

A car horn honked twice behind us. Tim's gaze went there first. When I turned and saw Auntie's Jaguar what I felt was resentment.

We piled into the backseat. Auntie pulled away from the curb and described a wide U-turn back toward campus. Tim was wedged into a corner, absently picking at the raised leather stitching covering the inside of the door. Sweat dripped down the sides of his face.

When we got closer I leaned into the gap between the front seats and pointed out Miller House. She made a left onto Lower University Avenue and a right onto Stuart. We passed the Computer Sciences building where my father taught, jagged glass edges making it resemble a giant clump of rock sugar. Heat from the air vents caressed my face.

Auntie assessed Tim in the rearview mirror. Her face was still with disdain. She took a little packet of Kleenex out of the glove compartment and tossed it back to him. He worked to tear the plastic wrapper and used a few to wipe his face.

"You can let me off anywhere," he said.

Auntie made a left onto Barrie and sped up, Miller House rising in the left-hand corner of the windshield. We ran parallel to a cycle path. Bugs flicked off little yellow lights buried along its borders. The greenhouse with its contained riot of flowers, creeping vines on fences, and she was turning into the long driveway.

Tim made a protesting noise in his throat but it died away. His fight was gone.

Auntie stopped in front of the little path leading up to the front steps. She flicked a switch and the doors unlocked.

"Wait," Tim said. He was staring at the stained glass windows on the second floor. "Just for a minute."

A crow alighted on the front porch banister, easily balancing its weight on thin wood. It turned its head and regarded the car.

"You don't know her," Tim said. His voice was clotted with phlegm. "She can be cruel."

"Don't," I said.

"She laughs at me. When I try to keep her from going out, doing the things that brought on the breakdown. Everyone thought I'd cut out but I didn't, I stayed, changed my life for her but she can't even..." He shook his head.

"What do you want me to say, Tim?"

He smiled bitterly. "I was the one who found her. Squatting in a shit-hole with guys who'd make your skin crawl. Bruises all over her body. No memory of a month." He opened the side door. Cool air trickled into the cabin. "She's the lucky one. She doesn't remember."

Auntie spoke. "Sometimes it's the best thing, walking away. The love may tell you otherwise but it's a lying voice. Keep doing what you're doing and it will turn to poison."

She adjusted the rearview mirror. Tim was frozen, staring back. "It already has. Hasn't it."

He got out and headed toward the house.

I leaned in and squeezed her arm. "You waited for me."

Her hand clasped mine. "Don't do anything," she whispered. "He'll fall apart on his own."

I tried pulling away and her grip tightened. "Listen to what I'm telling you."

* * *

Quincy sat up with Emily in the ground floor kitchen. Red-check-ered wallpaper and a mess of pots and pans in the sink. Quincy got up from the dining table when she saw Tim, openly relieved that he was all right. She didn't move toward him, however, stilled by the woman with the square of gauze taped to her chin, shrunken into a chair like she wanted to disappear.

Tim stared at Emily. He wiped his face.

"Apologize," Quincy said.

He nodded like yes, that's exactly what he should do. But he didn't.

Emily lifted her eyes to me. I was mostly hidden behind Tim in the kitchen entryway but she found me. For a moment everything grew quiet inside. She gave me a crooked smile. Her lower lip was bluish and swollen. Then the smile disappeared and she got up.

Tim frowned and looked down at the floor as she neared. Tension built like standing beneath power lines.

He whispered something to her very quietly.

Her left hand twitched at her side. She grasped it tightly with her right.

He leaned in toward her, whether on purpose or simply by instinct I couldn't say. She pulled her head back.

"I don't know who you are," she whispered.

"You know me."

"I remember this boy. Sweet and out of place. Stuttering a little the first time he asked me out." Tears spilled down her cheeks. "I miss him."

Tim's eyes shone with a fury that could no longer be denied. He did not raise his eyes to Emily because she would see that he missed that boy too, had not been ready to give him up. Losing your innocence came part and parcel with caring for someone ill. No matter the outcome you could never return to a time when you assumed things would turn out well. You'd peeked around the curtain, glimpsed the hideous frailty of the human condition, and it changed you forever. And you could never really forgive the one responsible.

When it was clear he wasn't going to answer, Emily maneuvered past him, up the stairs, gone. A door slammed a few moments later. Only then did Tim follow her up.

"Would you like some tea?" Quincy asked me.

"What?"

Quincy had a red sailor girl's dress on. Her hair was prettily arranged behind a headband. She looked ready for a cocktail party.

She nodded at the teakettle next to the sink. When I glanced at the stairs she said, "It's over for tonight."

I sat down at the table. She poured a cup, placed a tea bag inside, and brought it over. I watched tendrils of pale orange bleed out into the water.

"What do you get out of this?" I asked.

She gnawed her lip. "Oh," she said, sitting down opposite me. She took my cup and had a sip.

I rubbed my hands. I felt cold all of a sudden.

"You can sleep on my couch, if you want."

"Why? So I can watch them come out tomorrow like Ozzie and Harriet?" I folded my arms on the table and rested my head upon it.

"How does it feel?" she asked.

"Mm?"

"To have all the answers."

"Fantastic."

She drank some more of the tea. The kitchen clock ticked softly. The chair scraped as she got up.

"It's closer up the stairs than back home," she said, placing a hand on my back. "You didn't have to look for him."

Her apartment was cluttered yet sterile, like a stage set. Framed photographs of Jean Harlow and Marlene Dietrich on the walls. Empty cans of Tab and pastel-colored candies in glass bowls. The couch was off-white and only one of the cushions held a permanent crease from where she routinely sat. The kitchen had every appliance and utensil you could conceive of, but the refrigerator held only takeout containers and condiments. I could imagine a guy she'd hooked up with (Quincy was developing a reputation for being promiscuous) taking in these details and meshing them with the breathy whisper she used when describing naughty acts, the body that constantly adjusted itself to catch flattering angles. She was a master when it came to discussing inconsequentials and unyielding, through a tilt of the head or check of her phone, to anything beyond that. Even the floor was carpeted so she could walk between rooms with the lightness she so desperately craved.

In many ways we were still playing catch-up. What had happened between us on the first day of classes had so thoroughly pierced our respective facades that any attempt at regressing to it felt contrived. Yet neither of us was particularly smooth without it. I flipped through gossip magazines in the living room while she brushed her teeth. When that felt strange I joined her in the bathroom. She gave me her toothbrush to use when she was done. I didn't question it.

While I brushed she used makeup removal pads on her face, tossing them into an overflowing trashcan next to the sink. Her skin was criss-crossed with thousands of tiny lines, like she'd broken apart and someone had painstakingly glued the pieces back together.

The bedroom held pink linens and dolls carefully arranged on the vanity. The windows were open to reveal a dark expanse of sky and a sliver of moon sharp as an insult. We got beneath the covers, both of us still in our clothes.

Her contacts were the last things to go, placed in a little receptacle on the nightstand.

"They don't sleep together," Quincy whispered, turning in so her face was hidden against my upper arm. "Haven't...for a very long time."

"Ssshh. Go to sleep." The material of her dress felt scratchy against my skin. She sighed, and edged in a little closer.

7

Quincy and I went to class the next morning without checking on Tim and Emily. I'd like to believe it was because we were tired of the situation. It was preferable to the alternative, which was that I recognized the value of Auntie's suggestion to let things disintegrate on their own. The thought of a cold pragmatist pulling strings from within was repellent, but my personal likes or dislikes had little to do with it.

Liev, an Israeli student with a commando's build, was blind-folded and placed in a corner of the stage. I stared at the intricate tattoos covering his arms, unable to deflect awareness of the two empty seats normally occupied by Tim and Emily. Quincy sat beside me gripping a white leather handbag. A look from Gary silenced the class.

At first Liev shifted about on the floor. His jeans were pulled up to reveal gray athletic socks above black Doc Martens. But as the minutes wore on he stilled. Long, deliberate breaths made his chest swell and recede. I sat, impotent, thinking all I'd ever done was watch loved ones get carried away by the current without once wading in.

Gary signaled for Quincy to come down. She gave me a quick warning look to not do anything rash and, despite the worry line creasing her brow, went onstage. One of her heels clacked and Liev turned his head at the sound.

Gary motioned for her to remove her shoes. Stocking-clad feet whispered along the floor to where he sat. She leaned in and he whispered instructions. She picked up the props next to his desk, a bucket half-filled with water and a sponge. She moved cautiously toward Liev. The spotlight's glare caught her and made her seem discombobulated—arms, hands, scissoring legs.

Quincy's phone started vibrating from within her purse. I snatched at it without thinking, unzipped and pulled it out. The display read simply "Unknown." Awful thoughts crowded my mind: Emily calling from the hospital. Emily calling from the police station. Worse, not Emily at all but rather a public servant called to the apartment to manage the aftermath.

Quincy got close and Liev froze. "Who's there?" he called out, baritone spiced with an Israeli accent. On his arms were fierce protectors, dragons exhaling fire and soldiers carrying spears, but they were no good to him from behind a blindfold.

She dipped the sponge in water and wrung it out a little. Laid the bucket down. One of Liev's legs retracted to his chest. His hands were fists.

"What do you want?" Liev asked, voice losing some of its

strength.

Quincy thrust the sponge over Liev's head and squeezed. Drops fell on his shaved head and dribbled down onto his blindfold. He jerked sideways. "Stop!" Sliding along the wall.

Quincy followed, sponge tracking his head.

I'd found Tim rubbing his cock in a VIP stall and he'd asked me what time it was. A man like that didn't feel the weight of his actions. He could decorate a home, look after his girlfriend, take classes, and all of it was like skating on brittle ice. Because if he didn't feel their weight he was exempt from their consequences. It explained why he could raise a hand to Emily, mar that singular face, and actually resent having to apologize. What would he do if she went rogue again? Would he stop at the face? Or would he go further, doling out the sudden, focused wrath of a wronged child?

Quincy squeezed; the drops became a steady trickle. Though his blindfold was soaked through he didn't remove it. His breaths came fast, and then stopped.

Quincy was leaning over him. One of the straps of her dress had come loose. She was the aggressor in this exercise, but when Liev went quiet it changed. The audience stopped seeing her as Liev did, a malevolent abstract, and saw her as she was: a marionette with a prop.

Liev's fists opened up. His palms lay flat on the ground at his sides. The veins of his arms bulged and his body sprang up toward her.

"Take the blindfold off," Gary said clearly.

Quincy started to step back as Liev collided with her. They stumbled together, then his hand pulled the blindfold off and he blinked, taking her in.

"Good work, both of you," Gary said. He exchanged a look

with Liev. "Was that so bad? Giving up control for a bit?"

"Wouldn't do it again." He rotated a shoulder back, releasing some of the tension.

"I'd take the blindfold any day," Quincy said. "He had the luxury of not seeing what was going on."

Gary nodded, urging her on.

"Of...doing whatever he wanted." There was a note of envy in her voice.

Gary noticed her hanging strap and fixed it. "It's harder sometimes, being an observer. You think the remove grants you the ability to change things, but it rarely does."

I put Quincy's things back on her seat and made for the door.

"Where are you going?" Gary asked.

Quincy watched me, huffing with exertion.

"Bathroom."

I cut east across campus toward Miller House, utilizing the shortcuts through shaded areas I'd discovered when avoiding the gazes of strangers had meant more than taking the simplest route. My shoes squished fallen leaves, shorn branches overhead shaking in mock applause. I surprised a groundskeeper picking up trash with a thin metal stick and placing it in a carrier strapped to his back. The chirps of a few lone birds sounded above me, calling attention to those who had already left for warmer climes.

Cool air whipped at my shirt. I hopped a fence that went around behind the house, fingers crushing vines that leaked clear syrup. Through the front door and up the stairs, fear like a stone in my throat.

The door to their apartment stood ajar.

Inside, the air was thick with dust motes loosed from open drawers, pillaged cabinets, and unzipped luggage lying on the floor like bruised fruit. The coffee table held toiletries, AC adapters, CDs and DVDs shorn of their protective casings.

"Em?" I called out, voice sounding pitifully small to my ears. A faint creak from the bedroom.

I didn't want to go any further. Not without enlisting help. Terrible images flickered past my mind's eye, Em's body broken and unconscious on the floor, a gag in her mouth, the tools Tim had ransacked the apartment for, sharp with serrated edges, resting bloody and sated on the bed.

I turned the doorknob and pushed the bedroom door open.

Emily stood looking out the window, a pale blue nightgown on and nothing else. Her hair hung loose to her shoulders. She turned to me. Her face was puffy from exhaustion.

"He left," she said.

I took her face in my hands and kissed her. She was motionless. I pulled back a little. Her eyes were dark and cautious. She took a piece of the gauze bandage on her chin and peeled it off. An ugly, jagged cut, the flesh around it reddish-purple. I put my lips to it gently.

"Harder," she whispered. I licked it and pressed in.

Her breath came out in a shudder. Her fingers grasped my hair.

* * *

Afterwards we lay on the floor, clothes mostly off, breaths coming in rough unison. Her left arm was flung across my chest, fingers absently playing with the little black hairs beneath my belly button. She wore a large turquoise ring, possibly a loaner from Quincy, and I felt the band on my skin once in a while. Her salt taste was in my mouth.

"I'm waiting for the guilt," she said, staring up at the ceiling. Her torso had broken out in gooseflesh. Tiny red dots were beginning to appear on her breasts from my stubble.

"Come over me," I said.

Her legs went to either side of mine and shifted up a little so our faces were matched. Her hair fell like steady rain, blocking the room from view.

I brought my right hand up between our faces and splayed the fingers. Bent the middle joint of the middle finger, the two halves forming a wide V.

She nuzzled it.

"Broke it. When I was a kid."

She nodded. Our smell, sharp and musky, in the air. "I've got something like that."

She took the hand and placed it on her right knee. There was something hard and rigid beneath the flesh. Gently she made me feel the four bolthole scars at the corners, so old they were almost lost beneath new tissue.

"What does it feel like?" I asked.

"Like someone rubbing at the same patch of skin, over and over."

She dozed. Her pressure felt good on my chest. I wished she were heavier so I could feel it more. I wanted to go about the room collecting evidence of the day, placing strands of hair in zip-lock bags and swabbing at pools of saliva. Instead I hummed a song whose words I couldn't remember and told myself not to forget.

* * *

Mom shuffles down the hospital corridor in bare feet, shrinking away from other patients when they get too close. She doesn't really hear their groans and taunts anymore, but their arms, flaking skin and sharp yellow fingernails—she doesn't want to feel that on her. She continually scratches a low-grade itch but it's clever and keeps shifting about.

Beneath her gown are patches as angry red and glistening with pus as anything found on the bodies of others, but she doesn't know that. The showers are communal so she's stopped taking them. Sometimes it hurts to take the gown off because pus has bonded it to her body.

The bathroom stinks of piss. The tiles are cold on her feet, making her realize she's not wearing shoes. She makes a mental note to go back to the dormitory to get her shoes or at least some socks, bare feet are no way to greet the morning, but she'll have forgotten in a few moments. There are no hard edges in this place, no prods. You slide and slide, once in a while sensing the rate of descent, and then that's gone too.

Men piss in urinals with their drawstring pants fully down, flaccid cocks indiscriminately splashing wall and tiles. Women shit in stalls without doors, born multi-taskers exchanging gossip, picking at scabs on their legs and working nits out of their hair. Mom passes them until she stands in front of the large, rectangular mirror taking up most of the back wall. Her fingers grasp the edges of a basin shaped like a trough. Beside her, patients comb hair and brush teeth.

She stares at her reflection. She does not look away, barely blinks. Once this was impossible but Doctor Thibodeau's talks have been helping. Lecturing her for hours inside of a locked office, a steady, relentless flow, she was no actress, it was just something she'd made up and that was okay, admitting you're weak was okay, admitting you're a fat and disgusting piece of meat is okay, admitting your tits are flabby and your pussy hangs low is perfectly fine but you have to admit it, you can't parade around in denial.

You're no queen, he'd said. You're not special.

She observes her double chin. The men's whiskers along her upper lip.

She sees the lines on her forehead and around her eyes and mouth. She puffs air out her mouth and watches her cheeks jiggle.

She thinks she should clean herself up but can't remember where to start. She wishes she had some makeup but it isn't allowed. Patients aren't allowed to use scissors, and she'd have been mortified to ask a nurse to trim those little hairs. She could wash her face but the steps required to do so stack one atop the other and become a kind of kinesthetic collage: water through fingers through hair, fingers crumpling towels smoothing hair back.

The bathroom empties out. One of the last automatic hand-dryers times out and falls into silence.

She reaches for the faucet, hesitates, pulls back.

She walks quickly out of the bathroom, as if being chased by what she'd seen in the mirror. She's surprised to find the corridor empty of patients. Mornings are the active time, chatting, swallowing pills, playing ping-pong in the games room. She finds out why when she goes back to the dormitory to retrieve her shoes.

It isn't morning. It's night.

* * *

A phone was ringing. Emily stirred and lifted her head off my chest, eyes blurry with sleep. She rubbed at them, evening's gloom not aiding her efforts to focus. For a second I thought it was my cell phone. Listening closer I realized it was hers. She did too, and sleep falling away like chipped ice, she rolled off me and went over to the nightstand to retrieve it.

"Hello?" Voice lowering enough to make it clear whom she thought it might be. A long, warbling car honk came from the traffic along Barrie Street.

"Yeah, I'm home," she said. She sat down on the edge of the bed, making the springs creak. "No, he left. I don't know where." A pause. "I don't want to talk about it right now, Q."

The floor was chilly. I got up and started putting clothes on. No order to it, simply as I found them. I could have used a shower but wasn't about to ask.

"I'll see Gary tomorrow, what's the problem?" she muttered. "Why now?"

She was bent into herself. Tinny sounds emanated from the phone. Shadows entering through the window played across her body like a projector onto a screen.

"Meeting at The Kasbah? That's official."

My belt buckle made a noise when I fastened it. She glanced over at me. I couldn't have been more than a vague outline; mussed hair, fumbling hands, unformed chest.

"Neil's here," she admitted. "Tell him we'll be there in twenty."

We didn't speak on the walk over and barely touched. The air was cool and stung the nostrils. The ground glistened with wetness from a downpour that must have occurred while we'd been sleeping. Later I'd come to understand she was looking for some sort of reassurance from me that this was the beginning as opposed to an error in judgment, but I wasn't schooled in such things. I knew how to react to circumstances, not how to determine them. So when she thrust her hands into the pockets of her gray cardigan and sped up, I maintained the distance, thinking this one goes away don't think about it.

The Kasbah was a hole in the ground at the fringes of the 3 Points district. The ceiling dripped water onto a red carpet that squished beneath our feet. Red lights pulsed like the onset of a migraine. At center was a raised dance floor occupied by a middle-aged man, eyes closed, weaving to Arabic music. A woman with thick eyebrows sat at one of the rickety tables, wiping down cutlery and placing them in a plastic tray. In the back of the room, next to a bathroom with an "Out of Order" sign, were a couple of bruised-looking couches around tables with hookah pipes. Gary sat at one smoking away. Quincy sat next to him, nursing a drink and trying not to touch anything.

We took seats opposite them. I tried not to dwell on Em's knee touching mine. Quincy's gaze flicked between Emily and me, piecing together the details of what had transpired. Her primped hair and air of moral superiority irritated.

I took a sip of her drink. Vodka cranberry. Quincy nodded like I'd confirmed something.

Gary passed Emily the hookah pipe. She hesitated and then took a small puff, blowing out the side of her mouth.

"I've been permissive," he said to us. "You don't get to skip my class. Skip others, make up whatever excuse you want, not mine. Fail acting and you fail the program."

"I was worried," I began.

"You just left and thought what, I wouldn't notice?" He worked his lower jaw side-to-side. His mouth looked like a cored hunk of beef in the red lights. "After bailing you out with Jeremy this is how you show thanks?"

"I'm sorry."

"Yes, I know, Neil," Gary said. "You're very good at apologizing. I'm asking you not to do it."

"Why's Quincy here?" Emily asked.

All eyes went to Emily. She took another puff of the hookah.

"How come you two are here alone?" she continued. "Isn't that a little..."

"What?" Gary asked, unable to mask his surprise at the insinuation.

Quincy gave Emily an unconvincing look of disbelief. I took another sip of Quincy's drink, not looking at Em because if I did, if I watched her rub her eyes in seeming ignorance of how suicidal what she'd just said was, my chest would clench with affection.

"I was worried about Em and went to check on her," I said to Gary. "Tim's kind of gone off the rails lately."

"Gone off the rails how?"

His gaze went to Emily's bruised chin. She hadn't put the gauze back on. Her fingers went up a moment later, partially obscuring it.

"We'd been fighting," she said quietly. The brass end of the hookah pipe belched puffs of smoke. "Explosions over nothing, like where to hang a picture." She went to take another puff, thought better of it, and passed it to me. "The truth is things haven't been right with us for a long time. We both thought moving for college would be a fresh start, but the problem was never location. I guess, maybe, I was, and that wasn't going to change."

I took a long puff. The water in the hookah gurgled. My mouth filled with the taste of strawberries and cinnamon. My lips were wet with her excess saliva.

"You could have told him that," Quincy said. "Say before he moved halfway across the country."

"Who asked you?" Emily asked, like she really wanted to know. "Who told you to come with us? Who told you to do anything?"

Quincy's lips tightened like she was about to lash out, then broke apart in a thin smile. "You're right," she said, getting up. "I'm the stupid one." She looked at Gary. "You asked me to bring them, I brought them."

"I don't know where he went," Emily said to her. Her skin

looked drained. "He packed some things and took off."

The red light blinked off, sparing us the sight of Quincy's reaction, then back on. "I didn't ask."

"Sure," Emily answered. "You're here because of me. Keep telling yourself that."

A shoving match broke out on the dance floor between the middle-aged man and a short barkeep/bouncer. The latter reached for the other's legs, the former swatting at his opponent's chest. The middle-aged man's glasses went flying. There was an embarrassed moment while he crawled around looking for them while the barkeep and other patrons looked on. Finally the barkeep handed them to him. One of the lenses had cracked. Defiance sapped, the middle-aged man shuffled toward the door.

Quincy left. Gary warned us again about not missing class and followed suit a few minutes later. Emily started to make a crack about not letting Quincy get away but I tutted and she relented. She was blinking a lot.

"How much you wanna bet he stiffed us on the hookah?" she asked, poking at the smoldering tobacco remains in the bowl with a chipped nail. "Reads us the riot act then goes home with one of his students. Classy."

I signaled to someone for the check.

"I shouldn't have dragged you here," she said.

"Not your fault."

The barkeep came up with a bill. He was limping a little from the altercation. I gave him my credit card without looking at the final amount. Emily flattened out the wrinkles on the barkeep's shirt, which he accepted with the solemnity of a warrior. I watched the last embers die in the hookah bowl.

"I wish he'd just stay gone," she whispered.

"Don't say that."

"Why?" She lifted her gaze to me. Her eyes were almost black in the darkness.

I placed a hand on the back of her head.

She tilted her head as if sloughing it off, then released.

8

Dad is strapped to a dentist's chair naked. His belly droops over a sprawling thatch of pubic hair and a penis shriveled with cold. A metal helmet is affixed to his head, sensor lights blinking. His pectorals droop. His bare feet are turned inwards but it's the chipper, resigned smile on his face that transfixes.

"I tried to stay away," he says, words garbled through a mouth guard. "I really did." Drool spills down onto his lap.

"She needed to know someone was out there, waiting for her."

Light envelops the room, a wave of white fire that makes him seem pitifully small by comparison. Nurses stand in a rough semicircle behind him, weaving in time with music only they can hear. The light emanates from their eyes and out of their mouths.

Dad senses them and tries turning his head around to see but is restricted by the helmet. His chest twitches.

"Oh well," he says.

I step back and meet a wall. Low laughter from the nurses. I glance

behind me and notice a cartoonishly large red button lit up to be pressed. I
follow the electrical wires that snake from it to the chair Dad's strapped in.

"You do it," he says. "I won't have the quack tormenting your mother
do this too."

"No."

"Please, I never asked you for anything..."

"Dad..."

"Do this."

"Don't ask me." I swallow and try to shout the words. Nothing comes
out.

"It's already HAPPENED, don't you see? The moment I decided not
to scoop you up in my arms and run at the first sign of her changing this
was in the cards. It's not you."

The nurses begin to ululate, a high, piercing noise that echoes off the
walls and builds upon itself. Their light pierces my skin, corrupts muscle,
interrupts blood flow. It raises my right arm.

I try to tell my father that his is the only true light in the room, that
when he's gone there will only be darkness, but my mouth remains closed.

My hand slams the switch. An angry buzzing shoots through my body
into the floor and out.

The current pulls his lips apart, warping his smile until his cheeks
split open. The smell of cooking flesh fills the air.

* * *

Em and I ate waffles in bed. Blanket and sheets lay hopelessly tangled at our feet. Freed of Tim's rules she took a special relish in
eating with her mouth open, crumbs sticking to her naked body,
and washing the food down with slurps of black coffee. We didn't
talk much. Once in a while we'd pass the syrup or butter melting to

yellow grease in its dish.

When I couldn't eat any more I got dressed and opened the bedroom window. The sky was overcast and gave the illusion of things moving slower than they actually were. In the courtyard the scarecrow's arms, bent up at the elbows in perfect right angles, shook straw fingers. I could make out each one, catching thermals in the air I felt moments later.

"Jeez!" she exclaimed. "Are you trying to kill me?"

I turned around and saw her scrambling to bring the blanket back over her. It was a solid mass trailing sheets, and only moved up in increments.

I helped her get it all the way up. Cool air played on the back of my neck like fizzing pop rocks. After laying our plates and cutlery down on the floor, I knelt down off the side of the bed, lifted a part of the blanket, and dipped my head inside. So warm, the smell of our sex pungent and addicting.

I tongued her belly, picking up waffle crumbs that dissolved into sweet paste. She breathed evenly but her back arched at contact. When she took my head with both hands, forcing me to stop, I understood. When she touched me for longer than a few moments it felt almost unbearable. My body had never been touched like that before, and hadn't yet classified it as a good thing.

"Come back to bed," she said.

I sighed. "Can't."

"I can't get warm without you."

"I just need to check in at home. Change my clothes. I won't be long, promise."

"Don't promise."

I ran my hand up her torso, feeling the spread of her collarbone, the skin of her neck such a weak shell for the cartilage structure underneath.

"I keep expecting him to walk in through the door and pick up like nothing's changed."

"You're stronger than you think," I said.

"You have to say that."

I got out from beneath the blanket and rose to standing. She looked like the survivor of a hurricane or tornado, staring up amidst the detritus of her life.

"If I ask myself honestly if I could've gone through what you did, come out as intact..." I shook my head.

A knowing look came into her eyes. The freckles on her face somehow stood out more. "Why do I think that isn't true?" she asked.

* * *

The world didn't split apart into fragments once I left her. My footsteps pushed into the ground with usual pressure. I smoked several cigarettes on the walk back home and caught myself casting looks back toward Miller House like it was a talisman or proof. Nothing appeared to be different and yet everything was.

When people coming up the path got too close I cast my eyes downwards and wondered why. When I spotted a familiar shortcut through the MacNicol and Deutsch buildings that would have let me out at the planetarium and a short walk across the street to home I didn't wander off the path I was on. I didn't look people in the eyes and I didn't walk where they did—why? What was the point? Was I that much of a loser? Was I that pathetic Boo Radley lingering at the periphery, imagining myself superior—why had I lived this way? Why had I assumed people would greet me with a frown and a quick step back instead of a smile? Why had I acted like a coward when the woman dozing in Miller House was proof positive I needn't have done it for a single moment?

Did I want to sink? Was that it? Had I let myself sink because I knew a part of me would resist kicking back up to the surface?

I went up the front steps of the house, so mired in thought that I didn't notice the car parked at the curb a few feet away from my father's in the driveway. I didn't notice the squashed brown penny loafers next to my father's brogues in the foyer. The proportions of the room seemed off; walls a few inches closer, closet mirror warped and elongating my face. My cheeks were covered by a thin layer of beard.

"Young man!" a voice boomed from the living room. *Yung maaan.* I recognized it instantly as Ganguly Uncle. "Get in here and let me see your face!"

I was greeted by his jovially bloated body and apple cheeks in the living room. He wore a blue Hawaiian shirt and red suspenders that gave him the appearance of a used car salesman about to make you the offer of a lifetime. Dad sat beside him on the couch, taking me in with an expression I couldn't fathom or hold for more than a glance.

"Fun night?" Ganguly asked. What remained of his hair was slicked back and glistened beneath the living room lights.

"Oh, you know."

The window curtains were drawn back, letting in pallid gray light. Papers jockeyed for space on the coffee table with cups, pens, and paperclips. Many were marked in red ink and displayed my father's contained lettering and sharp lines.

"See, this is what we should have been doing at his age, Raja," Ganguly said, nodding toward me. "Out late, acting naughty with young ladies. Instead, what did we do? Eat too many *ladoos* and waste our eyes studying." He pried an eye open with two fingers. "Lasik," he said proudly.

Dad readjusted in his seat. "Wash and go to bed, you look tired," he said. Though he and Ganguly Uncle were roughly the same age, the heavy bags under his eyes made him look much older.

"Come now, some details," Ganguly said, rubbing his hands together. Long piano player fingers. "I've seen these *goras* on campus with the tight skirts, high socks ending just beneath their..."

"All right," Dad warned, busying himself with the papers.

Ganguly grinned like we shared a secret. "They have no shame, really none at all."

Dad showed him a document. Ganguly glanced at it briefly and tapped a set of figures. "If we claim Niladri as a dependent, that'll give us some leeway here," he said.

"How much?"

Ganguly scratched at the ridge of flesh that sprang up between his eyebrows. "Fair amount. It's easier to hold onto a house with at least one dependent."

Dad nodded and made a note with his pen. My face felt hot, like a dream where you show up to class without wearing any clothes. I shifted my weight forward, trying to get a better look at the papers, and Dad noticed I was still there.

"Are you hungry?" he asked. I shook my head.

"There are leftovers in the fridge. Pizza. Take some and go upstairs, can't you see men are talking?"

"Hold on," Ganguly said. "The Public Trustee lists him as a guardian along with you. Maybe he should be here for this."

"Don't make me tell you again, Niladri," Dad said.

"He could answer a few questions about life at home, how

you've worked to make Priya feel secure—"

"Leave my son to me," Dad said curtly.

Ganguly's eyebrows went up but he didn't press the issue.

"I'm not staying," I said to Dad, hating the shakiness in my voice. "I just need to get some things...."

"Then get them." He swallowed and licked his lips, spreading a dry paste of saliva.

I started toward the bedroom stairs. Pinpricks in the soles of my feet like they'd fallen asleep while standing. I heard Ganguly's low voice. "If Niladri doesn't show, the judge will assume you're hiding something. With the complaints Dr. Thibodeau's filed you can't afford any more negatives. Not with the Public Trustee pushing for full custody."

A low whistling in my ears. I wished I were outside and could look off into the distance but instead there were only the same artifacts: Tagore prints coated in dust, a vacuum in the upstairs corridor trailing a power cord. Each detail was an additional weight placed on my chest that made breathing difficult.

When I got to my room I closed the door behind me and stared at the bed. The small twin mattress that forced me to sleep on my side, legs pulled in so they wouldn't hang over the end. The pillow permanently dented by my head. The crusty sheets with their vaguely repulsive and comforting smell. I felt as if I hadn't had a good night's sleep in weeks.

Just thirty minutes. I'd set the alarm so I wouldn't overdo it.

Movement downstairs, then the creak of a lower step as someone started upstairs.

I opened the closet, shook out a sports bag lying on the floor, and began indiscriminately tearing clothes off hangers and shoving them in. I threw in a couple of sweaters from the upper shelf. There was a tan leather jacket with epaulets and buttoned front pockets, a found item from my father's wardrobe that he'd long since stopped wearing. The more I'd worn it the more the exterior scratches and inner lining rips had become emblems of my history, not his. I slipped it on.

The bedroom door creaked open. Dad stood at the threshold but did not step inside. He watched me open dresser drawers and throw in socks and underwear. My hands felt cold.

"You'll fit in more if you slow down," he said.

I didn't want to slow down. The bed, the room, was like quicksand. The small window in the corner offered no view of campus and even now Emily was starting to fade, the warmth of her touch ceding to decay in stasis that was this place. I vowed not to call it home again. I would not honor it in such a way.

"Are you safe?" he asked.

"I'm fine."

"Who are you staying with? I can't imagine you're going back and forth from Forest Hills every day. Or are you? Does she send her man to pick you up?"

His arms were crossed over his chest. His face was tight with anger but it was more for his own benefit than mine. When I left it would go slack and the mournful expression I couldn't stand would reappear: hopeless and irrefutable.

"She's got her hooks into you now, I suppose."

I zipped up the bag and slung it over my shoulder. "It's not her fault."

His gaze, magnified behind thick lenses, grew unfocused. "I guess not."

I pushed the dresser drawer back in its berth. My thumb lingered on the thin strip of edging brass. "I'm trying to do something. I know you don't believe it, but I have to try." I took a labored breath. "I have to, *Baba*."

I saw his arms lower at the periphery of my vision. "Wait here," he said, and retreated back into the hall.

I finished gathering my things. My pockets bulged with lighters and half-full packs of cigarettes. The strap of the sports bag dug into my shoulder.

Dad returned carrying two full cloth sacks and laid them on the bed. Objects poked out along their bodies; chocolate bars, rolls of socks and quarters, paperbacks.

"The *haram jada* fraud says I can't visit her anymore. He told the Public Trustee I'm dangerous." He tried to laugh. "Hospital security has my picture like I'm a criminal, Niladri."

I nodded, staring at the bags. One of them was perched perilously close to the edge of the bed, a nudge away from falling.

"Can you..."

"All right." Doing it was easier than hearing him ask.

"There's an extra car key in the garage. Park it in the driveway when you come back."

Downstairs I made small talk with Ganguly for a few minutes. He talked about the hazing his son had endured joining Sigma Phi Epsilon at Rensselaer, and how excited he was to have obtained membership. There was obvious pride in his voice—Atanu was an undergrad engineering student riding a partial scholarship—but reluctance as well. Ganguly was so close to our family, such a forgiving, positive presence...and sullen in groups. Those whom he loved reciprocated because they felt they were part of a select few, exceptions to a generalized disdain. He was no longer skinny and no longer stole, but this much would never change. Submitting to torture for the privilege of being one amongst many would never sit well with him.

Dad gave me a zip-lock bag containing a few slices of pizza. I took it and the bags, said goodbye to Ganguly, and went downstairs to the basement. Dad followed close behind, footsteps echoing a half step after mine.

In the garage I turned to him and asked, "They can't take the house. At best they can go after her things, what's in her name..."

Dad pressed a switch and the garage door trundled up. Beneath the clatter, "Our name, Niladri. Mine and hers. That's how we've always done it. They want to cut it down the middle."

* * *

A thin rain started as I drove south on I-33, dark spots on the ground eaten up moments later by the wheels of the car. Water dripped down exit signs and ones advertising food and lodging. It crept into the exposed innards of raccoons and the odd deer lying crumpled on the side of the road. Oversized sheaves of corn tied to streetlamps with dark red bows for Thanksgiving writhed like the remains of crucified bodies. I lifted my right shoulder to better hold the phone to my ear.

"Are you waiting for me to say something?" Auntie asked.

A Mack semi barreled past on the right-hand lane, cheerfully ignoring the rules of the road. Twin oval red lights and Betty Boop mud flaps.

"Did you think they'd go so far?" I asked. "The house?"

Tinkle of ice in a glass on the other end. It was barely afternoon. "I didn't. I wasn't sure what the Public Trustee would do."

"I can't"—grip tightening on the wheel—"I'd never have talked to them if..."

"It's out of your hands. You told them what you found. What they do now is up to them."

"Dad was having a...war meeting with Ganguly. I've never seen him like that before. He could lose everything."

"He had twenty years to take her name off the deed. Who's to blame for that? You?" She sighed. "I've said this to you I don't know how many times but you don't listen. This isn't your doing."

A sign for Exit 42 came up on the right. I put the blinker on and readied to switch lanes.

"Did you do what I asked? Hold off with the boyfriend?" I could hear her grinning. "Tim?"

"You're a worse gossip hound than any of the other *Mashis*."

"Well?"

I didn't answer until after I'd switched into the right lane. It was growing murky outside and the interior lights automatically came up, pale blue gauges and dials. Mom's care packages lay stacked on the seat next to me.

If I'd truly been concerned for Emily's safety why hadn't I knocked on their door the morning after their fight? Why had I let her remain in the presence of someone so unstable for an entire night and morning without lifting a finger? It was a question I hadn't asked of myself because I didn't wish to know the answer.

"Yes," I said.

"And?"

And Tim had fallen apart on his own, just like Auntie had predicted. And I'd crept in like a thief posing as savior. Because keeping her in harm's way for a few extra hours was a small price to pay in exchange for excising him from the picture.

"Nothing happened," I said, taking the exit.

The road described a wide loop. The brake lights of cars ahead of me began flashing on.

* * *

The high brick walls spanning at least five city blocks were more akin to a prison than a hospital. A plaque mounted next to the steel front gates read, "Dixon Health Care Facility, est. 1925." Shielded cameras roosted like magpies, endlessly recording a grim stretch of abandoned silos, a mechanic's shop besieged by wild grass, and crumbling factories with all but the highest windows broken. The neighborhood had gone to seed; the hospital flourished.

A camera found my car. The lens auto-adjusted to make me out through the windshield and a moment later the gates creaked open, revealing a brick path leading up a low incline to the Admittance building. I passed a security booth at left where a guard nodded and went back to his magazine. There was a soccer field where a few patients wearing identical plastic rain jackets chased down a Frisbee. Elm trees with foliage blazed fall orange and yellow. A children's playground that gave me a chill every time I saw it, tiny footprints etched in the sand. The path forked at the Admittance building, a three-story bunker with a flashing beacon up top attracting ambulances like a bug zapper. I went right and passed a series of smaller bunkers before parking in a lot facing one. I thought of nurses gathering up their little wards in the playground, necks red, faces stained with grime.

The stench of musty clothes and industrial cleaning fluid ruled inside Baker Pavilion. Pea-green walls spattered with brown stains that wouldn't come off no matter how much you scrubbed. A fire extinguisher encased in glass and warnings posted every few feet: No Smoking. No Loitering. No Groups Larger than 3 Without

Supervision. Each sign carried a cartoon demonstrating the infraction with a thick red line through it. My gaze flicked from object to object because staring straight ahead at the two steel doors that waited at the end of the corridor made me feel nauseous.

The corridor opened out to a small waiting area in front of the doors. In the right corner was a nurse's station, blue-tinted glass looking into a sprawling terminal with flashing lights and several tiers of surveillance screens. Two nurses played gin rummy at a fold-out table. A third, whom I had always called Nurse Khadijah, came out to meet me, rolls of black flesh packed into a white uniform. Wide smile revealing a chipped front tooth. She held out her arms, flesh jiggling.

"Every time you get six inches taller," she said, Jamaican accent like drizzled honey. She pressed me to her massive bosom. She smelled of clean sweat and peppermint lozenges. The sacks in my right hand glanced off her leg.

"What's that father of yours feeding you?" she asked. "I can feel your bones. Tell him to buy meat, red meat, the more the better."

Masked from the overhead cameras, I slipped twenty dollars into the pocket of her uniform using my free hand. "I know it's early to visit. Do you think I could…"

She pulled back to see my face, wide-set eyes squinting, upturned nose flaring in exaggerated deliberation. "Just this once," squeezing a cheek. Tight cornrows that looked like they hurt. "How can I say no to such a heartbreaker?"

She led me to the door at left, pulling out a thick ring of keys attached to a pocket with a brass chain. This door had a porthole window covered in wire mesh from the inside. Disembodied parts of patients walking past on the other end could be discerned: an earlobe, a neck jutting forward.

The door at right had no window. I did not look toward it but its presence did not leave me. The obscenity of that perfectly featureless door, like a face sheared off by a grenade, and what lingered beyond it did not escape the minds of anyone in the pavilion.

She slipped a long, slightly rusted key into the lock.

"How is she?" I asked suddenly, not wanting her to open it just yet. "I mean, how is she doing?" My arms ached from carrying the bags.

Slow turn as the tumblers fell. "Crying too much, fighting with the nurses, not participating in group activities." She glanced at me and I could sense the canny intelligence lurking behind the curiosity. There was a reason the other nurses quieted when she spoke. "Why is that?"

"I don't know."

Someone whistled a few bars of "White Cliffs of Dover" on the other side, a tremulous, mournful sound.

"She knows the game. Smile, volunteer where you can, and get that early release. Why's she making it hard on herself?"

She waited for me to say something. The buttons of her uniform pressed out when she breathed. I wanted nothing more than to run outside and take large, gasping breaths of fresh air.

"I'll talk to her," I said.

"Do that."

She pulled the door open. The stench grew overpowering. It was the smell of mental illness, of truth denied so long it had grown fuzzy and tumorous, eating out its host from the inside. Spit squirted into the back of my throat.

"She's Bed Thirteen," Nurse Khadijah said, eyes on an anorexic teen mopping the floor a few feet away. "Just put the bags underneath."

The floor was ceramic-smooth and reflected the fluorescents overhead. My shoes squelched on the wet surface. The girl shrank back as I approached. Clumps of hair were missing, revealing red patches of scalp.

"One part soap to three parts water, Tammy," Nurse Khadijah called out. "Is that what you have?"

The girl blinked and stared down at the muddy water in the bucket next to her. As I passed I noticed she wasn't wearing shoes. Suds clung to pert little toes.

The dormitory was a high-ceilinged room containing two rows of fifteen beds, headboards pushed back against the walls. It stood empty in the daytime in accordance with hospital rules, the only movement coming from the two barred windows on the far side, where the shadow of an elm's branches caressed the floor.

I went up the center aisle reading bed numbers tacked to the wall above each. Personal mementos were discouraged so the only differentiations were medical; an IV stand holding a bag of viscous gray liquid, intricate pulley systems for the broken and obese. I found Thirteen, bent down and slipped the two bags underneath. I got a strong whiff of urine from nearby and decided I'd done enough, I'd delivered the care package, I'd visit her later but not now. And I almost believed it until I straightened up and saw the restraints dangling off the side of her bed.

I found her in the common room with several other patients, sitting on one of the plastic chairs arranged along the walls. She stared up at a television bolted to the ceiling. Her face was slack. Her hands were clasped together, the thumbs methodically rubbing. There was a stillness to her eyes that frightened me, a level of atrophy beyond the phony emotions she'd display for the benefit of others. When the television flicked from commercials back to a soap opera she didn't even blink.

I knelt down in front of her. Touched her hands. Her thumbs stilled. A little noise of discomfort escaped her throat. Her eyes drew away from the television screen and traversed the room, past a gray-haired woman scratching her breasts through her robe and a stout little man with his head thrust back and a beatific smile on his face, finally settling on me. And for a moment, there was nothing.

"Hey," I whispered. I squeezed her fingers.

The noise in her throat grew louder, protesting.

"It's me."

"Niladri?" She coughed, loosening the phlegm in her throat. She blinked deliberately several times but her eyes would not focus. I squeezed tighter and then she squeezed faintly back.

"You should have called first." She pulled her shoulders back so the gown would drape better. "I'm not ready."

Thunder cracked outside and a moment later the television volume was cranked up impossibly high, a couple's pillow talk reverberating off the walls. I glanced around to see who had the remote but no one did; there was only a single camera taking in the proceedings overhead.

Mom closed her eyes and grimaced as though the racket were coming from within her. A grizzled man with the hunched posture of a war vet began shouting at the camera to turn it down. His face grew beet red and his shouting devolved into calling the nurses Nazis and niggers, but still the volume didn't change.

I got up, pulling at Mom's hands. She opened her eyes a little. I motioned toward the hallway and after a little encouragement, she rose. As we walked out I could feel the eyes of other patients settle on us like flies.

She froze outside the dormitory. "I can't go in. I'm not allowed."

I glanced back at the hallway we'd come from. There was no place to sit, just the anorexic girl mopping a little further along. "It's okay."

She plucked at bits of her gown with two fingers. Shook her head.

"Say I made you."

Upon entering she sat down at the edge of her bed, looking at nothing. I sat next to her, feeling the wood slats beneath the thin mattress.

"Dad asked me to bring you some things. They're underneath."

She nodded but didn't move to retrieve them. Her hands found each other, fingers knitting. She took shallow breaths through her mouth.

"Why are they still restraining you?"

She didn't answer.

"Nurse Khadijah says you haven't been participating in Group. That you've been off by yourself."

"It's better that way."

"They're watching you all the time, Mom. You can't do things like that."

"It doesn't matter."

"What do you mean?"

"Treatment at home doesn't work. So I'm staying here from now on."

"That's not true." I wiped my brow and it came away dry. "Who told you that? Was it Dr. Thibodeau?"

She smiled a little but her eyes were dim.

I grabbed one of the restraints. "Did he do this?"

"I forget sometimes. I'm no better than anyone else. I can't just get up in the middle of the night to check."

"For what?"

She nodded toward the windows. "The parking lot. Sometimes I can see the car, *Baba* inside."

Someone passed outside the door. She got up and went to it. Her entire body pitched taking steps, like a ship beset by gales.

* * *

A cold, driving wind blew leaves across the driveway of Miller House. Students milled about on the front porch smoking, voices rising when the sound of the coming storm rose to a shriek. The scarecrow had been nearly sheared from its moorings, skeletal beams showing through clumps of hay and plaid. Its head whiplashed and described agonized rotations.

Kegs had been set up in the kitchen and living room, spigots dripping foam. Furniture was pushed up against the walls to make room for a DJ spinning hip-hop, girls with their arms around guys with bored looks on their faces. I pushed past them to the stairs, side-stepping a couple making out, the girl's back pressed up so tightly against the banister that excess flesh pushed out between the supporting posts. Wallflowers lingered at the top of the stairs, plain girls wearing too much makeup and formless dresses.

Emily's apartment was empty, though most of the lights were on. In the kitchen I found a beef and macaroni dish stiffening in Tupperware. Empty plastic packages holding dried bloodstains from the meat. Carrot tops and green pepper cores clogging the sink. I popped a cover on the Tupperware container and slipped it into the fridge. I cleaned up, thinking—and hoping—Emily might return while I did.

I was trapped between where I did not want to be and somewhere new I couldn't yet feel. When I thought of my mother all else faded, became window dressing. There was nothing else. There was nowhere to go. There was only this, there was only this, THERE WAS ONLY THIS forevermore, and all the wishing in the world wouldn't change that. Mom would waste away and Dad would waste away with her. And I would watch it happen and do nothing save wring my hands.

The kitchen counter stood clear. Without Emily I possessed no claim to this place.

As I exited I made eye contact with Quincy coming up the staircase. Her face and upper chest were covered in sweat. Silver tinsel was wrapped halfway up one arm, and she clutched a green plastic beer cup.

For a second all she registered was a man's movement at Emily's door. I saw the hope alight in her eyes. Then she took me in and it faded. Others passed her on the stairs. She nodded toward a door at the far end of the hall leading up to the roof.

Emily was sitting on a lawn chair overlooking the greenhouse. She wore a hoodie, hand pressed to the back of her head to keep the hood from blowing off. Her legs were crossed. A foot pointed toward the flowers visible through panes of curved glass, stuttering color like Morse code.

My shoes scraped on the tarpapered surface. She straightened at the sound but didn't turn around. When I got close she uncrossed her legs and I sat down between them. Her hands draped loosely about my chest.

"I wanted to call you," she said, voice dampened by wind. "But I didn't want to be possessive."

"Forget about that," I said.

Her thighs tightened against my torso. And for the first time since leaving the hospital, I felt something other than mixed up.

"You can call me whenever," I said. "You don't have to worry, or be afraid that I'll judge you."

"You say that, but how do I know?"

I tilted my head up and met her gaze, deep and clear like an animal new to the world.

"You keep so much inside," she said.

"I know." The wind ceded to the babble of voices on the front porch. "I don't want to be like that. I...had a hard time of it, growing up. Maybe I learned the wrong lessons."

She touched her head to mine. "Whatever it is..."

I shook my head.

"You don't have to tell me."

"I want to." I took a deep breath. "Jesus, it would feel so good to just once."

Lightning filled the sky, an interconnected network of streaks displaying a pattern too complex to decipher. Afterwards I thought I could make out its image etched onto the clouds.

"Just give me a little time," I said. "I'll get there."

9

Over a month passed without word from Tim. Emily and I rarely left the apartment, so wrapped up in discovering shared eccentricities that his absence soon took on an abstract quality. Once upon a time we'd known a boy who disappeared. Today held more pressing questions. Should we venture outside for a walk and make snarky comments about fellow strollers? Should we go to a bar and make new friends and afterwards share notes about how easy it is when there's someone beside you offering priceless validation? We reveled in these little things but it did not feel smug. When you've spent the better part of your life considering yourself a freak with burnt-out synapses in place of social skills, finding a sibling soul inspires a readjustment of ego.

I spoke to my father on the phone once or twice a week, never about specifics or for longer than five minutes at a time. We chatted about the weather and good websites for recipes, and drew conclusions from a caught breath or unexpected tone. When the heaviness grew apparent one of us always ended the call, except that the heaviness remained, growing fat and tumorous beneath my skin. Emily grew attuned enough to my moods to identify it; I lied or pretended it was about something innocuous. In dreams it spread leathery wings and revealed scenes of my parents getting ECT treatments and being injected with serums that made their genitals swell and pus seep out of their pores. Cold and horrific though they were, the dreams also effected a cheap catharsis that allowed me to get on with the day.

But any thought of my mother and the utter lack of easy villainy or hope in her day-to-day life erased this benefit. I wasn't divining answers while I slept. I was merely spinning wheels, like a child fabricating monsters to drown out the sound of his parents arguing. For example, Dr. Thibodeau appeared in my visions as a cut-rate Josef Mengele, hooking up complex apparatuses and puncturing my mother's flesh with screwdrivers to "bleed out the sickness." What did he do in real life? Lecture her for hours on end? Prescribe pills that kept her meek and docile? Ensure the restraints were on tight? The point was I didn't know, and even if I did, I doubted any of it could be construed as malpractice. So I continued to wake up troubled, nothing resolved or better understood, burrowing my face into Emily's neck to soothe the itching in my gut.

All those issues I hid away were what Quincy no longer could. At first when she started reminiscing about Tim apropos of nothing I chalked it up to closeness. What harm in remembering an overwrought turn of phrase, an ill-advised haircut, or a doomed attempt at keeping pace with barflies? But it didn't stop there. Em found her on the phone berating Tim's parents for not reporting him as a missing person. When Emily brought up the fact that Tim had gone off the grid before, Quincy just gave her a withering look and said lost weekends didn't count, he was in trouble, and anyone who said otherwise just didn't want to be bothered. She pestered Administration and even tried to get Gary to organize some sort of search party.

I did my best to be quietly supportive...and stay out of the way. While I hoped nothing ill had befallen him, I couldn't say I wanted him back.

Quincy put on weight. When bulky sweaters couldn't cover it she resorted to fake eyelashes and Mafia wife nails, visual tricks to draw attention away from her expanding midriff. Her cheekbones disappeared beneath bloat. The string of men she'd bring back to her apartment trickled down to almost nothing. Though I'd never approved, it was better than passing her closed door and knowing she was inside, a slave to mounting obsession.

It became difficult to talk to her. Conversations started off fine but after a while the words would peter out and there'd be a loaded silence, like a cloud pregnant with rain awaiting only an inciting charge. Few things escaped her notice—my socks lying next to the couch, the dried remains of chili I'd attempted in the slow cooker, the Frank Miller graphic novel on Em's nightstand which I'd bought for her and she was gamely trying to plow through.

Initially these were fodder for innocuous teasing, like "You should really do a load of laundry for this boy" etc., but eventually it grew biting. Quincy was like a cat that had been content to bat a mouse around as long as there was food in her bowl, but now that the bowl stood empty, she extended her claws for the kill. She knew how much it hurt me to be thought of as an interloper, knew I couldn't really defend against it, and kept on regardless. She read every piece of evidence of a deepening relationship between Emily and me as proof that we'd forgotten all about Tim. So she railed against it, calling out every liberty I enjoyed, rolling her eyes or scoffing when Em and I shared an intimate moment to remind us that we were opportunistic shitheels.

What neither Quincy nor I could have anticipated was how quickly Emily would regain her old strength freed of Tim. Or how fiercely she'd come to my defense.

When the three of us hung out Emily would make sure a part of our bodies were touching. When Quincy started in on me Emily would refute with vacation resorts we'd fantasized about online, or how we'd manage it so as not to spend more than a week or two apart come summer break. Little details that solidified our relationship and made the past with Tim seem like just that. Neither of the girls openly argued, but as soon as it was just the two of us again Emily would vent, eviscerating Quincy's weight and psychological weaknesses, trying to make up for what she believed she was responsible for putting me through. She had an amazing, misguided ability to cast me as the hero in all situations.

The bile between Emily and Quincy grew, and on the day before we finally discovered what happened to Tim, it spewed.

The three of us were eating Chinese food and watching *East of Eden* when Emily's phone rang. She picked through open containers of dumplings and glazed ribs on the coffee table to retrieve it. A quick check of the display screen and she silenced the phone. Pressed a few buttons and tucked it into her pocket. Her eyes continued to watch James Dean contort his body into various grieving postures but it was clear she was distracted.

"Who was it?" Quincy asked. A paper plate holding only white rice was balanced on her lap. It was a trick I recognized but did not call attention to: eating like an ascetic with company present only to gorge yourself once they were gone.

"Mmm? No one."

Onscreen Raymond Massey stood watching his son whimper. His back was rigid, face lined with hard years and judgments. Dean put a hand out and Massey made no move toward it.

"Tell me," Quincy said.

"Wrong number," she said with an edge to her voice that made me look over. Her eyes said she was nearing the end of her rope with Quincy, and that finding an excuse to break things off was in order.

Quincy picked up the remote and paused the movie. "How long are you going to keep ducking him?"

"What are you talking about?" I asked.

Quincy's lips drew down in the beginnings of a sneer. I saw it on her face more and more, watching happy couples, watching skinny people. "Ask her."

Emily scratched her bare arm. She wore an old Adam and the Ants T-shirt of mine, the collar raggedy. "You have to stop this, Q."

"I always hated that nickname. So unoriginal. Couldn't you two have come up with something better?"

The food on her lap was in danger of spilling. I grabbed it and placed it on the coffee table.

Quincy's eyes, shiny in attack, lingered on Emily. "You've taught him to pick up. What's next? Cooking? Or is it pill dispensing?"

Emily took her phone out and tossed it at her. It hit Quincy's chest and tumbled down her bulky wool sweater to her lap, where it lay amidst a few grains of rice clinging to her slacks.

"I'm going out for a smoke," Emily muttered, and started looking around for my jacket. I tried to make eye contact with her but she wouldn't look at either of us. She slipped my jacket on and went for the door, patting the front pockets for the pack.

Quincy was scrolling through Emily's phone and jabbing keys with her thumb.

"Stop."

"She erased her call history. Saw me looking and knew I'd ask." She clucked. "Tricky."

I didn't say anything.

She offered me the phone. "Look for yourself."

"I don't want to."

Her eyes slitted in false compassion. "You trust her. Tim never did."

"I'm not Tim."

"He'd bend over backwards and she'd always have this look on her puss, like she was doing him a favor."

I rubbed my forehead. "I can't talk to you when you're like this."

She dangled the phone in front of my face. I snatched at it. She pulled it away at the last second. A wave of revulsion swept over me as I took in her squashed fruit of a face and moist eyes. I got up. She laughed but there was a pleading quality to it as well.

"Come on, I'm sorry." The phone and its erased call history taunted me to the door. "Take it."

Gary had picked up on the changes occurring in her. He'd set up exercises designed to highlight the excess weight she carried or her utter inability to connect with someone past an errant moment. Now, we'd all been subjected to humbling moments in class; being a victim to his moods came part and parcel with the insights he enabled us to glean about ourselves. But where Quincy departed from the class was in how relatively easy we were to hurt. A few jabs at the soft parts and our mouths would snap shut and our throats ache. Quincy, however, had created a shell so thick she'd convinced herself there'd be no penetrating it. Exercises devolved into haranguing sessions, spittle flying from Gary's mouth as he called her a fat pig, a dilettante, and that worst of insults, a phony. She just stood there, absently turning the rings on her fingers like a mother bearing out a child's tantrum. Afterwards classmates would attempt to commiserate, but she would have none of it and eventually they stopped trying. A quiet resentment sprang up between us and her. Who was she to stand apart? What right did she have to protect her innards when we'd laid ours out to be pecked at?

In class the morning after the confrontation at the apartment she was called up once again and told to sit on a chair onstage. Jasper, a curly-haired Swede sitting closest to the spotlight, went to turn it on but Gary stopped him with an upraised hand. Quincy watched him with the tired gaze of a woman past her years, once in a while adjusting her sweater around the midriff.

After a moment Gary crossed from behind his desk, took the empty chair facing her, and turned it so they were side-by-side. He sat down, leaning slightly forward, palms together. His eyes went to each of the observing students in turn.

"Sometimes I'll stay in this room after my last class, just sitting." He glanced at Quincy. "There's a peace to it, isn't there?"

Her body looked like it would twitch if you touched it.

"Do you know why?"

She shook her head.

Gary smiled a little. "You do, even if you can't put your finger on it. Think about visiting people's houses. Some feel sterile, like a hospital. Others feel lived-in, like they could absorb every laugh, every tear, the sum total of our craziness. This has nothing to do with tangibles and everything to do with the emotional traces left behind by others." He shrugged. "You don't have to agree, but do you understand?"

Quincy stared at the empty chair in the front row. The chair which had remained empty these weeks except for when students used it to hold excess bags and notebooks. The one which everyone had stopped noticing except her.

"Yes," she said quietly.

"Actors have worked on this stage for over forty years. Fighting demons, opening their hearts, discovering, magically, that they're not alone. That a complete stranger can somehow feel the same way they do. Forty years of building a tapestry from the most transient of arts, and when you sit back and take it in you get that it's not transient at all. What we show others creates the most amazing energy. One with the power to heal."

Quincy's mouth twitched.

"I don't believe in much of anything, but I believe that." He nodded toward the rest of us. "Some of your classmates came here to add their part. Others came simply to put their hands out and feel the glow."

Her eyes grew wary. She'd been waiting the entire time to see what kind of trap he'd spring and now she sensed it was upon her.

"There's no shame in it," Gary said. "As long as you know which you are."

"I'm trying."

Gary nodded to where Emily sat next to me in the second row. "She doesn't need you anymore. You see that, don't you? If that was the reason you gave yourself for coming here, it's gone."

Quincy was biting her lower lip, kneading the flesh. Her upper teeth grew stained with lipstick. "I don't know what you want me to say," she said.

"He's not coming back," he said.

"Who?" Quincy asked and immediately regretted it.

"And really, how pathetic can you get? Obsessing over a pampered—"

"Be quiet."

"A boy playing at being a man, who runs tail between his legs at the first sign of trouble—"

"Shut your mouth," shouting the last word and then going still.

Gary's face slackened, revealing for an instant the pain he felt pushing students in this way. The man knowingly served as a lightning rod for our fears, drawing them out so we could face them in the open and become not just stronger actors but stronger human beings in the process. The tragedy was that it had desensitized him. It was essential that someone strong be at the helm, and this was the price he'd paid.

"You didn't know him," she said. "He could be so generous. If you were kind to him he'd give you every last cent in his wallet, only if you were kind, and is that such a horrible thing to ask?"

I took Emily's hand but it was nonresponsive. There was a flat, injured look on her face, like she'd divined Quincy's words a moment before she'd said them. Her eyes flicked between the backs of those sitting in the row ahead, unsure of where to settle.

* * *

Shortly after class ended Emily confessed to me that Tim had in fact been calling her throughout his absence. Hothouse flowers bloomed in her cheeks as she admitted to receiving voicemails and text messages which, she emphasized, she'd never responded to. Her eyes tracked mine, gauging the minutest shifts. She needed a haircut, I thought, inspecting the blonde strands curling around her ears. Her index fingers hooked into the belt loops of my jeans.

She said she knew where he was staying in town. That was when I should have started arguing, telling her she didn't owe him anything and how miserable she'd been with him around. Friend or no, she had to think of herself now. Instead, I focused on the slight pull of her fingers on the belt loops, amazed that a woman cared enough to use me as her tether.

* * *

On the eastern fringes of town, in the shadow of Truman Bridge, stood the Oswego Boardwalk, a mile-long stretch of penny arcades, novelty bars, and souvenir shops now mostly boarded up for the coming winter. During the summer, when cops drank beer at outdoor tables and kids screamed on creaky rides, you could almost convince yourself the churning river lapping at your shoes between wood planks was nothing more than nature's exuberance. But when the sounds disappeared and the smells of cotton candy and cooking grease dissipated, all that was left was a mad boar bashing its snout against an enclosure. The planks shook and bled white foam. Storefronts huddled together like besieged townsfolk.

Em checked their addresses, squinting to make out numbers through graffiti.

"It's further on," I said, pointing to where the boardwalk curved away from the water to allow room for two of the bridge's massive cylindrical supports. Water gurgled and foamed all around them. Traffic roared overhead.

When I was a kid my parents would take me to the boardwalk at least every other Saturday. Dad and I would play arcade games, Mom would get some sun, and in the afternoons we'd reconvene for burgers. Dad snapped pictures *ad nauseam*, which neither Mom or I understood. Why continue documenting a weekly ritual? Still, we dutifully struck poses, Mom winking to the camera, hands on her hips as a thin sundress flapped against her thighs. When it was time to head home I think we were all secretly grateful that a piece of that golden light that never seemed to wane on those long Saturdays had been captured for posterity.

Em's head was bent into her chest like a roosting bird. Our shoes tracked foam.

We passed a homeless man staring up at the bridge intently. His beard was peppered with gray. He blinked slowly to better receive the ecstasy of vehicles belching exhaust.

"There," I said, spotting the sign for the Sunset Motel, set back a few hundred yards from the boardwalk. A collection of maroon-painted cottages clustered around a broken stretch of parking lot. Picnic benches littered with trash and a front office advertising cable TV and hourly rates.

I started toward it and Em touched my elbow. I stopped but didn't turn around. I kept staring at the motel sign, broken light tubes in the shape of letters, areas blackened by weather damage.

She put her arms about my waist and squeezed.

"It's right over…"

She turned me around. She was surprisingly strong when she wanted to be.

"You're not going anywhere," she said, hair whipping about her face. "I just found you."

Em found the right cottage and knocked. A coffee cup held crushed butts next to the door. Gray efficiency blinds covering the window rustled. I noticed the movement but didn't look in its direction. Somehow I doubted Tim would be particularly glad to see me.

The deadbolt slid back, the door opened, and there he stood, a little gaunt maybe but otherwise unchanged. He hugged Emily and ushered us inside. He smiled without making eye contact.

The walls were painted algae green. The room felt airless, claustrophobic. The carpet was stained with mildew.

"Check this out," Tim said, sitting down on the twin bed. The threadbare comforter held butterfly designs.

He tapped a coin slot affixed to the headboard. Took a quarter from the nightstand and slipped it in. Internal mechanisms groaned and the mattress began shaking. "I can hear it when people use it in other rooms," jittering in front of us like an out-of-focus image. "I don't know, it's funny."

Tim was barefoot. There were no books or magazines anywhere. A small TV rested on the dresser facing the bed, partially covered by one of his shirts. A fan circled overhead, endlessly churning stale air. I wondered if this was what he'd been doing these past few weeks, lying on a come-stained bed watching the blades turn.

"Thanks for coming," he said to Emily, then as an afterthought, "both of you." He tucked his hands beneath his thighs, like he was afraid they might fly off.

"Tim..." Emily began.

"When you didn't answer my calls I thought okay, she's had enough and that's fine."

She pulled the shirt off the television, revealing Tim's warped doppelganger on its glass screen. "I should have..."

"I wasn't expecting you to." He ventured a little smile. "I didn't think I'd get another chance."

She folded the shirt and placed it next to him on the bed. Hair fell over her face but I knew she was looking at him.

"I'll go get the car," I muttered.

"No, don't do that," Emily said. Her hand twitched but she didn't touch him.

Tim's eyes pleaded with her not to be cruel. He took her hand.

She didn't lean in, didn't pull away. They seemed frozen in an awkward pose.

"Whatever's wrong with me I'll fix it," he whispered. "But I'll never put you in that position again."

She exhaled like it hurt her.

"I promise, Em."

"Neil, will you help him with his things? I want to get out of here." She pulled her hand away.

Tim covered by getting up and saying, "No worries, I'll get it."

We walked more or less together to the bathroom. "Seriously," he said, fingers fluttering like a flamboyant queen, "you should see that boardwalk pick up nights. Whatever you want, skunk weed, queers, girls missing teeth..."

"Oh." Every move I made and every word that came out of my mouth felt out of sync.

He stopped at the threshold to the bathroom and turned to me. "Do you mind?"

His eyes roved across my face. He hadn't shaved in a few days and patches of light brown stubble dotted his cheeks.

I stepped back and he closed the door. A few moments later I heard him rustling around. Emily watched me as I neared. She opened her mouth to say something.

"He's coming," I said.

She nodded but her gaze remained fixed on the bathroom door. The shadow cast on the bed by the turning fan blades was the only motion in the room.

There was a smell like the innards of a crab after you'd ripped off its carapace. Beyond fear. Closer to shock, as raw materials began recomposing themselves for survival when survival itself had ceased to be an option.

"I'm going to check on him," she said. She moved forward and I took her arm.

"He's fine," I muttered, fingers pressing in tighter than I'd intended.

A car horn honked in the parking lot, answered a few moments later by a low wolf whistle.

Tim came out swinging a brown leather toiletry bag. "All set?" he asked, voice booming in the tight space.

Emily was looking at him strangely, like she knew she should recognize him but couldn't. Their eyes met and Tim's grin faltered. Just for a moment we saw the vacant sadness lurking there, and then it was gone.

"Grab that backpack?" Tim asked me, nodding toward where it lay by the dresser.

"Sure."

I retrieved it and Emily said, "We'll wait outside."

"What's the problem?" he asked.

Tim started toward her and Em put her hands up partway. Her gaze was on the dark splotches on the carpet but I knew what she was thinking about; the look on his face beneath the charade, a bottomless pit on whose edge we teetered.

"Just...get the rest of your stuff."

We stepped outside. The river's roar was loud and constant.

"I can't," she said, hands on her cheeks shaking her head. "It's the same pattern all over again."

"He doesn't know how else to be."

She glanced at the window. "I felt like I was losing my mind in there. Did you see him? Like it's fine, it's cool, we'll go back to school and it'll be like it never happened."

I came close and she pecked my nose. Her lips were warm.

"At least when I fell apart it was obvious." She chuckled, realized how inappropriate it was, and stopped. "What do I do with this?"

"Just be there." I felt like a hypocrite, dispensing advice. I shrugged.

Her face grew serious. Her nostrils flared as they always did when she was worried. She tapped my forehead with her index finger. "Don't lose me in there."

* * *

The three of us endured an excruciating car ride back to campus, Em and I up front, Tim in back silently evaluating the landscape outside the windows. Afternoon was turning into evening. I wanted nothing more than to curl up with Emily in front of the television but that wasn't an option. We hadn't even broached the topic of living arrangements. One thing I would not allow was for Emily to spend another night alone with him. I didn't care how pitiful he looked or what tricks he deployed. We were friends right up until he breached her safety.

Quincy had spared no effort for his return. Her coffee table held takeout from Señor Esperanza's, a rattrap of a taqueria the four of us had frequented (mostly as a dare) following a night of drinking. Stacks of plastic cups were laid out next to chaste bottles of pop. She'd even made a chocolate cake with vanilla frosting, and was so preoccupied with laying it out in front of him that it almost slipped off its platter.

Tim briefly glanced at it and reached for a plastic cup. "Where's the hooch?" he asked.

Quincy glanced at Emily. Tim noticed.

"Really?"

Emily took the cup and went into the kitchen to fix him a drink. Quincy fidgeted but didn't sit down. "Is it really you?"

He patted the seat next to him.

She sat down. The sheer black dress she wore tightened unflatteringly around her stomach. Tim pretended not to notice.

"You baked?" he asked, scooping a little frosting with his index finger and popping it in his mouth.

She smacked his hand lightly. "I tried."

"It's good."

Emily came up behind the couch and handed Tim his drink. He thanked her. Quincy cut him a piece of cake. Emily put her arm around my waist and for a moment it did seem as if things might turn out all right.

Tim took a few bites and noticed we were staring at him. "Sit down, you're making me nervous," he said to Em and me.

We gathered around him. He ate quickly, periodically washing it down with his drink. "I'll tell you everything that happened, every last crummy detail. But not tonight." He looked at each of us in turn. "Can we just hang out?"

I looked at Em. "Sure," she said, shrugging.

Quincy filled him in on innocuous news—who was hooking up with whom, the latest professor Gary had provoked. There was something almost soothing about such details, like reading an entertainment magazine from two years back and realizing the stories never changed. Soon enough, though, she began talking about what she'd had to go through in class. My heart went out to her as she described the torturous sessions Gary had put her through. Though she had reason, she never once painted him as an outright villain. As much of a shit as he'd been, as demeaning as his methods frequently were, Quincy sensed a purpose behind it. Tim wasn't as charitable.

"What's the matter with you?" he asked her. "How could you just take it?"

Quincy frowned. Large gold hoop earrings shook.

Tim's gaze ricocheted between Emily and me. "And you guys just sat there and let him?" I could see him working himself up. "Things are good and all of a sudden friends are disposable."

"It's not like that," Emily said.

Tim made to get up, then thought better of it. When he met Emily's eyes he shook his head and looked away.

"I'm just curious..." Tim began, tone making it clear it would be offensive. "How long did you two wait before hooking up? A week?"

Emily gave him a steady warning look.

"Not even that?"

"Does it matter?" I asked.

Tim took a sip of his drink, found his glass empty, and passed it to Quincy. "I'll have another."

"You can make your own drink," Emily said.

Quincy took it without protest. Cracking ice in the kitchen. Pouring vodka.

"I guess congratulations are in order," Tim said to me. The words were directed at me but their true target was clear. "You have no idea the kind of hoops I had to jump through with Emily in high school. Courtship rules she must have gotten in a book. No making out before the second date, no petting before the third..."

"Since when did you care about any of that?" Emily asked. She was blushing.

"I cared."

Quincy gave him the cup. He stared down at its contents.

"You look hungry," she said, opening up a few of the takeout containers. "Dig in, don't be shy. The guac's actually not half bad..."

"I'm feeling kind of tired, actually," he said.

"Oh Tim no," she said.

"Would it be all right if I lay down on your bed?"

"What is this, punishment?" Emily asked. She swallowed with difficulty.

"I'm just tired. It's been a long day."

He placed the cup on the coffee table, next to the food and cake and cutlery and soda pop. Quincy tried not to look disappointed.

"I thought I was doing you a favor," Emily said.

Tim rose and shoved his hands in his pockets. There was a panicked air to his movements. "I'm not hungry right now, thanks though," he said to Quincy and started toward the bedroom.

"He looks at me like I'm beautiful," Emily said, stopping him in his tracks. "Like just my being there is a gift. The worst part of my day is getting up in the morning because it means being away from his warmth. And what did I have with you except trying and getting rejected and then just not trying anymore?"

Tim walked the rest of the way to the bedroom gingerly, like he was worried a trapdoor would swing open beneath him, and shut the door behind him.

Quincy grabbed Tim's drink and finished it in a few gulps. "I think you should go," she said to Emily.

Emily blinked away tears, but she got up as though she'd been expecting it. Running mascara gave her raccoon eyes. Quincy brought things into the kitchen. I helped her. She brought out saran wrap for the cake and covered it up. It was quiet in the apartment.

"Smug," she muttered. "Finds a piece of happiness and thinks she can just hurt him like that." Frosting spread out against the inside of the plastic wrap.

She pushed the cake into the sink. It smashed against the sides and collapsed in on itself.

"I'll clean the rest. Go sit down," I said.

"It's hopeless and I don't care. Does that make me stupid?"

She turned on the faucet. Water dissolved the cake into brownish sludge. "He doesn't love me. I don't even think he likes me. Not that it matters." Wet saran wrap shimmered gaily. "I don't have the right equipment."

10

There was a message on my phone the next morning from Dad asking if I could run over a second care package to the hospital. I felt anxious at the thought but wasn't really surprised. My father had been exiled, and though I secretly believed it to be more a blessing than a curse, I wasn't ready to disappoint him by refusing. I told myself it was a small thing, easily done.

Telling Emily I was stopping home was actually the easiest part. She'd gotten up early, and the grim set to her mouth made it plain she'd be spending the day making amends with Quincy and her new ward. This seemed to be their way: acute flare-ups, followed by a period of calm. At least my absence would mean sparing Tim proof positive of just how completely things had changed in his absence.

Dad stood in the driveway next to a rusty moving truck, giving instructions to two men hauling things out of the garage. He wore an old windbreaker of mine with the hood up, giving him the appearance of an aging hoodlum. I came up behind him, crushing a carpet of rioting yellow and orange leaves underfoot. He nodded at me as he helped one of them load an elliptical machine into the back of the truck. The mover looked barely out of his teens and wore a permanent half-sneer. Dad clapped him on the back and the kid shirked it off, hitching up loose jeans on his way back into the garage.

"I'm getting rid of all of it," Dad explained. "Elliptical, stationary bike, rowing machine...rowing? What was I thinking? Your mother can't even set foot on a boat without getting sick!"

The windbreaker hung loosely on his frame. His paunch was nearly gone. His skin had a yellowish tint to it, like the onset of jaundice.

"Know what I think we should do with the extra space?" he asked. "Set up a game room downstairs."

"Okay," I said, forcing my gaze off him. My insides felt cold.

"A nice polished carom board. Or a ping-pong table, those are great for parties. I'll teach you the basics, it's easy."

The movers threw something heavy into the back of the truck, causing an enormous racket. Dad winced and looked about to say something, then remembered me and refrained. He took a deep breath and smiled, as if none of this were particularly important.

"Exercise was my big solution when she started putting on weight. I read all the books, bought the equipment, developed a training plan. I even worked out with her so she'd feel we were both in it together. Lot of good it did."

"Mom's not the exercising type."

"No, she's not." He took off his glasses and cleaned them. "I got tired of seeing all that equipment every time I went downstairs. Riding her like a gym instructor, forcing her to spend at least five minutes per machine when in the end she'd just eat more anyway...

what a waste."

He slipped the glasses back on and blinked several times. Sleep grit clung to the corners of his eyes.

"Dad, are you all right?" I asked.

He gave me a look that belied his words. "Don't you worry about your old man. I can still beat you in an arm wrestle any day of the week."

"I could have helped. You didn't need to hire movers."

"Why not? You're busy, go on."

He closed his eyes, stealing a moment's rest, and when they opened they were attentive and kind. It was the gaze that had held me in thrall throughout most of my life, the one I sought out by doing things that pleased him, punishing myself preemptively to avoid seeing it turn to disappointment. The gaze that said I was his son and there was no disputing it.

"I should have given you the tuition money," he said.

I shook my head. "It's okay."

"I didn't know! You're just like her when it comes to secrecy. How about a couple of hints that you were thinking of joining the drama program? I never even saw you practicing for the audition."

I peeled off a red leaf sticking to my jeans, shot through with bluish veins. "I practiced outside mostly. Walking around."

He shook his head wonderingly. "I spoke to your acting teacher. The illustrious Mr. Gary."

"He's insane."

"Yes."

We laughed. A helicopter buzzed past overhead.

"The man's alienated at least half the faculty so far, with plans to finish the job by Christmas. But he knows people, Niladri. Directors, producers. People who can get you work after graduation."

"You don't know him. He doesn't just do favors." I watched the older of the two movers, a squat man wearing a shirt open to reveal a chunky brass crucifix, trundle down the rear door. "It's taken a lot just to keep my head above water in his class. Every day it's some new test and the rules always change."

Dad crossed his arms over his chest and pretended to scrutinize me. "He seems to think you're one of the most promising students he's ever taught. Of course I wouldn't expect anything else, but..."

The older mover cleared his throat. When Dad turned to him he held up a pale receipt. Dad went over and they conversed quietly for a few moments.

"How much for the tools?" Dad asked, nodding toward the garage. "Industrial power drill. I've got a brand new socket and wrench set, plastic hasn't even been taken off yet."

"We don't take tools," the man said shortly.

The sun disappeared behind clouds, casting the driveway in shadow. Dad inspected the receipt as if he could change what he found there. He muttered something and the mover said, "That's *list*. You want to take your chances with someone else we'll unload. But hourly rate still applies."

A gust of wind flattened the windbreaker against Dad's back, revealing the curvature of his spine and thin flesh. He signed the receipt and the mover cut a check. His accomplice sat on the low stone wall edging the lawn, swigging from a plastic water bottle.

Dad slipped the check into his pocket and came over to me. "I put the bags in the side seat. I went easy on the chocolate, sure she's been gorging herself."

The movers got into the front seats and slammed the doors. The engine chuffed several times and caught on. A stream of exhaust shot out from the back of the truck and blew into the garage.

Dad began to smile, then noticed the expression on my face and said, "Once the trial's over it'll all be different. A fresh...a fresh start."

I nodded.

"Go, what are you waiting for?" He patted my shoulder. "Help me by living."

* * *

This time there was no warm welcome from Nurse Khadijah. When I entered the station I had to wait almost a full minute before she swiveled in her rollie chair to face me. Patients showering, eating, watching television were displayed in miniature on screens behind her. She stared at the bags I held in my hands like they contained writhing snakes.

"Can I see her?" I asked.

She began creaking back and forth in her chair, slow and regular like a metronome. "Pour them out."

"What?"

She nodded at the bags.

"I...why?"

When it was clear she wouldn't answer, I upended one of the bags, spilling a cornucopia of snacks, bras, and socks onto the counter. She poked at a package of Swedish Fish.

"Now take it to her like this," she said.

"Did I do something?"

"You didn't talk to your mother," Nurse Khadijah said.

"I did."

I could feel heat emanating off her body.

"I tried to," I amended.

"She had chocolate stains on the bed sheets. Wrappers and junk on the floor. She's not supposed to eat anything in the dormitory." She opened the package of Swedish Fish and began eating them. "Dr. Thibodeau took away a day's overtime from our checks. Said if we weren't going to do our full jobs then we wouldn't get full pay. Isn't that funny?" She chewed with an open mouth.

"I'm sorry."

She smacked her lips, affording a glimpse of partially chewed red paste between her teeth. "I didn't ask if you were sorry. I asked if it was funny."

She motioned for me to lay the other bag down on the ground. "If she acts right I'll bring them to her," Nurse Khadijah said.

It was getting very warm in the nurse's station. "Can I see her?"

"She's in the garden."

"It's barely forty degrees."

Nurse Khadijah swiveled back to the screens. A thick arm pushed the mound off to the side. Two socks fell to the floor.

"Doctor's orders."

Past the parking lot opposite Baker Pavilion stood half an acre of tilled earth bordered by fencing. Stakes had been put in at regular intervals. Clumps of dying vegetation littered the ground. In the distance stood an earthmover, sinister somehow in its silence. Beyond that a single figure bent over a spade, a speck of darker brown amidst the dusty brown landscape. I hopped the fence and started toward her.

Mom worked in spurts of furious action, digging out overripe purple cabbages, most with leaves eaten through by insects, then stopping to recover her breath. She had nothing but her gown on. Her arms and face were whitish with cold.

A nurse stood in the doorway of an equipment shed a few hundred feet away ensuring the punishment was carried out.

She was breathing so hard she didn't hear me until I was right behind her. I touched her back. She started and then redoubled her efforts, air hissing out between her teeth.

"I ate too much," she whispered like a litany. "I get fat that way, and *Baba* loves me less."

"Mom..."

"That's why he stopped coming."

Dozens of unearthed cabbages stared up at us like eyes with purple-white pupils. Her entire body was shivering.

"I'm no better than the rest. I forget that sometimes."

"Let me," I said, grasping the spade.

"I have to," she answered.

I peeled one of her hands off the handle. It was reddish and swollen. A sigh escaped my lips.

"You can't just come unannounced like this anymore," she said, shaking sweat out of her eyes. "I start getting used to not thinking of you and you come."

I opened my jacket and placed her bruised hand against my chest, warming it. She tried to continue working with a single hand, and paused.

"It's not fair," she said, staring down an endless row of raised earth with cabbage leaves poking out.

The nurse stalked out of the equipment shed. Mom's eyes went to her and widened. She pulled away from me and attacked the ground in a frenzy. Earth was tossed up everywhere, some raining onto the legs of my jeans. Her body constantly seemed on the verge of falling.

"I told him not to stop me!" Mom called out.

The nurse stopped a few feet away from where the excess earth was landing.

"Her hands..." I began.

Mom made a dissenting noise.

"Yes?" the nurse, Arabic with sharp features, asked. She took in my mother and I saw that she despised her, this pampered woman who did nothing except make their jobs more difficult. And I understood how truly frightened my mother was, living with patients she couldn't trust, overseen by nurses who could no longer be trusted to protect her.

I shook my head. "Nothing."

"She needs to focus," the nurse said.

I slipped off my jacket. "Can I give this to her?" I asked.

"I'm fine, I don't need it," Mom said. She wouldn't even look at me.

I laid it down on the ground next to her. "For later?" I asked the nurse.

She stared at me for several moments. Then she motioned toward the parking lot.

* * *

When I woke up the next morning my entire body ached. There was no position that eased it, the feel of torn muscle knitting itself back together beneath my skin. Even Emily's gentle touch hurt.

I wanted to curl into myself. I wanted to pull the bedroom curtains closed and try not to think.

11

A few days later Emily and I were coming down the stairs to the ground floor, discussing a good place to grab a decadent breakfast, when we were stopped by the sight of Auntie waiting for us below. She held a brown paper bag of bagels and two coffees in a cardboard holder. I saw the bright exhaustion in her eyes and recalled the series of messages she'd left on my phone which had gone unanswered.

Auntie smiled at me, prim and expectant. Emily came down the rest of the way and embraced her.

"I've wanted to meet you for so long," she said.

Auntie was thrown off by the contact. She tightened her grip on the bag, the contents seeping grease. "Me too," she answered. "I couldn't wait for that one to get over his nerves."

Emily took the coffees out of her hand and turned to regard me. "Well?" she asked. "Has the world ended now that I've met your mom?"

Auntie's smile evaporated. The sadness was like a cord of living tissue between us, hideously exposed to the elements. She tilted her head slightly, accepting of whatever answer I provided.

"I guess not," I said.

All throughout the day the three of us spent together I kept telling myself it was a joke, nothing more. Of course she's not my mother. My mother is...well, that didn't bear thinking about. In the car, headed to one home furnishing store after another, Auntie requiring only the barest sign of preference from Em or me to signal a salesman over, I waited for an opening. Only it never seemed to come. The two of them got along so famously—conversation flicking from a shared soccer-playing past to gardening tips to reveling in my clumsiness, my supposed sweet nature, the way my voice would shoot up an octave when caught in a lie—that my stepping in to clarify things would have caused instant embarrassment. And so I waited for Auntie to create a pause in the conversation and come clean. But that didn't happen either.

Come afternoon, Auntie's Fendi purse was filled with receipts for furniture, silver cutlery, and china plates, all for our apartment. A part of me was grateful for it; finally I would stop feeling like an interloper in Em and Tim's home. But the lie I'd told lessened it all, like enjoying a dinner out with your parents with a poor report card to broach afterwards.

Auntie, by comparison, giddily embraced her new role. She laughed frequently, a throaty chortle I couldn't remember ever hearing before. Her shoulders relaxed and for once her posture lost its inward set. She seemed taller, strolling arm-in-arm with Emily to browse shoes and try on makeup.

I tried to reconcile this woman with the one who'd get drowsy from drinking too much, relying on Arjun or myself to get her up to her bedroom. I knew her coming to Miller House was an act of desperation. She couldn't sit alone in that house anymore, looking out onto a backyard with a swimming pool and basketball court she'd never used a day in her life but had paid to maintain for the family she'd always wished to have. She couldn't keep waking up to the same truth, that the most precious things in life lay beyond the reach of will and firmly in the dominion of fortune. Will had given her the courage to refuse her parents'—my grandparents'— wishes to get married before immigrating to the States. Will had made her wealthy, rising to CFO of Schiller-Frost Pharmaceuticals before cashing out. And will was what ultimately thwarted her. It couldn't have been easy, seeing your pampered sister who had never really worked a day in her life piss away a happy marriage and close relationship with her son. It must have been like a burr buried deep in the meat of her arm.

"Don't be angry," Auntie said during a rare private moment, waiting for Emily to exit the bathroom at Lord & Taylor. Her eyes scanned my face fondly.

"I'm not," I said. "How could I be?"

"Tell her the truth after you get home," she said. "It'll be fine, you'll see..." She broke off, as if trying to remember what she'd been about to say.

I kept nodding, and then turned away from her. My chest ached. I clapped a hand over my mouth.

She put a hand on my shoulder.

"I wish..." Ready to confess to what made me both cling to and retreat from her; the sense that fortune had gotten its threads crossed.

"Shhh," she said. "Me too, *janu*." A moment later, "Dry your eyes. She'll be out any minute."

* * *

While the three of us had been busy furnishing the apartment, Quincy and Tim had been moving his things out. There was a synchronicity to it all I found cold—one coffee table swapped out for another, a few leftover CDs and DVDs as a kind of parting gesture of generosity. Emily pretended to be unaffected by it, sleeves rolled up assembling a cherry wood rocking chair, nails trapped between rosebud lips, but it must have hurt. It would have been easier if she and Tim could just make a clean break of it, but I knew that wouldn't happen. They had been friends before and they would continue on as such. The burden of responsibility would simply transfer over to her.

Later that evening we went over. Quincy and Tim were spread out on her bed watching *La Dolce Vita* and snacking from a tray of macaroons cooling on the nightstand. Quincy had continued on with the baking. Seeing her freely spill crumbs over a sky-blue pajama top, hair up in curlers, I thought that she had finally taken a step in line with her true spirit. After all, what good were fancy dresses and perfectly teased hair to a man who sat scrunched up against the headboard like a positioned marionette, skin the pallor of one who rarely ventured outside? The empty look on his face was that of a child who didn't yet understand how badly he'd been hurt. He ate and watched the movie and said hello to us and it was all the same to him.

Tim moved off to the far side of the bed. Emily wriggled into the nook between Quincy's breast and shoulder. Tim held up the weed tin and shook it in my direction. I went over to his side and started rolling a joint. Tim watched as I broke up the weed, mixed it in with a little tobacco, and spread it out on a thin piece of Zig-Zag rolling paper. I worked both ends until the mixture became a firm cylinder and licked the sticky inner strip, sealing the joint. Finally I tore a thin strip of cardboard from the inside of a cigarette pack, rolled it up tight, and stuck it in one end. Tim took the joint and inspected it, marveling at its smoothness.

"Does the filter do anything, or is it just for show?" he asked, pushing the tiny cardboard piece in further.

"Makes smoking easier when it gets down to the nub."

Tim rooted inside the weed tin for a lighter.

"By the window, please," Quincy said, not taking her eyes off the screen.

"Aw c'mon," Tim said, flashing her a coy smile. "Please?"

Her eyes met his and must have seen what I did: blatant manipulation. The disingenuous vacuity Emily and I had seen at the Sunset Motel, a kind of film masking all the thoughts and deeds he dared not express, had only grown in the following days, and plastering a rogue's smile over it made it all the more repellent. And yet she shook her head in good humor and gestured toward the window, accepting the pretense.

"Let's watch something else," Emily said. "I can't follow this movie halfway through."

"But it's tradition," Tim said.

Emily gave me a look that said Tim was exaggerating again.

"Don't you remember," Tim continued, "we took that 'Intro to European Cinema' class at the art institute."

"Wow, how many years ago was that?" Emily asked.

"I started drinking grappa, you said things like '*ciao*' unironically..."

"I did not." Her hands were crossed over her chest, fingers still carrying the scent of new wood and nails.

"Sure," Tim said, going over to the bedroom window and cracking it open. "It never happened. I made it up." He held the joint out to me, offering me the chance to take first puff. I took him up on it, blowing out a stream of smoke into a six-inch gap of night.

"It's just that was so long ago," Emily said. I could hear in her voice that she didn't want to harp on it but felt compelled to.

"Terrible, I know," Tim said.

"No," Em said quietly. She moved out of Quincy's nook and sat up in bed. Quincy kept her eyes on the screen. She absently flicked a few crumbs off her chest.

Tim took several large puffs of the joint then passed it over. "You guys don't have to stay if you don't want to," he said to me.

"What do you mean?" Emily asked.

"If you have somewhere you need to be, go for it," Tim said, insisting on speaking to me instead of Emily.

"I don't," I said.

I kept smoking, watching him stare out the window. A student rode his bike up the path outside the house, taking advantage of the rare lack of foot traffic to describe long, lazy half-circles. I didn't want to be there. Not when he was like this, jittery, pulling back rubber bands and letting them fly regardless of target. If it wasn't for Emily I'd have taken the opening he offered and gotten the hell out.

"What's the plan, exactly?" Tim asked, facing the girls. "Do I keep living here like a tenant Q doesn't want..."

"Don't put words in my mouth," Quincy said. She paused the movie.

"For how long?" Tim continued. "A week? A month?"

Emily pushed her hair off her forehead, drawing it out for an extra moment's deliberation. "Do you want Neil and me to move to another building?" she asked. "Will that make it easier?"

"Fuck it," Quincy muttered. She went over to the clothes closet, selected a dress at random, and went into the bathroom to change, slamming the door behind her.

"Neil and me," Tim repeated slowly.

"I'll move if you want me to," Em said. "But as a favor, not payback. We're even."

Tim shrugged. "Whatever."

"No," staring directly at him, "I tried. My heart, my soul, everything I had was yours if you'd only opened up the tiniest bit."

I finished off the joint. Emily and Tim didn't say anything more. When Quincy exited the bathroom dressed to go out we fell in line and followed. If a resolution existed, it wouldn't be found here.

Where we ended up was an undergrad dorm party in Devlin Hall, a moldy two-story bunker within earsplitting range of the bell tower. Inside were copious Jell-O shots and stupid attractive girls all too willing to engage Tim and me in conversation. Emily was an instant hit. The prowling guys could sense the soft, clear-lined quality she possessed even if unable to call it by its name. She was gracious and danced with them, even allowing a shy suitor to refill her beer glass. When she started feeling unsure of herself her eyes went out across the hall and found me. Just a second's eye contact, nothing more, but it was enough. Hours passed. The room pleasantly blurred. Every person I struck up a conversation with found me fascinating and a little dangerous. I traded flirtatious looks with little whores I'd never see again, effortlessly stepping between moments like a skipped stone.

Quincy disappeared upstairs. Tim tried to find her come night's end, and when he couldn't, enlisted me in the search. I sent Emily home with a few classmates that were relatively sober, and went on up. We asked a group of guys holding corridor races with two rollie chairs. A girl with bleary eyes who just shook her head and tried not to throw up. A few doors were open, couples passed out, a few post-coitus with the stink of cheap alcohol and cock wafting out. Finally we got a tip from an ousted roommate who, more out of a desire to get some sleep than play Good Samaritan, let us into his room.

A tiny living area and kitchenette, barely the size of a Miller House bathroom. Posters of Journey and Black Sabbath covering cracks in the walls, so thin we may as well have still been out in the hallway. Beyond a closed bedroom door came low bed creaks and a woman sighing.

Tim put his ear up against it, glanced at me, and nodded. His eyes scanned the threadbare carpet underfoot, trying to comprehend a feeling he couldn't name. When he didn't bang on the door I sank into a beanbag chair and started smoking a cigarette.

"I don't think you can smoke in here," he said.

I glanced up at the ceiling and pointed to the little beige smoke detector with its steady red eye. My feet hurt and I wasn't about to get up.

Tim brought a chair directly under it, went up, and removed its battery. There was a precision to his movements that depressed me. Despite the weed and the revelry downstairs he hadn't really been with us. He hadn't left whatever promontory that called to him so fiercely, nor drawn his gaze away from its peculiar view.

He sat down on the chair and turned the battery over in his hands. They were still going strong in the bedroom.

"Did I miss my chance?" he asked.

"About what?"

"Should I have barged in there? Kicked in the door and saved her? I don't have that in me. I'd feel like an idiot."

I ashed on the carpet.

"She's happier with you," he said. "When I first came back I thought, 'Just wait for it to blow over.' But she glows. I can see the smart-alecky girl who'd dare me to play hooky with her. Do you know what a miracle that is?"

His face grew still. "Go on. I have this."

"I'll stay."

"Go. You have someone waiting for you."

The campus paths held groups of revelers brainwashed into thinking that talking without listening and breaking things just to see them break was the pinnacle of anything other than hell. Just a few short months ago I would have been content with slinking away for home but things were different now. There were people who cared enough about me to notice my absence.

Spooning with Emily in the pre-dawn hours, trying to still my racing heart and brain enough to drift off, I thought this all came at a cost. As long as she felt my hand clasping hers she slept untroubled. But I'd caused the growing rift between her and her friends, and the fact that I'd done so unwittingly was irrelevant.

I had to put things right. But as the minutes ticked away I feared I did not possess the materials.

* * *

Tim's first day back in classes seemed to pass without incident. He stumbled through Modern Dance, avoiding his reflection in the wall mirror as all of us lacking a gymnastics background did. He feigned interest in Mr. Buchanan's long-winded speeches on Elizabethan theater, peppered at intervals with oblique references to the mysterious "forces" behind the death of Christopher Marlowe. Though we'd never verbalized it, either Emily or Quincy or I was always close by him, ready to fill in awkward gaps in conversation when students would come up to ask how he was doing. Of course the one place we couldn't protect him was Gary's class, but as it turned out we needn't have worried.

During Tim's absence Gary had taken to ignoring his name during roll call. On his first day back, though he was clearly sitting in the front row, Gary ignored the name again. Class continued, with students being called up for improvisations or to begin rudimentary scene work, but not Tim. Soon enough class was dismissed, and the worst seemed to be over.

First love, fed by unstable and quick-burning fuel, created a disconnect miles removed yet nearly equal in totality to what Tim was experiencing. I treasured Em's idiosyncrasies—the filthy jokes and mad cackling, the weird little dances and characters she'd come out with when we were alone. I felt as if I'd known her my entire life, and the fact that all of this came from within a lithe, salaciously underdeveloped body...I'd stopped using protection early on and, against her better judgment, so did she. If feeling every inch of her pussy and watching her bite her lip hard enough to draw blood when she was close to coming resulted in pregnancy, so be it. Nothing but the salty, musty taste of her in my mouth mattered. We went from fucking in front of the apartment window to jamming chairs against classroom doors and going at it on the desk, the floor. One time Mikas, the grim janitor who roamed Carruthers Hall like an uneasy ghost, found me eating her out and just stood in the doorway while Emily pulled her skirt back down (she was experimenting with girlier clothes) and I hunted in vain for my other shoe.

She was beginning to really know me. It was like living with a sleuth sometimes, when all you wanted was to quietly brood over some perceived slight or another and she pressed, relentlessly, until you came clean. So many of the tricks I'd used in the past to deflect attention fell flat with her. No, I couldn't just change the subject. Yes, she wanted to know why I was so angry, even if the reason was stupid. No, we couldn't avoid talking about the future; living in the moment was well and good but what we had deserved something beyond "we'll see." Worst of all was the fact that she was basically an open book when it came to her family, easily tossing in details about her parents' divorce or the four months she'd spent as a run-away following her breakdown. She'd taken the true meaning of a relationship, two souls sharing their lives, to heart, and though she was forgiving of my reluctance to reciprocate, I could almost see the sand slipping through an hourglass, each grain offered on credit which was fast coming due.

Was I being an idiot? Sometimes we'd be in bed chatting about nothing in particular and the desire to come clean about who my mother really was and the schizophrenia that had become the fourth member of our family grew very strong. Yet I never did, and it had nothing to do with fears that she'd stop loving me. She wouldn't. The best I can explain it is that by confessing I felt like I would lose some crucial, unacknowledged part of myself.

Thanksgiving came and went, first a small dinner at home with Dad eating store-bought turkey and Caesar salad, followed by a list-less hour watching random shows in the basement. Afterwards a second meal at Quincy's which, due to Em having gone back home to L.A. for the weekend, was filled with odd silences and aborted attempts at small talk. I couldn't call attention to the faltering situa-tion, couldn't make an innocuous comment without Tim rolling his eyes. At least Quincy had the solace of cooking to keep her busy. I just had his baleful gaze, interrupted only by a reach for the nearest wine bottle. I went back to the apartment early and avoided them for the next few days until Emily returned.

Tim started falling asleep during classes. When a professor shouted to wake him he'd jerk his head up, blink about at tittering students, and pretend to pay attention for the next few minutes. Sleeping turned into skipping, first just a few then entire days at a time. Quincy became a master at juggling two sets of notebooks per class, at getting two copies of all paperwork. She grew irritable over trifles and stepped with an uncommonly heavy gait, as though relishing one of the few things that remained within her control.

And Gary continued to ignore him. Of all the indignities Tim had endured this was the only one painful enough to prompt him to pretend otherwise. Every time Gary's eyes looked right past him the hapless grin remained frozen on his face, the apology he should have offered on his first day back caught between his teeth. He kept showing up, though, determined to see his punishment through. And then came a Friday afternoon where Gary was ribbing a few students about their dating and fashion choices, calling up others for a light improvisation, when Tim couldn't endure any more.

"I need two more," Gary said, sauntering up to the first row. Hands on his hips, surveying us like a general.

Tim cleared his throat and said, "I'm here." He straightened up a little.

"Liev," Gary said, "stop flexing your arms and get down here."

Liev stopped chatting with his partner Mark and rose.

"Gary," Tim said, a pleading note creeping into his voice, "at least say you see me." He sat about three feet away from where Gary stood.

Liev came out onto the stage, masking his discomfort with a head scratch. Those already called paced and whispered quietly among themselves, anything to avoid being co-opted into the brewing conflict.

The back of my head tingled a warning. There were no snarky comments or veiled insults to get a rise out of Gary. Only those brown doe eyes staring up, seeking mercy.

"Tu Li," Gary said, looking over at a shy Vietnamese girl in the back row. Her gaze in turn went to Tim. "Now, please."

"Is this it?" Quincy asked Gary from where she sat beside Tim. "Anyone who doesn't fall into line disappears?"

Emily and I were sitting one row up from them. When Quincy began speaking Emily touched her shoulder to discourage her from getting involved. Quincy shrugged it off and shot her a single, furious look. There could be no mistaking it; she understood we'd left her to mend Tim by herself.

"He knows he did wrong," Quincy said. "He'll do whatever it takes, just..."

Gary raised an arm, four fingers and a thumb made to look like a bird's beak. Opening and closing it; a talking puppet.

Tim pressed his hands into his thighs and came to standing. He stood nearly at eye level with Gary.

"I shouldn't have just left," he said quickly. The spotlight's glare made the decadent curls atop his head glow like a fallen angel's. "I want to make it up, just tell me."

Gary looked at him casually, as if the whole thing were nothing at all. There was no recognition in his eyes, no empathy or forgiveness.

As Tim kept looking at him his head pulled slowly back. His eyes dropped from Gary's face to his expansive torso. The thumb of his right hand hooked into the pocket of his jeans and pulled them down a little. He seemed to be wilting beneath the man's gaze.

Tim tried to step past him for the door. Gary blocked him with shocking alacrity. Tim stepped back and Gary closed the distance until their faces were inches apart, their breath mingling. His eyes crawled over his student's face.

"What have you done with Tim Webster?" Gary asked.

"Let me go, then," Tim muttered.

Gary repeated what he'd said and Tim tried to shove him. His hands hit a solid wall of flesh and slid off like beads of water.

Gary shoved him back, hard. Tim fell over his own chair and landed hard on the floor. His right leg was caught between the chair legs and he rattled it, trying to extricate himself. I got up along with several others, wanting to help him, but he got free and backpedaled toward the far wall. Gary closed the distance.

"Stop it!" Quincy shouted.

Gary came up over Tim's body, legs like concrete pillars flanking his torso. Tim tried to get up and Gary pushed him back down with the flat of his hand. Again and again it happened as the rest of us looked on, horrified.

A low, mewling noise was coming from Tim's throat. A dog with broken legs. A cat starved to the point of delirium. It seemed as if he'd been making that noise ever since we'd found him at the Sunset Motel and we were only just now hearing it.

Gary grabbed Tim by his shirt and hauled him to his feet. There was almost something tender in the way he did it. Spit dribbled out the side of Tim's mouth.

"Stand up," Gary said.

Tim's head lolled forward onto Gary's chest. Gary shook him. "Stand on your own two feet."

Emily stood frozen beside me. Quincy sat where she was, fingers of her right hand burrowing into the meat of her left arm.

"I can't," Tim pleaded.

Gary's face twitched. "You won't," shaking him brutally on the last word. Tim's shoes hovered an inch or two above the ground.

"Tim...."

The mewling intensified.

"I can't help you."

Gary let go. Tim fell.

* * *

A scraggly-looking cat hung about Miller House, a Siamese mix with orange patches of fur along its body. One of its eyes had been clawed out and the other, to compensate, glared with a witch doctor's intensity. It hated people and hissed if you got too close, but relied on us too; our bits of discarded bagel and pizza crusts, our combined presence that kept true predators at bay. Often when I'd go out onto the front steps for a cigarette I'd see it scrounging around.

That night I found it sniffing at the scarecrow's feet. Its ears went up as soon I neared, its eye focusing on the open can of tuna in my hand. I laid it down on the grass, then backed up to the steps and sat down. I busied myself with smoking and looking everywhere except directly at the cat. When I heard the wet eating sounds I allowed myself a look. Its head was completely lost inside the can, the force of its hunger causing it to shift along the grass.

All I could think about was Tim's body crumpling to the floor and the rest of us just watching it happen. Afterwards he didn't head to Administration to file a complaint. He did what we did: gathered up his things and headed to Voice class. That was the truly grotesque thing; dutifully doing vocal exercises next to someone who'd been crushed and pretending it never happened. I despised Gary for turning us into co-conspirators. He'd exposed the abscess and then just let it seep.

Yet even that was avoiding the truth. Because anyone could see Tim needed help. Em and I had seen it and had purposefully done nothing, choosing to spin wheels upon wheels, tumbling further into our own private world as he free-fell. It's just a phase. He'll snap out of it. Let's not make it worse by blowing it out of proportion.

The moon's light was on me, clear and hard like an interrogator's lamp.

Fuck Tim. Let him rot. I hadn't had the benefit of friends between the ages of eighteen and twenty-three. I didn't have the luxury of a trust fund that allowed me to pick up stakes whenever I wanted. I fell and I fell and I fell some more, and while most of my peers intoxicated themselves and clung to the illusion of immortality like children, I realized there was no end to how far you could fall. Our senses are tuned to discern shades of darkness beyond what you ever thought possible, and any chance of returning to the light would mean climbing painstakingly up, digging your fingers into a sheer rock face until your fingers were worn away to the bone.

I'd needed breaks like this more and more often. The speed with which I went through cigarette packs was proof enough of that. All that I wanted was waiting for me upstairs, yet it was only alone that I felt like I could breathe freely. I'd kept the defining circumstance of my life a secret from Emily, and every word I spoke drew me further and further away. I'd allowed her to be misled and it was too late for correction. When I opened my mouth to speak, the words didn't matter; it was only babble filling the airless space I'd created and was now forced to maintain.

She didn't really know me. She knew an actor playing a role with the desperate conviction of a mouse lying very still in its hole as an exterminator swept a flashlight past. Yet even if the light found me, and the air curdled with the smell of poison gas, I'd keep spinning lies atop lies, keep smiling a toothy smile, because if it was between that and bringing Emily to the fount of nightmares for a visit with my mother, there was no choice to make.

The cat finished eating and looked up at me. A sharp gust of wind passed through the yard, nearly toppling it over.

From the south end of campus, the bell tower began ringing. "Go on," I said.

The eye, glossy yellow in the darkness, bored into me. Past me.

I flicked my cigarette at it and it drew back. I went back indoors but the feel of its gaze on me lingered.

Like I'd been marked.

* * *

Early the next morning I came downstairs, on the hunt for a Pop-Tart or something equally sugary in the main kitchen to begin the day. Miller House became a mausoleum during daylight hours, hanging dust motes and dirt tracks left over from the daily exodus of students. At the foot of the stairs lay a stack of filled laundry baskets for the woman who came once a week. In the sink a pan held congealed pasta sauce, mushroom heads poking out like boils. I found what I'd sought in the cupboard, quickly swallowed it down, and had started back upstairs when my gaze was caught by two forms on the living room couch.

Tim slept beneath a quilted blanket. Quincy sat next to him, hair a tangled bird's nest, day-old makeup crusty on her face. She had a fashion magazine open in front of her. When the sun flared through the windows she slipped on a pair of aviator sunglasses, which gave her the appearance of a cokehead or mourner.

I sat down on the arm of the couch.

"What do you want?" she asked, slowly leafing through pages.

"We still have a few hours before class starts."

She made a disbelieving noise. "Think we'll be skipping that one."

I nodded upstairs. "I can look after him for a bit. If you want to take a shower, or..."

"Don't do me any favors."

Tim frowned in his sleep, creasing a perfectly unlined face. The index finger of his left hand twitched, as if fending off an aggressor. His arm pulled in closer to his body.

She put the magazine aside and sighed. She wore a teal blouse that was much too small for her now, buttons along the center on the verge of popping. "He starts getting stir-crazy if we stay in the apartment. He feels miserable when we're around other people. So where does that leave us?" She started rubbing the joints of her fingers.

I took her hand and began doing it for her. "So I was playing soccer with my dad one evening. I was seven. He was trying to teach me how to get the ball down to the ground. It got hard to see but I didn't ask to stop. We'd been playing for over an hour, and that kind of attention..."

"Prime currency," Quincy said, rolling her neck to loosen it.

I nodded. "Soon the only thing I could make out was his shirt, hovering in the air a quarter of the way downfield. One of those tie-dyed jobs, God knows where he got it. I guess he couldn't see me that well either because he kept lobbing them over my shoulder. I ran them down, but it got exhausting. Finally I saw the ball coming, way up, and reached a hand out to grab it." I stopped what I was doing. "The ball caught my middle finger and bent it back, fracturing it."

Quincy watched me. "Did you cry?"

I shook my head. "I ran the ball down, kicked it back to him. We played a while longer. I felt nauseous and my hand felt on fire but I didn't say anything. Not once during the next month, sleeping with my hand propped up on a pillow because it hurt too much to move."

"Why'd you do it?" Quincy asked.

I grunted. "I thought he'd get mad at me. I've always felt like I have to make up for some terrible thing I've done. Maybe I do, but not getting treatment for a broken finger wasn't part of it."

Tim's eyelids stirred and opened. He stared out blindly for a moment and began blinking rapidly, puzzle pieces of the room clicking into a discernible shape. His lips were tinged blue, like he'd been eating popsicles.

I squeezed Quincy's hand. "When you carry the weight of being wrong around wherever you go, it gets tempting to just add to the load. But this isn't part of it, Q."

"Part of what?" Tim asked.

"Nothing," Quincy said quickly, getting to her feet. "I need a shower."

Tim looked worried. "Oh, I'll come up."

"No," she said firmly. "Stay with Neil. I'll be back."

The hair on the back of his head was dented from the couch cushion. He rubbed his eyes and asked me where everybody was. I picked up the remote and started flicking through channels. There was a tension in the space between us, one which Quincy had felt without cease ever since he'd returned. It was what an animal feels upon coming across wounded kin, an instinctual desire to get away as it seeded the air with blood-scent.

He fell asleep again soon thereafter. After a time, I dozed too.

When I came awake the light in the room was very bright. Tim was leaning forward and I had a clear view of his neck. The veins bulged.

I started to say something when a trapped noise came from his mouth and he shot up, scanning the floor, the couch, me, like they were all closed to him.

"Hey," I said.

He waved vaguely at me and started toward the stairs. He watched his own footsteps to avoid faltering.

"She'll be back," I called out, and started after him.

"I'm gonna see." Hand on the banister for support mounting the stairs. A prince to whom everything had been given except the crucial atoms for survival, inchoate desperation in his eyes. "Just..."

He reached the second floor and went right past Quincy's door to the roof exit.

"Tim!"

I reached the exit just as the door slammed shut. There was a pull in my gut that opposed my arm reaching out to push the door open and follow. A watchful presence letting me know this would be my last chance to let him self-destruct.

Thick flakes of snow fell and dissolved on tarpaper. Newborn drops of water glittered like pearls between me and where Tim stood on a raised ledge on the far side of the roof, hands at his sides, evaluating the drop to the driveway below.

He turned to face me when I got to within ten feet of him. His chin was angled up, a shadow of his former smugness. His eyes were dull.

Snow touched my face and melted, pinpricks of cold.

"There's nothing," he said.

"No," trying not to look at his heels jutting out over air. "It gets dark. So dark sometimes we can't see. But you're not alone."

His shirt rustled. Car tires screeched in the distance.

I had the impulse to step toward him and he raised his hand. "Stay there."

I knelt without breaking eye contact. He took shallow breaths through his mouth. Water soaked through my jeans.

"You're one of the few friends I have," I said. "I tried...so hard to make them. Maybe too hard, a people pleaser, you know?"

He closed his eyes. The tips of his ears were red.

"Nothing worked. I'd echo what they liked and ignore all the warning signs but there's only so long you can keep that up. Eventually they pull away. And the sick thing is you're almost relieved. You don't have to try and be something you're not anymore. But it's not that way with you."

"That's what you think."

"You think you're this terrible person but you let me into your life when I had no one. I won't ever forget that. Tim...."

"Stop speaking."

"Whatever you were looking for in that motel, whatever you think you're missing...it didn't stop me from caring about you. It didn't stop Quincy or—"

"Don't say her name."

The sky moved into partial shadow then lightened again.

I got up very slowly. "You can push me, insult me, do your worst. But I'm not leaving you here."

He looked back over the ledge and his body began shaking uncontrollably. I stepped in and wrapped my arms tightly about his waist. He called me an asshole. His body strained against me. I think I apologized.

He clasped the back of my head, fingers digging into my scalp. "Don't tell," he sobbed.

"I won't."

He kissed me on the mouth. Stubble ground into my chin.

When the worst of the shaking eased he allowed me to pull him off the ledge. I shoved my hands in my pockets to warm them.

He put two fingers to his lips. "Wanted to feel...just once."

When Quincy found us on the roof a half hour later we were sitting with our backs up against the ledge, smoking. The snowfall had thickened and partially covered us like monuments. Her eyes went from Tim to me, trying to divine what had occurred.

"I was looking all over," she said finally.

"Needed some air," I said, brushing snow off my knees. I could still feel his lips against mine.

She crossed her arms over her chest. The collars of her black coat were up like a countess trying to go incognito. Thick black stockings covered her legs.

Tim flicked his cigarette over the ledge. I imagined it turning end over end as it fell, meeting the driveway in a shower of orange sparks.

"Sorry, Mom," Tim muttered.

I laughed until it became impossible to stop. Tears leaked out the corners of my eyes.

* * *

I cooked dinner for the four of us that evening, butter Parmesan rotini, veggies spritzed with balsamic vinegar on the side. It was a relief to settle into the familiar preparatory actions, salting water to boil, peeling carrots, and chopping jalapeños. It meant I didn't have to hang out on the couch and watch how grotesquely unchanged everything was. Emily rolling a joint. Quincy thumbing through playlists on her iPod. And Tim watching TV and chatting with them about inanities. What had almost happened I couldn't even think of directly, yet it seemed to have temporarily brightened his spirits. It was the hope in Emily's eyes taking him in I couldn't stand.

Quincy noticed the jalapeños and ribbed Emily about not being able to take it. "What'll Neil's mom think? White *and* she can't take spice? That won't do."

Em grinned at me. "She called this morning."

The knife paused mid-chop. Pepper seeds clung to my fingers. "Who?"

"She wants to have us over for dinner tomorrow."

I didn't think it was possible for me to feel anything else that day. But the thought of having dinner in Auntie's house, each dish meticulously served by Arjun, made me feel soiled.

I laid the knife down. "It's a long drive."

"I said yes," Emily said.

"Your dad teaches here, right?" Quincy asked. "Don't you all live on campus?"

I nodded without looking at her. Finally the truth would come out. It would be uncomfortable but really, who cared? It was nothing when compared to the dullness in Tim's eyes as he'd stood out on that ledge, as though his soul had already fled his body.

"Not exactly," I began. "I mean, we do, but..."

"His mom and dad don't live together," Emily said. She gave me a reassuring smile. "She told me. Hope it's okay."

Quincy yawned and sunk deeper into the couch. "Welcome to the club. Does anyone stay together anymore?"

I finished chopping the jalapeños and threw them into a bowl filled with veggies. Thinking one couple, despite catastrophe, had.

Tim cut out after dinner. We'd barely spoken to each other the entire night. It was getting late and Emily was taking a shower. Quincy and I were on the couch finishing a second bottle of red wine. Blur's "Tender" was playing on her iPod connected to the living room speakers. She had good taste in music.

"You get used to it," she said. Her leg was crossed, a bare stockinged foot touching my thigh. "Notice things about them you never did before. It's like the protective shield is gone. You see them as weaker than you ever thought possible. And the hurt that comes from that somehow makes them easier to love, too."

She looked down at her glass and sloshed around the dregs that remained. "I had a younger brother. Did I ever tell you that?"

I shook my head. Emily was humming the song's chorus in the bathroom.

She smiled. "Weird little Charles. Face always buried in a book. He got glasses before he was ten. Shortsighted, can you believe it? He would do this thing where he'd put his face an inch away from mine when I was sleeping and just stare until I sensed something and came awake. God, I hated it." She forced herself to finish the glass and set it on the coffee table. The rim was stained with her lipstick. "And then he was gone. Leukemia. And for months afterwards I'd swat out at the darkness of my room, sure he was staring at me."

She edged closer to me and rested her head on my shoulder. "My parents kept going, for me. They tried, but..."

I pressed my lips to her forehead. The song faded out and the silence before the next one began seemed very large.

12

One of Auntie's gifts was a gleaming silver armoire whose doors opened to reveal full-size mirrors. It was designed to make getting dressed easier, and it did, but there was a funereal quality to it as well, carefully tying a tie and slipping a herringbone blazer on next to a woman pulling up stockings and pushing newly blow-dried hair off her face. The foot of space between us smacked of alien formality, one which had no place in an apartment littered with cast-off socks and underwear. When I brushed my fingers against her back the skin was cool to the touch.

"If you want to get in her good graces, ask to take leftovers home," I said, watching my mouth form the words in the mirror.

"I thought she had people to cook for her."

"She does. But she'll make an exception for this."

Auntie had been cooking nonstop ever since inviting us over, multiple pots bubbling delicacies while she meticulously went over place settings and what kind of alcohol to keep on hand. This morning she'd gotten up and micro-managed Arjun as he cleaned the house. The last few hours would be spent in her room, trying on a selection of saris before deciding on official entertaining garb. I knew this as surely as I knew it was a mother's place to host her son's love interest for the first time, and that no amount of explaining after the fact would ever erase the stain of such thievery.

"Zip me up," she said.

She wore a fitted gray blouse with a white ruffled skirt that flared out at her hips. I zipped up the latter and smoothed out a few wrinkles in back. She fanned her face with one hand to control the blush spreading across her cheeks.

"Will you look after me? Make sure I don't say anything dumb?"

"You never do."

"I'm serious."

I nuzzled the back of her neck. Her fingers settled her hair to keep it from getting mussed up.

I imagined my mother watching television in the common room, nursing her bruised hands. A hundred indignities awaited her throughout the day but what we were about to do, had she known of it, would have been the only one she couldn't abide.

Three quick car honks sounded outside, followed by a protracted fourth. It was Quincy's code, used when she knocked on our door nights. Em and I went over to the window, where we saw her standing next to an idling Lincoln Town Car in the driveway. Thin layer of snow on the ground. Packed bags at her feet.

When we came out a uniformed driver was loading the bags into the trunk. Quincy stood where she was, hands on her hips, staring at Emily as she approached. Her face looked wan from too little sleep, ends of her hair stringy from a recent bleaching. Artificial blue pupils stared from their sockets with an almost manic intensity.

She'd settled on a course of action and had only to endure this last.

Emily took Quincy's hands and shook them. "What are you doing?"

Quincy's body absorbed the shock. In place of answering, she turned her face toward the backseat of the car. Emily and I saw Tim's silhouette through tinted windows, a face turned away from us even at the end, a child cowering in his room from parents he'd angered.

The driver slammed the trunk and got back into the driver's seat, keeping his eyes lowered throughout to avoid the scene taking place.

"Why now?" Emily asked.

Quincy took a deep breath, noticed the coat Emily had thrown on, a bulky black leather jacket, and smiled a little. "Change the coat before going over to his mother's house," she said.

"I need you," Emily said.

Quincy put her forehead to hers. "I don't think so." She glanced at me and whispered something I couldn't hear. Emily nodded like it was good advice, body swaying slightly. Exhaust from the car's back pipe stained the snow beneath it the color of ash.

"Let him go," Emily said, pulling her head away. She looked past Quincy to Tim. "You want to go, run! Leave her out of it."

"I want to," Quincy said.

"I know things are bad," Emily said, fingers fluttering at Quincy's chest. "But they'll get better."

Their eyes met, each searching for a truth that escaped the other.

Emily turned away and ran back toward the house, head down fending off tears. I tried to reach out to her as she passed but she shrank away. Quincy watched her go, blood slowly draining from her face. Tim stayed in the car.

I came up close and embraced her. I felt how rigidly she held herself, the only way she could see it through. The collar of her coat was redolent with perfume.

"How long?" I asked.

"Until he loses the hysterical edge to his laugh. Until I stop having to check on him in the middle of the night." She allowed herself a sigh. "The driver's dropping us off at the airport. I figured we'd just pick a destination and go."

I tightened my grip, pressing her into me.

"Don't you want to know what I told her?" she asked.

"It's okay."

"I asked her to give you time. She wants to know...just everything about you because it makes you real in her eyes. She sees that you're keeping secrets and doesn't understand how hard it is for people like us."

"People like us," I echoed, shutting my eyes.

"Broken."

"I've seen how you care for Tim," I said. "No one who feels like that is past love."

She tried to pull away but I held her fast. "I won't lie to you," I said.

She tried to take another breath and it caught in her throat. The car revved.

"He was so small, dying in a hospital room with tubes sticking out of him and I couldn't even visit him. He died calling for his sister."

"Shh."

"And I wasn't there."

Tim was watching me from the backseat. A scarf was wrapped tightly about his throat. He slowly raised a hand to me.

"You're here now," I said.

I watched them leave. When I could no longer see the car I went back inside. Emily was sitting at the foot of the ground floor stairs, picking at the handbag resting on her lap. She'd changed into a more sedate wool coat.

"Are they gone?" she asked.

I nodded.

Her lower jaw jutted out. "Oh."

I took a step toward her and she immediately rose. She took car keys out and tossed them at me. "We should go."

"Em."

"I'm not going to be late."

Around back was a parking lot that held Emily's car, a blue Audi S4. I turned the key in the ignition and the engine started smoothly. I waited a few seconds for it to warm up, staring at the logo stitched into the center of the steering wheel. Emily buckled her safety belt and laid her head against the side window, staring straight ahead.

"They'll be okay," I said.

She sighed. "Got a good vibe from the whole situation, did you?"

She put her palms to her eyes and pressed in. "I'm sorry. I won't be like this when we get there, I promise."

"It's fine."

"No." She looked at me and swallowed back the tears.

I went south on Barrie Street. The greenhouse whipped past on the right, condensation clinging to the insides of the glass panes, obscuring its contents. I had sprayed the windshield with cleaning fluid and turned the wipers on to remove specks of ice. Emily cried softly beside me.

I could picture every detail of what lay in store for us—Auntie meeting us at the door, Emily being charming if a little distant throughout the meal, dutifully asking for leftovers afterwards. I would drink too much yet still insist on driving us home and sometime before pulling back into the parking lot I would feel the heaviness in my chest as something precious and humiliating within me was snuffed out...only I could no longer pretend it was due to circumstances beyond my control. I was taking us there. I was participating in the lie. I was knowingly drawing myself away from love.

I came to the intersection of Barrie and Stuart, the last one before campus gave way to city proper. Raleigh Hospital was across the street, a beige structure that looked made out of giant Lego blocks. By the sidewalk to the left was a fire hydrant that had been opened, water trickling out onto the road to form a puddle crusted over with ice. The traffic light in front of us blared red.

I swung the wheel to the right and stepped on the gas. A van honked behind me. I sped up, running west on Stuart, past a series of weeping willows flanking a parking lot and the Computer Sciences building where my father had devoted his life until his wife had required it. Emily began to notice that we were heading back onto campus.

"Is this the way?" she asked.

I weaved between cars, constantly glancing to the right for the battered sign for Albert Street. I narrowly avoided hitting the back bumper of a sedan, slamming on the brakes less than six feet from impact. Emily jerked forward in her seat. The jack rattled in the trunk.

"Neil, slow down."

I turned right onto Albert and time was molasses now, every bit forward slowed by an invisible hand. Lawns covered in snow. Sewer grates overflowing with slush. Mailboxes with steel-reinforced bases to safeguard against hooligans wielding bats. And then my driveway like all the others, Dad's car dusted with powder, the wheels partially covered.

I parked at the curb. Dad had neglected to take in the clay flowerpots flanking the front steps and some had cracked, burnt orange chips lying at the base of frozen earth still retaining the pots' shape.

"Your dad lives here?" Emily asked. Seeing the missing siding, the overflowing gutters. The screen with a broken hinge periodically flapping against the front door.

My gaze went to the living room window, certain I'd see my father's face peering out in uncertain welcome.

"I live here."

Inside was quiet. Dad had spread out newspaper in the foyer to catch slush from his boots, one of which lay on its side like a landed fish. I righted it, catching a pungent whiff of his foot. We took off our shoes and went deeper inside.

The coffee table had been swallowed in paperwork. It was gloomy. I drew the curtains back but it didn't really help. Dust balls clung to the bottom of the curtains. My father had sat here, so engrossed in preparing for the coming trial that he hadn't even noticed it.

Em stood in the living room with her hands tucked in coat pockets. She hadn't brought her handbag in. I wondered if she'd taken a look at the house and thought it would have been too gaudy.

"I think he's sleeping," I said. "We can come back."

"We're already here."

She studied the scrawls in red ink covering the papers. It looked like the ramblings of a madman.

I kissed her cheek. "I'll bring him down. Don't worry, he'll love you."

She shifted her gaze to me, a question in her eyes.

"I'll stop you before you say anything dumb."

I went up the bedroom stairs, registering the cool, faintly spiced air as though for the first time. She was seeing me, I thought. The words, finding no precedent, echoed within my mind.

All the bedroom doors were closed. I opened my father's and stepped inside.

He lay with his back up against the headboard, glasses askew, sections of newspaper on his chest. The nightstand lamp was on, blazing in defiance of the glow entering through the gaps between closed window blinds.

His eyes were partially open, staring at a spot in the middle of the bed.

I shut the door behind me. I will always hate myself for having the wherewithal to do that.

I sat down on the edge of the bed next to him, staring into his face. His skin had a greenish pallor. I turned off the lamp, sparing him.

I gathered up the newspaper and dropped them down on the ground. Soft friction noise as they settled.

I took off his glasses and placed them on the nightstand. I'd taken care not to touch his skin and placed a hand over his eyes to get it over with. The feel of it traveled up my arm into my body.

I laid my head on his chest. He was beginning to stiffen. "*Baba*," I whispered.

Eventually I heard Emily calling for me downstairs. I retraced my steps back to her. The volume of the world had been turned down low. My heart pounded in my ears.

"He's not feeling so well," I said, slurring the words. "We should come back." I started past her for the door.

"Hey," she said, touching my arm. Unbearable, like bone scraping bone. "What's the matter? Is he all right?"

"Fine," I said, pulling my arm away.

December 9 - 26

13

Spiked vines burst from my father's chest and envelop my head and neck. I try pulling away but they're knotting me to his corpse, a steadily mounting pressure in tandem with dim pain as the spikes burrow into my skin. The vines swell with my blood. I can feel them questing inside me, pushing aside organs and strains of fat to deliver seeds. They sing with activity, a low vibration traveling up my spine. My throat fills with them, miniature vines growing as they push up into my mouth. My arm twitches to claw at them but it's been eaten away, a memory of a limb...

* * *

I'm on the bathroom floor clutching my throat. My vision pulses sickeningly in and out. Sweat streams into my eyes. I wipe it away with the back of my hand. I'm naked. I try to use the toilet to haul myself to standing, slip, and slam my jaw against the seat. I laugh because I'm still dreaming, must be, just haven't tripped the right switch in the landscape to bring me back to bed with Emily.

Hands on my back. I swat them away without looking, just another monster to prolong this. My jaw's aching that's not right I shouldn't feel that.

"Neil?"

I giggle. A clever monster. Sounds just like my girlfriend. "What's happening?"

The pressure in my bladder releases. Piss streams out in a warm flow, puddling around my knees. The familiar stench.

It doesn't back out of the room. Doesn't even shout in surprise. A hand, a claw, touches my head. I start to shiver.

* * *

Night became day. More snow fell. I was in the passenger seat of Auntie's car, inspecting the swelling along my jaw via the rearview mirror. Purple shot through with reddish streaks. My eyes belonged to a stranger. My features had shifted into a pattern I did not recognize.

I'm not here, I told myself. When I wake up, I'll be somewhere else.

Auntie came out of the house, glanced down the street, and got into the car. She carefully removed the leather gloves she'd used to touch the body and laid them on the dashboard. The stitched fingers looked mangled.

"I'll take care of it," she said, using Bengali because the words were softer that way. "All the arrangements. I don't want you to go back in there."

"But it's my house."

"Please." Her lips were pressed together. "Let's go back to

mine. We can call the police from there."

I reached out and straightened the fingers of the gloves. Auntie watched me do this without comment.

"What will I tell Mom?" I asked. "That won't make it harder, I mean." I looked at her. "You tell me that and I'll do anything you want."

Her eyes lost their guardedness. She rubbed her lips, using it as an excuse to look away. "Emily was in hysterics. Thank God she called me first. You can't go back to her until you're in control of yourself."

I reached for the door handle thinking *when I was ever?*

"Please, *janu*, I'm your family. Let me help."

Over the next few days she made preparations for my father's cremation, notifying family in the U.S. and overseas, arranging to host a few old friends from his Presidency College days who couldn't let "Rock Raja's" passing go unnoticed. Everyone she spoke to uttered the same condolences and Auntie answered in kind, deploying euphemisms like kind, sacrificer, and generous when both parties knew it to mean gullible, martyr to a lost cause, and bankrupt. My name was dropped frequently and I soon stopped hearing it. I ate whatever was put in front of me. I nodded out at the dining table and living room. I spilled things. Neither Auntie nor Arjun ever complained about this; whoever was nearest would simply clean up and help me to bed.

A police officer came for a statement, hat in hand, nodding at my edited recounting of events. I described finding the body in great detail and left out Emily being in the house. When I stopped speaking he thanked me for my time. For some reason I couldn't understand the phrase and asked him to repeat it. The officer gave Auntie a sheepish grin. She ushered him out.

Arjun helped me carry out one of the obligations of an Indian son grieving for his father—shaving my head. His hands worked with the speed of a master craftsman, first cutting with scissors, then spreading shaving cream on my scalp and razoring off the bristles. I watched them cascade onto my shirt.

"Tell me," he asked.

I lifted my eyes to the mirror. Beneath a dry scalp were my father's sad, wounded eyes. Same spreading out beneath the nose to a wide mouth. Behind me, the walls of the bathroom were white with thin yellow stripes.

"It's good," I said.

"Do you want me to save the hair?" he asked.

I shook my head. "Just throw it away."

I started to get up and he tutted. "We still need to wash the head."

"Forget it."

"It'll rash otherwise."

He quickly started the water running and laid a towel out on the counter. He turned my chair around, leaned me back, and went to work. The calloused fingers that rinsed and shampooed had done everything from performing makeshift facials on Auntie to cooking her meals and cleaning her toilets. The gentle yet firm pressure he applied made it easy to give yourself over to him.

"I was young when I lost my father. He was a shopkeep, rarely home. Little more than a shadow growing up but I knew him when he burned."

He dried my head and began rubbing in a balm that smelt of cherries.

"Everyone knew your father," he went on. "His heart was open. You could confide anything and it would stay safe because his trust in you was as deep as that in himself."

I nodded, thinking that was true. Had my father existed in a world of parallel spirits he might have been king. Instead he'd come into contact with liars and charlatans, within his own family even, and he never developed the skills to manage that. Every betrayal stung as deeply as the first.

Friends of the family, all referred to as either Uncle this or Auntie that, paid me visits. It seemed like a processional at times, middle-aged women bedecked in brightly colored saris and so much jewelry that embracing them was like hugging a metal statue. Their husbands lurked behind like bodyguards, apologizing for not coming sooner and not spending enough time with my father. They kept glancing at each other like it was a piece of group choreography. I had the urge to push someone or start cursing, just to see how they'd react.

Auntie entertained them in the living room, holding court with an easiness that surprised me. I'd rarely seen her in groups, but it was clear by the way the other women deferred to her that she was intimately familiar with the minutiae of their lives—which Indian import store sold cashew *bhujia*, which daughter was behaving "questionably" at college and needed a talking-to. It was hard to watch Auntie dispense advice and make tongue-in-cheek jokes about an Uncle's "thriftiness" and not think of my mother in the old days. Few would argue that she had been the undisputed queen of this social circle, garnering a free pass from close scrutiny due to her mystique as a former movie starlet. In those days Auntie had been the slightly off sister who drank men's drinks and asked inopportune questions of them when she'd had too much. She was a threat, and nothing Mom did could stop the other women from gossiping about her, the hungry way she appraised their husbands when she didn't think anyone was looking, the steel that resided at her core that all who interacted with her sensed, and which short-circuited intimacy.

When Mom's illness became impossible to hide it had all changed. The women had descended on her like wolves tearing into the runt of the litter, calling attention to when she sweated profusely, or fell silent listening to the voices, when she faltered performing the thousand domestic tasks Indian women were expected to know by heart. There was an obsessive quality to it, as though on some level they were exacting revenge for having been duped so brilliantly. Auntie never participated in these attacks but it must have been a relief not to have to bear their collective wrath alone. Few people truly felt the paralysis that came with not being wanted. My mother, up to that point, never had. Now she would learn.

They asked her to sit down while they stood. They started nodding their heads in agreement whenever she opened her mouth. They served her food early, when the children ate, and invited her to go upstairs for a rest before they started. In the wake of Dad excommunicating Auntie my parents' calls to friends started going unanswered. Their invitations ignored. And yet, in a feat of willful ignorance Mom and Dad kept on, doggedly making conversation where there was none, ignoring the self-satisfied air of doing a good deed those who periodically attended their *nemontons* carried. As I sat on the couch next to Auntie I realized that the support network my parents had relied on ever since moving to the States needed little time to grieve my father's passing. To most of them my parents already existed solely as a series of distant memories.

In the late hours, when Uncles' collars were damp and the living room air was thick with cigar smoke they'd cling to their dearest possession: offspring. By this time I'd be resting in an upstairs bedroom but I would always leave the door open to hear. As in all other aspects of Indian relations, this too was privy to rules of engagement. They'd start by praising a son or daughter for good marks or a kind act, followed quickly by a complaint negating it, such as lack of talent in sports or particularly noticeable baby fat. It was their way of gaming a system that upheld humility as the chief virtue. When it was Auntie's turn she'd speak of me as though I were her flesh and blood. Only there were no little manipulations present in her speech, no compliments dispensed as reluctantly as cash tips.

She said she loved me but didn't understand me. And that it was a good thing. She'd been sure of many things, the life she wanted, how she'd go about getting it. She'd planned and taken all the necessary measures. And she'd gotten all except that which lasted. She had comforts but no husband to keep her warm at night. She had idle time but no children to occupy them with. She'd grown desperate and tried to force these things but it always ended in disaster. Scar tissue formed. It became easier to ignore the absence than face how it was eating you from the inside.

Now she understood little. Not what would happen next, or how to prepare for it. And it was all right because someone needed her again. A sparrow had flown into the house and for once she wouldn't try to cage it. She'd let it do what it would, provide whatever shelter it needed, and listen to its song that made her heart swell in its mystery.

* * *

Rain pissed down onto the banks of the Oswego. We stood in a loose semicircle around a pyre, my father's body wrapped in white cloth at its center. The ground was muddy and slick. The air tasted faintly of rust, compliments of a textile factory a quarter-mile downriver.

Ganguly lit a torch. It took several tries but he finally got it going, flames flickering like moans. Some of the women began to ululate, a high, trilling noise that floated out over the water and echoed.

Auntie nudged me forward. The skin of her face looked white around the edges, like what bordered a cut after you'd pulled the scab off too soon. Drops of water spilled down the part in her hair and off her nose. Her hand touched mine, just for a moment, and lowered.

I took the torch and came up close to the pyre. Ice floes the size of cars crawled past on the river. I pulled a scrap of cloth out and touched the flame to it. It blackened the cloth then lighted and raced toward the pyre. It hissed when touching wet wood and for a moment I was sure it would go out and I couldn't do it again, if I did it again I'd look into the center of the pyre and begin to scream but then a yellow-blue sunburst and logs began to burn.

Flames quickly charred the rest of the cloth. Bits of it flaked off, revealing pinkish cheek, a bent elbow. Two massive logs atop the pyre cracked and collapsed inwards, throwing a cloud of cinders into the air. It tore off the cloth covering the upper half of his face.

His eyes were two pools of liquid.

I dropped the torch onto the ground and pulled a smoking log off the pyre. The volume of the world had gone down but I still heard people shouting. Cinders touched my face and neck, distant flares of pain.

Ganguly grappled the log out of my hands. He turned into me, using his large frame to block the pyre from view. The raincoat he wore was soaked to translucence. Soft black eyes took me in with the solicitousness of an older brother.

"They shouldn't see," I said. The air was gray about us. "Not like this."

Ganguly looked back and saw what I had. Sparing a moment's glance at those standing safely at the periphery, he poked and prodded the pyre until logs obscured his body again.

Afterwards everyone came back to the house—my house, I kept reminding myself. The women unwrapped enormous plates of food in the kitchen. The men sat with me in the living room, magically cleared of papers and other signs of my father's last days. Auntie puttered between the two groups, bringing fresh drinks and periodically catching my eye to see where I was at. It was difficult to follow the various conversations. One Uncle would start talking about how he'd spent weekends with my father prowling around the girl's colleges in Kolkata, no clear objective in mind, just to be near their weird intoxicating presence, then another Uncle would interrupt with a great deal on stereo equipment from a particular online store. I felt certain I could invent a wildly implausible tale, like how my father liked to dress up in a bear costume and scare little children, and their only reaction would be nods and pitying looks back and forth.

An Uncle next to me rose and Ganguly sat down in his place. He waited until Auntie had completed her latest round and passed me his drink. It looked milky like a White Russian.

"Quick," he muttered. It tasted chalky.

Without exchanging a word the other Uncles followed suit, passing their drinks down to Ganguly, who gave them to me one at a time. It became impossible to distinguish between drinks after the fourth or fifth. The blur came quickly and was as welcome as slipping into a hot bath. Throughout it the Uncles never stopped their patter, and it occurred to me, with the clarity of an insight that can never be retained, that each had struggled to hold his head up in a world that seemed intent on humbling a man, and that if they were to discard the formalities and reveal them it would hold us all rapt in surprised recognition.

Auntie returned carrying a platter of onion *bhajis*. A quick look at the empty drink glasses on the coffee table, along with the one I still held in my hands, told her what had occurred, but she pretended not to notice.

"No more," Shankar Uncle said as she laid the platter down. His drink was intact in his hand. The base of his neck was knotted with muscle and his suit jacket was carefully folded over one knee. "I have cholesterol to think about, woman!"

"Then don't eat them," she answered.

Auntie gathered glasses. Shankar Uncle plucked a *bhaji* off the platter with two fingers. He ate quickly and rubbed the excess grease off on the sides of his glass.

"Who made these?" he asked, an edge to his voice that made it sound closer to a demand. "Was it Swati? Have her give Reba the recipe."

Auntie took him in. The military posture he insisted on maintaining though it had been over thirty years since he'd been in the service. The carefully trimmed mustache and the flashy silver watch on his wrist that glimmered, betraying cheap materials. His wife Reba was well versed in worshiping him, not speaking to him unless spoken to and keeping her head tilted toward the ground. When she'd battled the skin cancer that had left marks like liver spots on her hands she had allowed herself to be shuttered up at home, letting him tend to their shame in privacy.

"I made them," she said.

"You?" he crowed. "Since when? Did Arjun have a heart attack?"

She didn't answer. But something changed in her eyes, a patina like a thin layer of ice beneath which lurked a depth beyond color.

Shankar Uncle nodded like she'd played into the joke. "They're good," he said, and invited the others to try.

Uncles laid *bhaji*s out on napkins and gulped them down in single bites.

Once Auntie was gone Shankar Uncle winked at the others and said, "Let's be fair. Sonia's good, but her cooking skills can't hold a candle to her sister's."

No one said anything. Shankar Uncle worked out a wrinkle on the sleeve of his suit jacket.

"Some women get an embarrassment of riches," he said. "The looks, smart talk, and the food." He shook his head fondly. "The wonders she could perform with a simple plate of *dal* was like magic. God knows how long she spent cooking but I'd always look forward to coming here. A dash of brown sugar in savory goat, jackfruit in chicken stew...genius."

"What do you want from me?" I asked.

"Eh?" His hand stopped working his suit jacket.

I grabbed a saltshaker near the platter and sprinkled it over the remaining *bhajis*. I held the platter out to him.

"It'll be better," I said.

"I'm fine, thank you." The words clipped and obligatory.

"Eat it when he offers you," Auntie said, returning with drinks.

Uncles took their respective glasses. Ice tinkled.

"I'll have it," Ganguly said, reaching for the platter.

I pulled it away from his grasp and rose. I went up to Shankar Uncle, who laid his hands out flat on his thighs. His knuckles were pronounced.

"Go on," I said, touching the platter to his chest.

His jaw muscles flared as he bit down on his teeth.

I tilted the platter and the *bhajis* landed on his lap, streaking it with grease. Uncles made abortive little noises.

Shankar Uncle made no move to clean himself. "Look at you," he said.

"Niladri..." Auntie began.

"The food's not good enough for him," I said.

"I didn't say..."

"We know what you said." I looked at the other Uncles. All except Ganguly averted their gazes. "We all know."

I stepped back and felt very dizzy. The platter dropped onto the carpet. It grew very quiet in the kitchen, the magpies sensing commotion.

Auntie and Ganguly brought me to the bedroom stairs, then he took me the rest of the way up. He had a very firm grip. By the time he helped me into bed his shirt had come untucked.

"If you need anything I'm just downstairs," he said.

I pulled at the covers, untucking them from the sides. My room too had been thoroughly cleaned and made anonymous. "Do you hate me?" I asked.

He crossed his arms over his chest and assessed me. A few belly hairs poked out beneath his shirt. "Absolutely I do."

"You were the only one who kept coming around. Even when her food began to taste like the poison in the air."

"It wasn't so bad." He went to the window and closed the blinds. "I can't relax with those people. But I always could here, whether your mother was having a good day or no." He tucked his shirt back in and buttoned his jacket. "They never attacked, your parents. I don't think they knew how."

"There's two free beds in the other rooms if you'd like to take a nap."

He smiled and shook his head. "We can't all be as lucky as you."

I closed my eyes but there were only gears upon gnashing gears behind the surface of my eyelids. I was an automaton that would carry out the wishes of an intelligence beyond comprehension or control. How comforting to think so.

"I stole so much from her," I whispered. "Even this."

* * *

I drifted in the twilight between waking and sleep. It winked away and my heart was racing. It felt like a depth charge had sunk down ever deeper, past the pretty water dappled with sunlight, past where the temperature dropped and snapping fish lingered at the periphery, finally touching the riverbed and exploding in a burst of sediment.

I got up and scrambled for the door. The room was suffused with shadows, so many it was impossible to distinguish one from another. In the hall I registered the quiet downstairs, turned left, and entered my mother's room. I found the light switch and hesitated, frightened for a reason I couldn't say.

I flicked it.

The room had been completely stripped. A bare mattress and pillows. A vanity cleansed of glued photographs, perfume, and cosmetics. Clorox and Pledge had beaten the sour smell into submission.

I'd wished for this every time I passed by the door and heard Mom talking to herself. When I'd knock late at night, driven to distraction because it was all I could focus on, she'd temporarily grow quiet. But it would always start again. And when the humming that was not humming rose in volume and her cadences grew unfamiliar I prayed she and everything in that room would just disappear. No explanation. No rehabilitation. Lanced like a boil.

But seeing it offered no relief to my heart. Just the emptiness of falling without finding anything to hold on to.

Auntie sat at the kitchen table sipping a cup of tea. She'd removed the pins from her hair and it flowed loose to her shoulders. The look suited her, easing the hard planes of her cheekbones and jaw. Her face was newly washed. When she saw me she smiled, a crooked thing, infusing all the blemishes, the crow's feet, and discolored patches of skin with a kind of dignity.

"Come sit by me," she said.

Once I was seated next to her she took my hand and kissed it. Up close I could see little strands of gray within her hair.

"The fridge is packed. You'll have enough food for the next month."

"When did everyone leave?"

"An hour or so ago. Ganguly was last. He always was a lingerer." She gave me a sly look. "Tell me the truth, how much did they give you to drink?"

"I don't know," I muttered.

She nodded like I'd confirmed her suspicions. "I'm going to get up in a few minutes and make you a plate and I don't want to hear any fuss about it. I won't have my only nephew turning into a drunkard. At least not without a full belly."

"Is that what I am? Your nephew?"

She was quiet for a few moments. Our reflections warped and conjoined against the patio glass, shot through with incandescent streaks from the light fixture overhead.

"You're my family," she said simply.

"Who asked you to empty out the house?"

"Would you have wanted others to see the house that way?

That...cave *Dee Dee* hid in? How your father could have let her sink so far..." She shook her head, revealing a flash of gold in one ear.

"Why my room? And my father's?"

She sighed and I knew his room had also been subjected to stripping. Before I'd even had a chance to come to terms with what had happened all evidence was removed. While I'd wasted precious days she'd set a plan in motion.

"Arjun took care of it all," she said. She saw the worry on my face and laughed. "Everything's in storage."

"You should have told me."

She looked about to say something, then tilted her head and let it pass. She brought her cup over to the sink and rinsed it out.

I took the thumb and index finger of my right hand and pinched the skin of my left arm as hard as I could. The dart of pain cleared away some of the cobwebs.

She began taking saran-wrapped dishes out of the refrigerator. "You held yourself like a man."

I would have screamed an obscenity were it not for the certainty she wouldn't react.

"I'm proud of you, *janu*," she said.

* * *

I excused myself after dinner, telling Auntie I needed to clear my head. She had settled into the living room couch with a Rohinton Mistry novel and a couple of sweets, only raising a hand in acknowledgment.

Who was this woman? Had she always existed somewhere within that tightly coiled body? Was this what she'd been like before years and circumstances had intervened?

My reactions driving were delayed, the smooth interplay of acceleration and braking giving way to jerks and stops. On the highway I rode the rightmost lane. Every passing car was a potential crash, every patch of black ice a reaper's grin. It was as if I'd undergone major surgery and now had to relearn tasks taken for granted.

This time Nurse Khadijah led me deeper into the pavilion than I'd ever been. Beyond the bathroom was a series of unmarked rooms on both sides of the corridor, a few standing ajar to reveal examination beds and dusty office equipment. Nurse Khadijah methodically flashed a light inside each of these before closing and locking them. The armpits of her uniform were soaked through with sweat.

I noticed that none of the rooms held cameras and asked her about it.

"Doctors work with patients in them," she answered, tucking the thick ring of keys inside a pocket. "No need."

"You never wonder?" I asked.

"What they get up to in there? I like my job, thank you very much."

We passed the cafeteria, a maw of molded steel and plastic in the process of getting hosed, mopped, and sprayed by a group of patients. The entire far wall was composed of yellow-tinted glass and looked out onto the rear of the hospital grounds. I was surprised to see none of the patients slacking and taking in the view, until I noticed the nurse observing from the kitchen.

Finally we came to a set of stairs leading down to a lower level. A single, flickering fluorescent bar was the only source of light. The concrete was slick, subject to a leak somewhere overhead. A steady, slightly irregular pounding noise came from below.

"She's stopped speaking," Nurse Khadijah said. "Not a word since last Wednesday." She cleared her throat. "I don't know what happened. I went through the videos, couldn't find a thing."

"Maybe she realized it wouldn't matter."

Air hissed from between her nostrils. "I've seen this before. She's getting to the bad place. When she gets there not you, me..."

The fluorescent bar winked off, then sparked grudgingly back to life.

"Go on," she said, and nodded toward a witness camera. "Wave if you need help."

Water dripped through ribbons of hanging insulation to sizzle against naked bulbs. Row upon row of washing machines tumbled hospital gowns and undergarments, suds lending the scene a grotesquely domestic air. Patients pushed loaded laundry carts, stepping carefully to avoid stacks of rotting wood beams and masonry. Joplin's "Piece of My Heart" came from an unseen radio and mingled with the groaning machines.

Against the far wall stood a massive contraption belching fart-smelling steam. Lights blinked along its rusty haunches. A conveyor belt extruded from its center, angled down to a long table manned by patients.

A back twisted with scoliosis. A bony arm ending in yellowed fingernails. A shoulder twitching with metronomic precision. My eyes took in these details but could glean no context. All of these broken people, shunted aside by loved ones, forced into activity because it was just as good as anything else. A few had the bloodless look of those not long for the world yet even that held no greater meaning. Their light flickered weakly and would be snuffed out. Another patient would take their place.

The contraption buzzed. A load of clothes was carried out by the conveyor belt and dropped onto the table. Patients grabbed at them and began folding, sliding completed articles down to a man stacking them into a laundry cart. They had been taught to do it in a way that valued efficiency over presentation. My mother, almost lost in a cluster of patients in the corner, did it as she had always done, using one hand to create a precise crease and the other to actually fold. When the overseer, a hawk-nosed female patient with the jittery eyes of a mania victim berated her for not going fast enough, Mom nodded and kept on unchanged. Sweat dripped from her forehead onto the table. The stream of clothes was endless.

I went up and touched her arm. My fingers left an impression behind on her skin. Her cheeks sagged, like she was losing weight faster than her body could adjust. Her mouth was partway open, sucking in the moist air and pushing it back out.

"Mom."

She didn't pause folding. Her hands were lobster red from the heat. Hawknose gave me a dirty look but held her tongue.

"I know you can hear me."

She blinked several times. Her eyes had retreated deep within their sockets. I wanted to touch her again but didn't want to see her flinch.

There was no way I could tell her about my father.

A filled laundry cart was rolled out and replaced by an empty one. Garments thudded against the inside of the clothes dryer like a giant knocking.

"Tell me what to do," I asked.

Mom scratched her hair. The nails were chewed up.

"Should I steal you away? Where would we go? India? Home? Where can we go that the poison wouldn't follow?"

The patients nearest us edged away.

Hawknose had stopped working and was watching me intently. Her lips were crusted with dried saliva.

"Do you think I wanted it this way?" I grasped her elbow. Her arm tensed. "I'm the one who has to live with it. Who has to see you in this shit. You can hide. You've always just hidden, you *child*."

She pulled her arm away, sending a gown fluttering to the floor. Hawknose clapped her hands. "Attention," she shouted. "Attention!"

"I'm not going to keep saying sorry. I've done that my entire life. I hope you fucking die here."

I broke down. "Please, just look at me."

Her hand reached out for more clothes. Her fingers touched a gown and slid off. She turned her hand palm up and stared as if she didn't recognize it.

"You got sick after you had me. There was something so... wrong in me that it twisted you forever. And I can't ever make it right. Can I?"

Hawknose was up in my face shouting something. Spit pattered on my face.

"I just have to watch," I whispered.

Mom closed her eyes and frowned, like a sleeper beset by a nightmare.

Hawknose put her hands against my chest, frail bony things, and pushed. "You go," she said.

Mom yanked her back by the hair. Hawknose grunted and almost fell. Patients stared.

"You don't touch him," Mom said.

Hawknose rubbed her head, eyes moving quickly between Mom and me. "Now you've done it," she said, backing away. Her gaze went to the nearest camera.

The clothes dryer buzzed. More clothes dropped onto the table but work had stopped. There was a sudden clatter behind us, followed by the jangling of keys. I turned to see Nurse Khadijah, with a speed completely at odds with her size, darting through the rows toward us.

"Wait," I said, trying to come between her and Mom.

Mom raised her hands. She looked like she was going to throw up.

Nurse Khadijah sidestepped me, reaching into her uniform for a small can. She raised and sprayed it in Mom's eyes.

Mom screamed and fell to her knees, fingers digging into her eyelids. Nurse Khadijah pulled out restraints and looped them around Mom's wrists. I grasped a bit of her uniform and tried to pull her away but she was immovable. We were both coughing from the spray.

Nurse Khadijah hauled her up to standing. Mom retched.

"My fault," I said. Needles stung my eyes.

"Get back," Nurse Khadijah said, one hand on Mom's wrists, the other at her pocket. The nurse's eyes looked bloody. She glared at the other patients but they had already pulled away.

The two of them started forward. Mom took quick, hopping steps to keep pace. I tried to follow as best I could through blurred vision. I glanced off a patient's stomach, cold flab and pliant. I was saying unintelligible things, pleading.

Up the stairs, past the cafeteria and treatment rooms, past the common room where a couple shuffled to Sinatra like children turned mad seeking the attention of distant parents, to the door leading out of the pavilion. One of the nurses opened it from the other end and I realized, with dawning horror, where Mom was being led.

"Stop! Just listen..."

Nurse Khadijah brought Mom out into the corridor. The second nurse ran for the unmarked steel door, the one no visitor's eyes lingered on yet whose presence was felt in the belly of every patient. What resided behind the door was what kept the truly disturbed from carrying out their fantasies, and spurred those capable of recovery back out into the world with a cowed gratitude.

A soundproofed cell containing a cot and a toilet. A single light triggered by the door.

Mom moaned.

"I'm here," I said.

Nurse Khadijah dragged her in.

"Feel me here."

*　*　*

I waited outside that door for what felt like hours while Nurse Khadijah settled Mom inside. Intricate phrases of threat and abuse formed in my mind but when she finally exited they abandoned me. I caught a glimpse of the cell walls as the door closed behind her. They were covered in what looked like white upholstery. Deep scratches had been gouged into the surface.

A few of her cornrows had come loose, hair frizzy like steel wool. Her body reeked of perspiration. She smoothed out her uniform, betraying a slight tremor in her hands.

I brought my wallet out, took all the money and offered it to her. My eyes were locked on her chest.

She turned in, executing the old motion to hide the bribe from the cameras. Only instead of taking the bills she put her mouth to my ear and said, "Three days," like it was an act of mercy.

"She can't last that long."

"She'll have to."

The bills slipped out of my grasp onto the floor.

"It's Isolation or she goes back in with the others. They've turned on her."

"I don't understand."

She nodded toward the pavilion door, where the faces of patients were crammed up like barnacles against the porthole window, watching us.

"Beg, borrow, steal. Just get her gone."

* * *

A spotlight turns on and crawls across the stage until it finds me. There is a microphone angled at my forehead. I am six years old and terrified.

I open my mouth to recite the Tagore poem I'd memorized and painstakingly rehearsed with my mother for the past two months, the final presentation for Bengali Sunday School. Not a sound comes out.

The audience begins to whisper amongst themselves. I see my father in the front row smiling hard at me, willing me to succeed. A man leans over to say something to him but his eyes never leave me. A loud chair creaks.

"I want my mother."

Laughter in the audience. The whispering grows louder.

My father looks away. I start feeling lightheaded. The spotlight pins me to the ground.

The crack of floorboards behind me—someone's come to take me away. I turn my head and see her, black sari simultaneously caressing and obscuring her figure. She steps into the spotlight alongside me and looks out. Her eyes are clear and sharp. The laughter fades.

She adjusts the microphone for me. I put my hand out and she clasps it. We get through it together.

14

An icy wind rocked the car as it journeyed across the bridge. I tried to think but all I could picture was my mother alone in that cell, muttering to herself to keep her imagination at bay. She was like me: she could create monsters out of the ether. And when the darkness began to resolve itself into bristling shapes, when she heard the faint scratching of claws against the cement floor and shouted for nurses who didn't come, what then?

I bartered with God. I would stare at the sun until the whiteness signaling permanent damage corroded the periphery. Weave the car into oncoming traffic, if only He would erase my ever visiting the hospital. But all the hand-wringing achieved was a momentary easing of guilt. It afforded my mother nothing.

Sloppily pulling into Ganguly's driveway resulted in my knocking the metal trash can over. I parked the car quickly and got out to right it but was too late. The front light came on. He came out to find me dragging the dented remains in from the street. An arched overhang composed of shingles, one of the sole decorative elements to the simple ranch house, protected him from the elements. A metal rooster affixed to its peak spun wildly.

He motioned me inside.

"I should have called," I said, stepping into the tight foyer. Family pictures were enshrined in frames along the wall. A brass bench with floral print cushions on the right side.

"Nonsense."

I sat down and took off my shoes. The bottoms were encrusted with snow.

Ganguly started to say something cheerful and meaningless when he saw the expression on my face. I was too exhausted to pretend otherwise. But having him bear witness to it was like holding a mirror up to my shame.

"You were sleeping," I said, noting how his hair stuck up wildly at the fringes of his bald pate. He wore a wifebeater peppered with holes and pajama pants with Star Wars characters on them, perhaps one of his son's castoffs.

He sat down next to me. "Not long."

I watched slush from my shoes dribble into the gaps between wood slats. My feet throbbed.

"We could watch some TV," he said, covering a yawn. "I think there's a James Bond marathon still going on..."

"How bad is it?" I asked. "Really? Dad told me almost nothing."

He leaned his head back against the wall. A photograph of him and his wife Poonam was at eye level. He stood behind her, a rigid hand on her shoulder against the uniform blue background of a portrait studio. The camera had captured her smiling, transforming plain, slightly crooked features into something beautiful. It took a few moments to register the faded look of prolonged battle in her eyes, or that her shoulder-length locks were a wig.

"He didn't want you involved," Ganguly said.

"I'm asking. You don't have to tell me, but I need to know."

I watched him stare at the picture. He took a deep breath and slapped my thigh. "A drink first."

He got up with a force of will I could admire yet never fully comprehend, stepping gingerly past the stairs leading up to the bedrooms, not wanting to wake a family that no longer slept there.

* * *

The numbers blurred in front of my eyes. When I blinked they lifted off the page then settled back into their respective columns. Irrefutable evidence of the cancer that had been growing within my family. I pushed the nearest pages away, revealing stacks of filled folders on Ganguly's desk.

"What am I supposed to do with this?"

The furnace turned on in the adjacent boiler room with a low roar. There was a tiny rectangular window in the basement looking out onto the backyard. Snow swept up against it, leaving behind intricate patterns like the route of worms in wet earth.

"This is everything I have," Ganguly said. He chewed his lips, inspecting the folders. "There's an order to it."

I noticed a statement with the familiar MasterCard logo in the upper corner and picked it up. My eyes went down the page to the total balance: $28,456.32.

"This can't be right," I muttered. "Dad would never put this kind of money on a credit card. At eighteen percent interest? No way." Staring at the number made me feel itchy.

"I checked. It's right."

I began sifting through the documents for other credit card statements. Visa, Discover, Amex, then shadier ones like Wells Fargo and Sunoco and Macy's and something called Real Value Discounts. I studied the purchases he'd made.

"He was using them to pay for groceries, gas. Essentials," I noted.

Ganguly nodded and pointed out a few transactions. "These are cash advances. He's been using one card to make the minimum monthly payments on another."

I stopped counting balances after reaching $100,000. "He was maxed out."

Ganguly rubbed his face, pulling down his cheeks until he looked like a funhouse mirror version. "Medication. Stays at the hospital. I'm not even counting the money the Public Trustee gouges each month for services." He tsked, baring front teeth stained red from eating too much *paan*. "They came in acting like saviors. We're experts. Let us take care of her needs. Instead they just took."

My gaze lingered on a cable charge. "It got shut off last summer," I said.

"The cable?"

I nodded. "For almost a month. When it first went off I tried poking around behind the TV. When that didn't work I asked Dad to call Time Warner."

"And?"

I shrugged. "Dad said the TV was the problem, not the cable. He unplugged everything, dropped it into the trunk of his car, and said he was going to get it fixed. I'm sure that's where it stayed until"—I scrolled through transactions—"the fourteenth of July. When we got our TV back, good as new."

We laughed.

Ganguly shook his head. "If it had gone on for a year or two, he could have managed. But it's been over twenty years since she first got sick..."

"He could have told me. We would have...I don't know, tightened our belts."

He motioned for me to get up and took a seat at his table. He began slipping papers into folders and reinserting them within stacks. Deprived of Poonam's countervailing force, the house had swelled with clutter. Legal books moldered in the corner. Cardboard boxes filled with old stereo equipment, vinyl records, Atanu's old toys.

"You don't understand," he said. "Every time you came home to an empty house he blamed himself. He didn't care how much debt he ran up, just so long as you didn't want for the basics."

"And now?"

He looked at me steadily. "The vultures have come to collect."

* * *

It was the quiet of early morning when I returned to Miller House. The ground floor stood empty. Every creak on the stairs going up was a reminder that I'd become an intruder. I used my key to enter the apartment and spent a few moments taking in how unchanged it was since I'd been there last. Over a week had passed since Auntie had rescued me, during which time I'd ignored the countless voicemails left on my phone by Emily and formulated elaborate excuses that went unexpressed. When I looked out the living room window and took in the inane beauty of the frozen campus, ground covered in a glaze reflecting the sun's rise, barren trees at intervals like lost soldiers trying to reunite with their battalion, I marveled at my audacity. Like the sun and ground and trees I labored beneath a delusion. To think that Emily could possibly believe something like food poisoning or the onset of flu as the reason behind my being torn apart from the insides—it was insanity.

She slept over the covers, one arm over her eyes to block out the sun. She wore one of my wrinkled dress shirts, no bottom. The hairs of her pussy, a crudely groomed patch between slim hips, glowed with low heat.

I came over to her side and began pulling the covers out from under her. She muttered something indistinguishable and snuffled. I gently wiped away snot glistening beneath one nostril.

When I'd gotten the sheets free I undressed and got in next to her. I sidled up close. She sensed me and turned to one side. I draped an arm over her and adjusted so my body cupped hers. Her skin broke out in gooseflesh and warmed mine.

I slid my hand beneath her shirt and kneaded a breast. A faint sharp odor came from her armpit. I angled my face in and sniffed, wanting it on me.

My movements grew frenetic. Still sleeping, she took my questing hand and put it between her legs. Squeezed her thighs, holding it in place.

Once I'd wanted nothing more than to jettison the life I'd known. But it wasn't until I'd found my father lying in bed like a spent wind-up toy that I'd gotten a glimpse of what things would truly be like without its signposts. The descent I'd experienced wouldn't ever stop. I'd just keep sliding, edges growing ever darker, fingers along a glassy surface until one day I'd find myself in a place not unlike the Sunset Motel, judging the twisted people whistling at johns driving slowly past, not realizing I'd become one of them.

I didn't want to end up like that. No matter what my sins were,

I didn't deserve such a sentence.

* * *

She lies facedown on the floor with her eyes shut. Her throat aches from shouting. The smell of shit is in her mouth. She can't see the toilet in the dark but knows it's full.

It's a kind of offering, her being on the floor. A way of giving the voices that whirl inside her head a place in the real world, hopefully tempting them out. They can have the cot. They can caress the padded walls, smearing them with ectoplasm. And in return, all she asks is that they leave their poor, exhausted vessel, lying stiff on the ground like a snapshot of a war victim, in peace.

They tell her Niladri isn't waiting outside. He said he would. But he grew tired and left. I don't want him to wait, she whispers. It's bad enough he has to see his mother in this shame.

Raja promised he'd never leave you, the voices say. He brought you here when you became too...potent, then held your hand and said he'd be waiting in the parking lot, each and every night, until you got better. And he did. For a time.

She tries to recall details about what he looks like. It scares her that she can't remember.

Where is he now? the voice asks.

I don't know.

He didn't abandon you when you stopped rutting with him, blaming the medication. Or when you accused him of sleeping with the tarts that attend his classes, actually going so far as to visit him in his office and scream until Security was called. Can you imagine that nebbish sticking his cock into a teen? He'd run for the hills, tail between his legs, even contemplating such an atrocity.

Her hands go to her ears and press in. The constant rustling of the voices expands.

Why would he abandon you now?

I don't—

Don't tell me you don't know, cunt. Your son wishes you'd die here but your husband never did. Why did he leave you?

She stops breathing.

The blackness becomes a living thing that wraps tightly about her. She cedes the last of her will to it and is carried along by the stream of voices. Blackness fills her mouth and leaks out the corners of her eyes. Yet even at the last she deflects it onto every person she's ever known.

THIS was what she'd seen in the eyes of the witches she'd called her friends before they'd turned on her.

THIS was what had taken hold of her boy and turned him into a stranger.

And then, as suddenly as it began, it stops.

She waits a very long time, body twitching at false signals. She lowers her hands in increments, waiting for a returning whisper or chuckle. There is only silence.

This is when she would begin to weep or huddle into herself until sleep overtakes her. She'd been victimized by the voices so many times before but it never hurts any less.

Not this time.

Inside there is a stillness. She ponders the question that remains unanswered. Because Raja wouldn't have left her. Not of his own volition.

Which left very few possibilities. All of them bad. She doesn't think she can contemplate them, but slowly she begins to.

* * *

Emily had left the bed by the time I woke. I took the sheets and lifted them to my nose, breathing in the odor of our mingled bodies. I wanted to escape into that smell but the chill in the room and hushed voices coming from the living room made it impossible.

I opened the armoire and put on a fresh pair of khakis, boots, and a green cashmere sweater. I dug the sleep grit out of my eyes and inspected my face in the mirror, trying to discern if I possessed the strength necessary to carry out the gambit germinating in my mind.

It was no coincidence that Nurse Khadijah had decided to separate Mom from the other patients for three days. Two days from now was the Public Trustee trial that would determine whether she would be leaving the hospital or committed indefinitely. I didn't know how Nurse Khadijah had found out this piece of information, and didn't really care. What mattered was that the woman in charge of keeping my mother safe had felt the situation had devolved to the point where forced isolation was the only option left. There would be no reprieves following the trial, no trump cards laid down at the eleventh hour. If the trial were judged in the Public Trustee's favor my mother would be reintegrated with the general population and eaten alive.

Gary sat on the living room couch picking through joint roaches in the ashtray. Emily sat on the love seat. She still wore the coat she'd worn to retrieve him, shoulders flecked with snow. She had the pinched look of a woman who'd been taken advantage of.

Gary lit a roach. A low crackling. He exhaled and held it out to me.

I stood a few feet away from them, resenting their carefully constructed little scene. When I shook my head he shrugged and took another puff.

"The stuff you kids smoke these days. Bush league."

"Then don't smoke it," I muttered.

A gust of wind blew snow up against the windows. No one reacted.

"Look, I'm sorry I missed classes," I said. "I'll make it up—"

"I didn't come here to guilt trip you, Neil," Gary said.

Weed smoke reached my nostrils and made me feel like I was coming down with a headache.

Emily shook hair out of her eyes and picked at her fingernails.

"What is this?" I asked her. "Some kind of test?"

She stared at me blankly. "What?"

"A *test*," I repeated, injecting bile into the word. I looked to Gary. "To make up for missing classes? Is that it?"

"She's worried about you," Gary said.

"I'm okay," I said.

"How?" Emily asked. Her hair was greasy. She hadn't even paused to take a shower before running for help. That was what finding me in her bed had triggered. "How are you okay?"

"I had to take care of some things," I began.

She gave Gary an acknowledging look.

"Family stuff."

Gary crushed out the roach. "I don't think that's going to fly anymore."

"Well, it's not really any of your business," I told him.

"Is it mine?" Emily asked. Her fingers stilled. "Where've you been? I didn't know whether you'd gotten into an accident, or..."

"I thought things were going pretty well."

She looked like I'd slapped her. "You take what you want and leave. You make me feel like a whore sometimes."

I started for the door. She got up instantly, like she'd been expecting it.

She stopped me when I was less than six feet away, gazing into my eyes with a clarity that made me want to smash her face in.

"Tell me what happened," she said.

My eyes crawled over the freckles of her face, flaring nostrils, the tiny scar on her chin from where Tim had hit her. I couldn't organize them into a whole.

"I won't come here anymore."

"I don't want you to go!" she shouted. "Just let me in."

Her hand went to my chest and felt my racing heart. I swallowed and tried to look away but her head was right up close. The moment stretched out like taffy, and split apart.

She lowered her hand.

I stepped around her and paused. Her breaths came unevenly.

"Don't do it," Gary said quietly.

I slipped running up the driveway to where my car was parked and fell hard on my knees. The familiar twin hammer strokes of pain I'd felt countless times trying to pull off tricks on my BMX as a kid, followed by it liquefying and spreading up my thighs to pool at my groin. Slush and grit were on my hands.

Had my soul shattered on the frozen macadam no one would have been able to put the pieces back together. There was no logic to them, no overriding sense of purpose or unique human quality announcing itself as they were arranged. Just trivia, a talent for mimicry, pragmatism lurking beneath a caul of sentimentality.

* * *

Ganguly's basement became a base of operations. We carefully moved all the folders to an empty corner and pushed the desk off to one side. What remained was a single chair and a tall lamp Ganguly angled over it.

"Sit," he said.

I watched him pace in front of me, hands crossed behind his back, belly jutting out like the prow of a ship. He pulled a small tin from his shirt pocket, extracted a *paan*, and popped it into his mouth. Its sweet, minty smell infiltrated the air between us like incense.

He stopped and turned on his heels toward me. "Why are you here?"

"For my mother. She's alone, and—"

"Alone?" Ganguly asked, turning the very idea into something juvenile. "But she's not. Our office is there for her."

I didn't say anything.

The floor creaked as he came up over me, partially blocking the light. "Is it the money?"

"No."

"No?"

"If it was about money I'd let her stay where she is. I know how expensive medication can be, especially long-term..."

Ganguly tutted. "You sound like an accountant. Speak from your heart, Niladri."

I swallowed and said, "I...care for her."

"Well, that's wonderful," he answered, chewing loudly. He started walking back across the room. "And your father? Did he care for her too?"

"Of course."

"And where did that get him?"

I leaned forward. "What's that supposed to mean?"

"You can't show frustration," Ganguly said, gesturing for me to sit back in the chair. "So much of the judge's decision will come down to character."

I turned the lamp so its glare fell beyond my feet, then rested my head back against the chair. "I never saw a more devoted man. He spent every free moment talking to her, taking walks with her, reminding her in a hundred different ways of the world outside her head."

Ganguly tilted his head up and scratched his neck. "And did you do the same?"

"I..." did everything I could to stay away from her. Considered every day that didn't end with me disrespecting or calling out her frailties a good one.

"How many treatment meetings did you attend?"

"Not many."

"Not any. Isn't that correct? How about patient-family outings? The beach party this past June, for instance."

June was the month I found out I'd been accepted into Raleigh's Drama program. Vague desires and fantasies of living in a beach house on the West Coast had become validated by an acceptance letter two paragraphs long. I'd taken walks lasting hours, craving unspoiled vistas to use as a canvas for my future life. A father having a water-gun fight with his young daughter made that suddenly a possibility for me. A backyard barbecue became a get-together of close friends, all of whom contributed meaningfully or deeply to the world in some fashion, yet still made time to crack a few beers and eat my handmade burgers. My body may have been trapped in the here-and-now but my heart resided firmly in this place of soft edges and swooning emotions.

"No," I said.

"Your father attended every treatment meeting. Took time off work to lay a blanket out and get a tan with your mother on the beach. And yet, for all that, he failed."

"He didn't."

Ganguly rocked forward and back on his heels. "You consider four relapses in five years a success?"

"You weren't there."

"Neither were you," Ganguly answered. He stood a foot or two away from me, belly button pressing out against his shirt like an all-seeing eye. "By your own admission you didn't really take part in anything. Yet now we're supposed to believe that you'll magically succeed where your father—"

"He couldn't take her spasming on the bed because of the pills. Going a week without being able to shit. She needed his help going to the bathroom. She'd hobble like a ninety-year-old."

Ganguly swallowed the last of his *paan* and licked his lips. They were crimson from the juices. I imagined his entire insides looking like that, a tincture before an X-ray scan.

"Let's take a break," he said gently. "Would you like a glass of water?"

I nodded.

He brought one over and watched while I drained it.

"Sorry," I said.

He shook his head and tried to pawn it off like it was nothing. "That's why we rehearse. So you can say these things here and not in front of a judge."

I gnawed a finger. "It's not that I didn't care. I want you to know that."

"You don't have to explain."

"I would have participated if I didn't know it would end with her back in the hospital. My father could just...block that out."

"He still saw Priya underneath."

"Yes." I couldn't.

15

Snow was piled up in drifts in front of the house and along the steps. Several of the neighboring homes had put up Christmas lights, blinking cheerfully beneath a clear afternoon sky. It was a neat neighborhood, filled with good and judicious people who had diligently shoveled out passageways to their vehicles.

Auntie's Jaguar was partially buried in the driveway like a wounded beast waiting for a victim to come within striking range. Ice coated the windows and obscured the cabin. The thought of Auntie having stayed in the house all this time, drinking tea and flipping through photo albums, made me uneasy.

I grabbed a shovel from the garage. Auntie opened the front door a crack and peeked out while I cleared the terrace. Her face looked a little puffy from sleep. She smiled warmly.

"Do you need help?" she asked.

A gust of wind ruffled the collar of my jacket and died down. I shook my head.

She leaned against the doorjamb, yawning once in a while. She must have been chilly in just a long-sleeved black top and slacks but didn't show it.

"Don't worry about the car," she said. "I'll take care of it tomorrow."

I broke up a patch of ice with the steel end of the shovel. "Show me your hands," I said.

She gave me a strange look, but complied.

I came up close and peered at the nails. "Nice and manicured," I said. "You're going to risk that shoveling?"

Her eyes searched mine for clues to my absence. Her hair was freshly washed and framed her face prettily. The foyer shadows were kind; she could have passed for a woman in her late thirties instead of one nearing fifty.

"Should I worry about you?" she asked.

I rubbed my hands to warm them. She got some ski gloves out of the foyer closet and gave them to me.

"I'm just tired," I said, slipping them on. They were neon yellow and blue. They'd belonged to my father. If Auntie hadn't been watching I'd have pressed the interior of a glove against my nose and breathed him in.

I pulled my lips up into a smile. Patently false, like one proffered by a ticket-taker or Jehovah's Witness.

Auntie had known me since birth. She'd held my tiny body in her hands and watched me blink and take my first breaths. And yet she nodded, believing the smile without question. "I'll make some tea. Don't be too long."

True to her word, a cup of milky tea with extra sugar was waiting for me when I came in. She put out some biscuits which I ate ravenously. I hadn't eaten all that day.

The house was a fraction of the size she was accustomed to. Here she had none of the comforts she'd grown to rely on, yet her vitality had increased tenfold. She wiped down counters and set out newspaper for my wet boots as if she'd been taking care of a family her entire life. She hummed little scraps of Bollywood songs. And she was talkative, divulging one family tale after another like a stopper had been pulled.

How she'd been walking home from school with my mother one afternoon as teenagers in Srivilla, a Calcutta suburb, when they'd come across a swimming competition. Mom had taken one look at the prize and lined up with the other swimmers. Never mind that she was still wearing her uniform. Or that she couldn't swim. When the starter's pistol rang out she took a running dive...and promptly began to drown a quarter of the way down the length of the pool. It had taken five men to pull her sodden, flailing body out of the water.

How the sight of a garlanded elephant had surprised my father on his wedding day, munching on the flowerbed outside of his parents' home. During an Indian wedding few things were as important as the groom's entrance. Usually a black Ambassador car or a pony would suffice. But he was marrying above his station, and their father had taken an instant liking to his manners and straightforwardness, so...the pachyderm. Never mind that my father had suffered his one and only panic attack in a zoo, and gave dogs the distance usually afforded to wild bears. Getting him onto the creature's back had taken hours. Upon reaching the cricket field lit up with torches, redolent with the smells of five open-air kitchens making food for nearly a thousand invitees, he had waited until people surrounded the elephant, leapt off, landed badly amidst congratulations, and pushed blindly into the crowd, certain one of its massive feet was about to stamp him out.

She spoke of how obstinately her parents had gone about trying to find a suitable boy for her. Despite her protestations, or the business degree she'd garnered, right up until she took the first airplane voyage of her life to emigrate to the United States. It was always the same; a man dressed to the nines, chatting too loudly with her parents in the living room like he'd just decided to stop by. Auntie was polite. She tried to be demure. Yet when they asked to meet with her again she was forced to refuse in no uncertain terms. This was how it was with Indian men; leave the slightest opening and they'll inevitably wriggle on through. It would be different in America. She'd be on equal footing there. Only what she'd found was a barter system. And she lacked whatever quality they required to make a purchase.

She lay lengthwise on the living room couch, a toe periodically flicking the air for emphasis. When her mouth grew dry she'd take a sip of water from the glass resting on the floor next to her, drawing it out to savor what she no doubt wished was Macallan 1938 instead. Soon enough her eyelids grew heavy and the pauses between recollections stretched out.

Auntie never allowed anyone to see her sleeping. Her bedroom at home was kept locked from the inside. It was a something everyone close to her knew, yet no one ever broached. And yet I found myself sitting cross-legged on the floor by the coffee table, finishing off a second plate of cookies and listening to her snore.

For me, she was willing to betray herself.

* * *

Shadows crept up the street, invading the lookout holes and parapets of a snow fort strategically built between two parked cars. Witnessing evening drape itself over campus had always lifted my spirits, bringing with it a sense of limitless possibilities and experiences waiting to be tapped. Yet my mother did not even know it had occurred.

Auntie muttered. A leg extended completely, then retracted. Her weight dented the cushions, an afterimage that would remain after she had risen.

I knelt down next to her and touched her shoulder. She sighed. Her eyes opened bleary and slow.

"How long have I been sleeping?" she asked.

I shook my head.

She lifted a hand to her cheeks and began pushing the flesh back. "I look a fright."

"No."

"Liar."

I stopped her hands. She gazed about the room like she didn't recognize it.

"You were drowning," she said. "I could see you thrashing in the pool. I was the only one inside the house. The patio doors...I banged on them, threw myself against them, but they wouldn't budge."

"It's okay."

"No." Tears came into her eyes; she shook them away. "I saw you...go under."

I pressed her to me. She sobbed without restraint. It had been so long since someone had witnessed it she'd forgotten how.

"You're the only family I have," she said. "My one hope."

"Auntie..."

"No, not Auntie. You're not my nephew and I'm not your Auntie. Those nothing words."

She pushed me away at arm's length. She shut her eyes tight and opened them, appealing to me with all she possessed.

I swallowed the stone in my throat. "Auntie..."

"No."

I lowered my gaze.

She slapped me across the mouth.

"I won't," I whispered. "Not ever."

She got up, teetered momentarily, and regained her balance. She went upstairs. I listened to her gathering her things. She came downstairs shortly afterwards and stood watching me from the living room entryway, clutching a travel bag in one hand.

"Does it help you to blame me?" she asked.

"I don't," I answered.

"That cunt." Her lower back was twisted. "Freak."

"She's my mother."

"You lost your mother years ago."

She went into the foyer and put her shoes on. I walked to within a few feet of her. "She never would have left you," I said. "If you were a vegetable falling apart on a hospital bed she'd have been at your side."

She buttoned her jacket. Tied her hair back, concentrating to not botch it.

"You deserve to be alone," I said, once she was gone.

* * *

I am sitting in front of Mom's vanity mirror taking in the sight of myself in a muted black suit. There is a yellow rose on my lapel. My face is cleanly shaven. But it's the glow of happiness, as unmistakable and intangible as the spark of prescience before the roulette ball lands on your number, that transfixes me. I'm dreaming, I tell myself. But it doesn't feel like one I've ever had.

The bedroom door opens and Mom enters, letting in a hubbub from downstairs. She's skinnier, though not entirely back to the idealized form she usually takes in my visions. Swathed in a yellow sari that matches my rose, she is smiling, almost erasing the unnerving stillness to her gaze, or the calloused hands from a punishment she'd carried out in a hospital garden once.

She tiptoes toward me. "Are you nervous?" Grinning like it would be a treat if I was.

"A little," I say.

I start to feel warm beneath my suit. A breeze wafts in through the open window, carrying with it the faintest hint of honeysuckle.

"That's good," she says, bending forward to inspect my face in microscopic detail. "It's a bad sign if you're not."

She pinches my cheeks, hard. I cry out and swat her hands away.

"You're pale as a ghost!" she exclaims.

"I like it, leave it," I mutter, glancing at the mirror to gauge the damage. Sure enough, twin clusters of red in the shape of her fingers are rising to the surface of my cheeks.

Her arm comes out, covered in a fine layer of brown hair ending in enough gold bracelets to still a jeweler's heart. I take it and come to standing.

"Don't be nervous," she says again.

I kiss the part of her hair. I can feel her heart beating beneath the clothing.

"I wish he could have been here," she says. "It would have been his joy, Niladri."

"I know. I do too."

A piano begins playing downstairs. It's a classical piece I don't recognize and has the effect of quieting the guests. We walk out of the room arm-in-arm. Upon reaching the threshold to the stairs she sets a slow, deliberate *pace geared for viewing.*

The entire ground floor is packed with guests. Their heads tilt up to watch us, Uncles and Aunties, faces I recall from elementary and high school, Tim and Quincy glimpsed briefly near the living room. It's all too much to absorb during the seconds it takes for Mom and me to come all the way down. What I'm left with as guests begin clearing a path for us to the open patio door is a great wave of encouragement, so powerful that were my legs to buckle it would have carried me the rest of the way outside to where Emily stands next to a priest and photographer.

She wears a frilly white dress with a yellow bow. It's very bright outside and she's squinting to make us out...

* * *

The car was freezing. I started the engine and waited for it to warm up enough to put the heater on. I rubbed my chest and arms, whistling scraps of whatever had been playing on the piano. The entire dream felt like déjà vu.

Outside, the hospital grounds were a photo negative. The lights had gone off in Baker Pavilion hours ago and what remained were glimmering steel bars over windows, the periodic splashing of headlights against a wall when a patrol car passed on its rounds. There were only a few other cars in the parking lot. Sometimes I imagined there were others like me inside them, crouched down low to avoid detection, playing the torturous game of when to look at the clock next.

When I switched on the heater I snuck a peek. Mom had one day left.

* * *

Cars and taxis were parked haphazardly in the driveway of Miller House, exhaust plumes mingling like the voices of carolers. A steady stream of tenants came out with legitimate and makeshift luggage, garbage bags filled with clothes, presents wrapped in construction paper. The mass exodus of Christmas vacation had begun.

Inside looked like a bomb had been set off. The chattering voices of students on cell phones confirming travel arrangements with their parents, combined with those exchanging phone numbers and promises to stay in touch, were like screws boring into my temples. I'd only been outside of this for a few days, yet it felt like I was returning from a journey they could not possibly comprehend. No one spoke to me on my way upstairs. No one seemed to even register my presence. I was grateful for this small mercy.

Apartment doors stood open. Emily's was closed. I still possessed a key yet had given up the right to use it. When I thought of how ill she'd looked sitting in the living room with Gary, and considered that I had been the cause, it almost broke my resolve. But I knocked.

The door to the roof banged open and a stocky guy wearing a cap with earflaps came out, dragging a jury-rigged television satellite behind him. He made a friendly clicking noise passing me and entered one of the apartments. A sign for a fallout shelter, three orange triangles within a black circle, was pasted on the wall next to his door.

I couldn't be sure, but I thought as I stood there, staring into the peephole, that I saw the light flicker within Em's apartment. I didn't knock again or make any sudden movement. My heart was full with the wonder of the dream. I tried to project it outside of myself and through that tiny lens. I believed what we had was stronger than the past. It was warm and embracing, proof of God's love.

If she'd let me in I'd lay my entrails out and beg her to be gentle.

The door never opened.

I went home and methodically laid waste. I emptied the contents of entire kitchen cupboards onto the floor. I smashed two dining room chairs to kindling. I tore pictures off the walls and stamped on the faces of noble Indian peasants. Cupboards without food. A table lacking chairs. Emptiness has no gradations. We'd suffered with a gaping hole at the very center of our lives and nothing and nothing and nothing. If I lost the trial I'd burn the house down.

I drank beer in the basement where Dad and I had watched TV on Christmas mornings. He'd sip tea and follow a cricket or soccer match, relishing my growing impatience. After my foot had tapped for the thousandth time he'd sigh and scoop me up onto his back. We'd mount the stairs quickly, passing the green plastic tree in the living room with white doves within its boughs and presents scattered about its base, up to the bedroom my parents still shared. Mom slept with her mouth open. Lustrous black hair spread out like a fairy tale heroine.

He'd hold my body a few feet above her. Every once in a while he'd dip or spin me and I'd try not to shriek and spoil the game.

"Count," he'd whisper.

One and he lifted me so high my hair grazed the ceiling. Two and he swooped me down fast, stopping inches from her face. Blood rushed to my head. Three and he let go. There was a perfect moment suspended between them. Then Mom's hands shot up and caught me an instant before collision.

She cracked an eye open. "Got you."

I tried to recall details from the dream but it split apart, grew abstract. The smell of beer and my own body was repulsive. I tried to crack open a window but didn't even make it halfway across the basement. I crawled up the stairs. When they swayed too badly I stuck two fingers down my throat and made myself vomit. Ropy yellow syrup came out.

My head glanced off the patio door. I reached up and unlocked it somehow. Pulled it open partway. The cold was like a bludgeon but it faded.

I crawled out, hands pushing through a crust of ice into snow like wads of cotton. The ice stabbed my skin and spurred me forward. My knees and legs seized up, becoming leaden anchors that made the going more difficult. This was my penance. Beyond the lip of the patio would be all of the wedding guests and Emily and my mother, patiently waiting. I'd see them and make a joke like finally or thanks for making it easy. Stagehands would come out and strike the snow and blowing wind, pull back the winter backdrop, and expose midsummer like honey.

What I found were metal bars separating me from the empty expanse of the backyard. At its perimeter a fence nearly covered by snowdrifts. A birdhouse slanted by its weight.

* * *

A guard came out of the Security booth and waved for me to pull over. The hospital gates creaked shut behind me. I rolled my window down as he approached.

"Is there a problem?" I asked, enunciating each word carefully. I kept my gaze forward. The beacon atop the main building flashed out in a wide arc, illuminating a night sky congested with clouds.

The guard chewed gum and didn't answer. He wore a thin windbreaker and an I.D. badge listing him as Momhamed Marzouk. His hair was choppy and short, likely self-cut.

"Late for a visit, no?" he asked finally.

I glanced at the dashboard clock. "I still have a half hour left."

He tapped his fingers along the roof. "You were here yesterday."

"My Mom's in Baker."

"Baker," he said, like it meant nothing to him. He leaned in through the window. "I was working yesterday, did you see me?"

"No."

He sniffed me, smelt the booze. His chin was covered in moles. "I didn't see you leave."

"Could you back away a little please?"

He gave me an obsequious little smile and pulled his head out.

An ambulance pulled up behind me, lights doused. The driver sounded his horn.

The guard waved me on. But when I glanced in the rearview mirror I saw him point a flashlight at my license plate, noting the number.

It would be my last night at the hospital.

I parked the car, got out, and started toward the pavilion, hands shoved deep in my pockets. I wore three sweaters and a parka but my chest still felt like a slab of meat in deep freeze. I glanced back and saw my footsteps in the snow, a meandering path. Whorls of snow played between cars and atop them, seeking entry.

I went around the side of the pavilion, a gloved hand feeling the stone, counting steps. Thirty and I was at the nurse's station. Thirty-six and I stood in front of the two doors. The cartilage of my nose ached. Exhalations were sole points of warmth.

I knelt down, pressing both hands flat against the wall. I touched my forehead to it and began whispering reassurances only she could understand.

16

I was at the nurse's station early the next morning. Nurse Khadijah was working alone. She saw me and her face grew grave. There was no checking the clock, no apologetic shrug or deflecting words; we were beyond that.

We walked to the unmarked steel door together.

The smell of urine came out in a blast. The light came on to reveal Mom lying facedown on the bed, one arm trailing on the ground.

I pushed past Nurse Khadijah.

"Mom?" I asked, brushing hair off her face.

She made an unintelligible noise. Her skin was covered in cold sweat.

Nurse Khadijah and I helped her sit up. There were food trays by the door with partially eaten cups of yogurt and sandwich halves. I spotted a bottle of water and brought it over to her. Mom drank greedily, eyes periodically squinting up at the light as if she couldn't quite believe it existed. Her face was etched with lines from the pillow.

"Can you get up?" Nurse Khadijah asked.

"I don't know," Mom said. Her voice was hoarse. "I don't think so."

I took her hands and rubbed them. I went up her arms, bringing circulation back to numb flesh.

"They spoke so loud," she whispered.

"Ssshh."

"They were dragging me under."

I dug my fingers into her shoulders, loosening hard knots of muscle. Her body swayed with the motions. Her bottom lip was swollen and flecked with blood.

"I couldn't breathe. I thought...dark things. Anything to make them stop."

"You don't have to..."

She grasped me by the back of the neck and pulled me close. "I thought of you. My boy. And it stopped."

We held each other. The totality and peace of it—I'd nearly forgotten what it was like.

Nurse Khadijah jangled her keys. "It's time," she said.

Mom's breath caught in her throat.

"Please," I said, "I just need a few more hours."

Nurse Khadijah's eyes grew hard. One hand was tucked into a pocket, ready to respond to adversity. Enormous false eyelashes batted as she inspected my mother.

"I don't think you can get up."

Mom started to say something and I squeezed her hand. I grew aware of the tiny camera lens staring at us from the upper corner of the room like a nesting spider.

"We should take you to the infirmary," Nurse Khadijah said. She looked at me. "Won't be longer than a day. Two max."

"That's all I need," I answered with a confidence I did not feel.

"I'll have the paramedics bring in a stretcher for her." Nurse Khadijah nodded toward the door. "Go to it."

* * *

The courthouse lobby held a massive stone sculpture of an eagle at its center, wings flared in descent, brutal spike of a beak jutting forward toward its prey. Its eyes were hollow white orbs. People entered through revolving doors and quickly branched off down one of the snaking corridors. Wall-mounted screens displayed stock tickers, the aftermath of an earthquake, a commercial for air freshener. Someone knocked into me and continued on, muttering under his breath. The revolving doors sounded like street sweepers.

Panic was a low constant itch.

Ganguly stood in front of me saying something. I nodded dumbly. His voice was drowned out by all of the background noises. I couldn't decipher it.

He led me down one of the corridors, turning his shoulders to get through congested sections. Mouths spoke, hands held cell phones to ears, papers were exchanged. I should have been able to put it all together, but the more I focused the more it all fell apart.

Ganguly laid his briefcase down on a table next to a room marked "2A." Glancing at me briefly, he pulled out a bottle of Aqua Velva, poured some into his palm and slapped it over my cheeks. He tucked in my shirt and hiked up my pants. He undid his tie, raised my shirt collar, and began looping it around.

"Remember what we practiced," creating a wide Windsor knot.

"We should have done more but it's okay. *Shut the door to errors and the truth will be shut out too,*" paraphrasing Tagore.

He brought my collar down and fastened the top button.

"I don't want you to go in there," I said, dropping my gaze to the table. "When you hear..."

"What? The testimony you gave?"

A man in his early thirties peeked his head out of the courtroom, saw us standing there, and retreated. The door he'd opened swung closed on its hinges. Its thick oak planks seemed more appropriate to an Inquisitor's chamber or dungeon.

"Scoundrels tried to use it as leverage for a fast settlement." Ganguly buttoned up his gray double-breasted jacket. It was a little less faded than the trousers. "They called it 'inside information from a family source.' Who else could it be?"

"And you still helped me?"

He closed his suitcase and picked it up. "I knew why you did it. But I wasn't about to tell your father."

* * *

"He's the big hero, right? Only what does he do but buy into her lies? Hiding the pills he should be giving her, bottles and bottles because he's too much of a pussy to force her to take them..."

Auntie whispered something beneath the recording's hiss.

"No, you want to know the truth?" My voice was shrill, barely recognizable. "He's weak. As long as he can trot her out in front of all the Aunties and Uncles, and slurp tea and pretend it's the dead good old days, he doesn't CARE if she recovers."

The prosecutor shut the player off. The judge, sitting on a raised dais in the center of the room, Ganguly and I standing at a table to his right, the prosecutor's assistants to his left, all watched her pick up the tiny device and hold it aloft. It was a manufactured moment for a piece of evidence requiring no such trickery. Body hidden beneath a power suit several sizes too big, feathered red hair at odds with a dour expression. After several seconds she laid it in front of the judge.

Ganguly cleared his throat. "Your Honor, Mr. Kapoor..."

"That would be Raja Kapoor?" the judge asked, clicking through documents on a computer screen. His hair was white at the temples and his face had the pleasant inscrutability of an English professor.

"Yes. He passed away earlier this month. The situation described in that recording has changed."

"And we're all sorry for the loss," the prosecutor said, walking over to her desk on the far side of the room to check notes. "However, we have no reason to believe this pattern of negligence will end under his son's care." Her shoes left behind faint imprints on the maroon carpet.

The judge looked at me. "You're the son?"

I nodded. "Niladri Kapoor."

"Your Honor, if anything, that statement is proof of his resolve to do better," Ganguly said.

"Please," the prosecutor said, employing the tone of a mother berating a child for the twentieth time. "He was looking to get out. Considering what he described I don't blame him." She gave me a look dripping with false concern. "Yet now he wants to take over?"

The judge tapped the screen with a pen. "I've been going over Ms. Kapoor's treatment regimen. I have a few questions."

"Of course," the prosecutor said. She signaled to someone in the back pews. A tiny man stepped out into the aisle and came forward, stopping between the tables. He was fastidiously attired in a V-neck sweater, red bow tie, and herringbone slacks. His hands were creamy white and smooth like a woman's. Those hands were what I remembered most from the times I'd met him, flaccid grasping my own, pointing out signs of deterioration on my mother's face while she smiled vacantly beside him.

"Perhaps I could be of some small service," he said in a Quebecois accent.

"Dr. Jean Thibodeau?"

He tilted his head agreeably. A mop of blond hair flounced atop his head like Tintin.

The judge slipped on reading glasses to better make out the computer screen. "She's currently on Solian?"

"Yes."

"And before that, Olanzapine."

"Indeed." The doctor chuckled. "She's been a challenging case."

"Palperidone, before that Quetiapine..."

"For the insomnia," Dr. Thibodeau said. "Quetiapine for RLS." When the judge didn't answer he added, "Restless legs syndrome."

"I'm aware of what it stands for." The judge took off his glasses. In the quiet of the courtroom the sound of the frames clacking against his desk was quite loud. "Maybe she should have cut down on the coffee instead."

Dr. Thibodeau smiled but his eyes had grown wary. Two fingers picked at a loose thread on his trousers as he tried to determine whether the judge was an ally or threat.

"It's just that typically there's a progression in prescribing meds, a narrowing field of choices." The judge shook his head. "I'm not seeing that here."

"Well, as I said, it's a difficult case."

"Challenging was the word you used."

The prosecutor stepped up next to Dr. Thibodeau and placed a friendly hand on his back. "Your Honor, the doctor has taken time out of a busy schedule to join us today…"

"And I appreciate it," the judge answered, watching one of her assistants pass along a scrap of notepaper to the doctor.

Dr. Thibodeau scanned it briefly and said, "In addition to severe delusions, Ms. Kapoor—"

"They're not delusions," I said, unable to stay quiet any longer.

"She believes she's a movie star, Your Honor," Dr. Thibodeau said. "If that's not delusional thinking…"

"There's truth to that, Your Honor," Ganguly said. Beneath the cover of the desk his hands were tight fists. "She's been in several movies. Not a movie star, certainly…"

"Egotism," I said, recalling a line we'd rehearsed, "but not delusion."

"What else?" the judge asked Dr. Thibodeau.

The doctor folded the paper and slipped it into his pocket. "Prolonged periods of anhedonia…"

"Inability to experience pleasure?" I interjected. "She's trapped in a hospital."

Dr. Thibodeau gave me a pissy look. "Am I going to be subjected to this throughout, Your Honor? I thought I was here to answer your questions, not his."

The judge leaned back and crossed his arms over his chest. The American flag sagged on a flagpole behind him.

"Also, if I can add…" Dr. Thibodeau said, ignoring the prosecutor's signals not to, "this kind of disrespect has been going on for years. I have literally hundreds of emails from his father suggesting alternative therapies, voodoo potions…"

"Like having her garden in the cold for hours?" I asked.

"It wasn't hours," Dr. Thibodeau said, and quickly realized he'd given himself away. "She tells lies, Your Honor. Trust has always been an issue with her."

Ganguly nudged me.

"I've visited her more during these last few months than I have...ever," I told the judge. "She's aware of what's happening to her. Understands the consequences."

"Just more games," Dr. Thibodeau muttered.

"What if it's not?" Ganguly asked the judge.

"We don't deal in hypotheticals here," the judge said.

"She's terrified," I said. "She can't last much longer in there." I nodded toward the prosecutor. "Whatever they tell you, she can't."

"This is absurd," Dr. Thibodeau said. "The woman's ill. She requires hospitalization."

"I can see that," the judge said, nodding toward the computer screen. "Quetiapine, doctor? I can't remember seeing that on a treatment sheet since the eighties."

Dr. Thibodeau began to blink quickly. "If you're challenging my methods..."

The judge waved him off. "Nothing as dramatic as all that."

The prosecutor laid a file on the judge's desk. "Your Honor, these are recommendations from former patients who are more than willing to attest to the doctor's abilities. If you'll turn to page three, you'll find the very moving story of Sarah Reeser, a thirty-six-year-old mother with bipolar disorder who..."

"It must be difficult, dealing with so many patients," the judge said, not having once looked away from the doctor. "It's not private practice, after all."

Dr. Thibodeau's concave chest struggled to puff out. "No, it's not."

"With a patient like this, who frustrates at every turn..."

"I'm trying."

"I don't doubt that."

There was an awkward pause during which each waited for the other to speak.

"I'd like to thank Dr. Thibodeau for making the time to speak here today," the prosecutor said.

Dr. Thibodeau grinned, a wet thing like a leech's mouth.

"Thank you, doctor," the judge said.

He left without looking at anyone. He paused at the door. On the other side lay respectability and the casual hauteur that comes with holding lives in your hand. For a few moments we'd been privy to the blundering child operating the machinery, but once he left the courthouse it would be gone.

He'd fucked with my mother. He'd fuck with others. And he'd continue on until the human wreckage became impossible to ignore.

The judge looked at me. "Where were we?"

The right words, as it turned out, came easily. They'd only lacked an avenue. They'd only required a purpose.

17

It was over quickly. The judge made his ruling, wished me good luck, and left through an exit behind the dais. The prosecutor nodded at us and poured herself a glass of water. Her assistants began briefing her on the next case.

Ganguly had stepped in once it became clear the judge was siding with us, negotiating financial details with the prosecutor as if they were traders on the stock exchange. Numbers were rattled off. The words "acceptable agreement" were overused to the point of meaninglessness. I couldn't understand all of it, but what it basically boiled down to was that the Public Trustee would receive the bulk of my inheritance as a payout for their troubles. In exchange they would sever ties with my mother, making the prospect of getting her admitted to any psychiatric facility in New York State nearly impossible.

Ganguly touched my hand and smiled.

"Is that it?" I asked, unable to believe it.

"I still have to receive the official agreement from them, probably in the next day or two, but..."

I hugged him. My body felt brittle, a patch of ice besieged by sun. "Thank you."

"There, there," he said, giving my back a brisk pat. "It's fine."

I wasn't in much shape to drive. Ganguly offered me a lift back home. We'd won, I kept telling myself, watching Christmas shoppers peruse storefronts downtown and drop money into the bucket of a Salvation Army Santa. The idea was so foreign in the context of my family. There were hopes dashed and promises broken. I understood those. But accepting what had happened would mean inviting in the idea of the worm having finally turned for us, and I wasn't there yet.

There was a half-full bottle of vodka in the fridge. I doled out two shots in coffee mugs. We clinked and drank it down. Ganguly beat his chest like a Viking.

"What now?" he asked. The house was in shambles but he pretended not to notice.

"Sleep." Plate shards stared up at me from the floor. Curry powder in the air tickled my nose. "For a week."

"No one says you can't sell the house."

"I know, Uncle."

"Priya can always go to an out-of-state hospital."

"Yes."

He drained his mug and laid it on the counter. "I'm an old man. We enjoy talking to ourselves."

* * *

I slept for nearly twelve hours, getting up only to use the bathroom and call Nurse Khadijah for a status update. The infirmary was pretty strict with visitors, but a few minutes could be arranged tomorrow. I thanked her and hung up. Sleep had allowed my body to begin feeling the true extent of its injuries. My back twinged when I turned to my side. My teeth felt sensitive; I ground them during times of stress.

I began clearing out the worst of the wreckage, tossing splintered chair pieces and crushed loaves of bread into a garbage bag, lost in thought like the caretakers who cleaned the college grounds. This place couldn't remain the backdrop to my own personal passion play anymore. Somehow I had to transform it into a home, a safe place that honored my father's best impulses.

I needed money. I needed a job. I had to learn what bills were due each month and ensure they were settled.

And I wouldn't be alone.

The campus seemed deserted. Those few traversing it kept their distance. Christmas lights on trees gave it the appearance of a metropolis following a deadly plague. The moon, nearly full overhead, seemed cowed by the lights and frequently obscured herself behind clouds.

Carruthers Hall smelled of chlorine. Most of the lights were on. A freshly cleaned floor offered a warped reflection. As I passed classrooms I imagined students hiding behind desks and with their backs up against the wall, participating in an elaborate prank designed to frighten the wits out of a classmate. Several times I cast a look over my shoulder, certain I'd see one of them creeping behind me with a mischievous grin. But of course there was no one.

Until I reached the far end of the hall and heard Gary calling out instructions from within the auditorium, voice echoing like the wrath of a distant god.

A low thrust stage invaded ten rows of seats covered in red cloth. Gary stood at center, gazing up at an intricate grid of stage lights and calling out commands to a stagehand that made some flare and others recede. Dense crimson suitable for Macbeth's contemplating murder. Pale, shimmering blue heralding the denouement of a Tennessee Williams play.

He ignored me for several minutes. Then he told the stagehand working in the mezzanine they'd resume tomorrow. All except the soft yellow houselights blinked off.

"I didn't know you'd be here," I said, touching the lip of the stage.

He stared down at me. His face was expressionless.

"I didn't have a choice," I told him.

"About what, exactly?" He sighed. "Semester's over, Neil. What do you want? Credit for the classes you missed?"

"That's not what I..."

He hopped down off the stage and gathered up a notebook and thermos resting by one of the chairs.

"It's bigger than you or me," I said.

He rubbed his chin. He hadn't shaved in a few days and the gray bristles made him look older. "I know about your mother. Broad strokes, anyway. I understand why you'd try to hide it, but it's no mystery. Most of the teachers know she has problems."

"Good," I think I said.

"See, I want to say what you're doing's right. But I can't give you that."

I wanted to walk out of there. But I was held prisoner by the words issuing from his mouth.

"I have a daughter who's thirteen who barely knows me. She lives with her mother in Cincinnati. I used to visit during the holidays then stopped when I realized it was more for my benefit than hers." He fiddled with the thermos tab. "You falter as a human being and the worst of it is you don't even feel that bad. Because when you find talent in a student, the joy of that discovery is so strong it makes everything else seem...less." He spared me a quick glance. "I appreciate your coming but all I can see is someone throwing that away."

I could have refuted it. Promised him I wouldn't let the undertow of circumstance pull me under. But it was all I could do just to figure out the next few steps. I had no idea what lay in store for me beyond that.

The only thing Gary couldn't accept were lies, and I wasn't about to speak them, no matter how noble the intentions.

Later I found out he was as good as his word, providing Administration with the fake grades necessary for me to continue on in the program. He even convinced many of the other professors to allow me to retake midterms and move forward from there.

But I never did go back.

* * *

Ganguly called the next morning to say the papers had arrived. They were so dense with type that I didn't really look them over, just signed at the bottom. He made a copy and faxed it over to the Public Trustee's office. I slipped the original into my pocket. I couldn't avoid the niggling feeling of having forgotten something crucial, a detail that threatened to overturn everything that had been accomplished.

"I'm going to be traveling for the next few months," Ganguly said, checking emails at his desk.

"Where?"

"The motherland, to begin with. There are friends of mine and your father's I haven't seen in almost ten years. After that, who knows?" He stole a glance at the boxes stacked in the basement corners, filled with objects he no longer used yet couldn't quite bring himself to discard. "No matter how long I worked down here there'd always be Poonam's snores to fall asleep to come night." He flicked the screen off. "I think it's time I..." He didn't finish.

"I'll miss you."

He nodded. "Me too."

Before I left he offered me a part-time job managing the office affairs in his absence. Though he was adamant and wouldn't change the subject until extracting a promise from me to think it over, I couldn't accept. I was far too indebted to him already.

*　*　*

The infirmary was a model of pristine efficiency. Nurses zipped between rooms and a janitor painstakingly buffed a floor marked with arrows leading visitors to different sections. There were no wandering spirits, no smell of urine or feces. Apparently if you were still human enough to have a breakdown, you were granted humane treatment.

I found her room easily enough. The door was closed, affording her a luxury she hadn't enjoyed since August. A small table next to it held booklets and an arrangement of artificial pansies.

There was no reason for the dread, not anymore, I told myself, and stepped inside.

Auntie stood over Mom's bed, hiding her face from view. Long black coat. Black gloves clutching the metal railing.

As I came forward the air grew thick. I saw two things simultaneously: tears streaming down Mom's uncomprehending face, and her hand, reaching out for her sister's and not finding it.

"It's not true," she said. Auntie looked ill.

Mom looked to me. "She's lying."

Auntie's jacket was open to reveal a purple blouse tucked into a high gray skirt. No jewelry. I thought of her preparing to come to the hospital and deliberating over what she could wear that might be appropriate.

I took Mom's hand. She clutched it tightly. The covers were pulled up tight to her chest like a child. Her body writhed slowly beneath it.

"Don't blame Niladri," Auntie said. "I asked him not to tell you."

Mom spat in her face. "He's not," she said. A bitter, knowing look came into her eyes. "You've always been jealous of what we had. You wallflower, is this the best you can do? Spreading lies while your sister is in the hospital? You disgrace."

Beads of spit glistened on Auntie's face. She made no move to wipe them away. Her grip tightened on the bed railing. It took all she had just to remain standing.

"He loved you," she said. "More than life."

"Get out." Mom raised her head off the pillow. Her teeth were bared. "Go back to your hole."

"Mom, it's not her..."

Auntie shook her head briefly.

"You're a liar," Mom said to her, openly begging.

I took Mom's head and forcibly turned it toward me. Her body was tensed like she was in the grip of a seizure. She made indistinguishable noises of discomfort. Eventually her eyes found mine.

When I thought to look up, Auntie was gone.

* * *

Mom was released early the next morning. A warm front had crept in during the night, thawing the hospital grounds to reveal muddy stretches of grass. Adventurous patients trekked through it, inspecting soccer goalposts and baseball diamonds like they were artifacts from a lost civilization. A few nurses watched them by the infirmary entrance, brown and black faces angled up toward the sun. Christmas had come and gone and one of them, perhaps unwilling to cede the holiday completely, still wore a green elf's cap with a little bell that chimed when she moved her head.

She had asked that I not be present when she was discharged. It was a courtesy my father had first extended and one that I was happy to continue. Unlike times past the request had not come with overblown promises of the happy life to come, no ceaseless fidgeting and furtive stashing of pills in her purse. In many ways we'd gone through the committal together, and what words couldn't communicate, a look now would. I didn't need to be by her side while she signed discharge papers and received a patronizing lecture about "successful readjustment."

Like her, those things I cherished most lay beyond the reach of facts. It resided in the pauses between conversations, in revelatory moments found in dreams you struggled to maintain in waking life. It lay in the secret gratitude toward anyone who'd ever cared for you, each one of whom refuted a belief, deep within, that you did not deserve it. To rob her of those things, or to aid others in the task, amounted to matricide. I would fight, tear off my skin to spite it, but never lie down and allow it to happen. Her struggle was my own.

She came out wearing jeans, a teal sweater, and an old parka. She carried the red bag my father had delivered to her back in the fall. Her hair was pulled back in a bun. She'd lost weight and her skin looked washed out. The nurses, whose eyes were trained to selectively identify those wearing hospital gowns, barely registered her.

She plucked the cigarette I'd been smoking out of my mouth and threw it on the ground. "Filthy," she said.

Her gaze possessed the same clarity as when she'd been released from Isolation. I wanted to plead with her—hold onto it, you don't know how long Dad and I have waited to see it again—but knew that wasn't the way of it.

I took her bag. We started toward the car. She slipped on a wet patch of grass but regained her footing. She glanced back at the nurses to see if they'd noticed.

"They don't care," I said, putting an arm around her back.

I slipped the key into the ignition. She put her hand over mine.

"What's wrong?" I asked.

She was breathing fast. "We never wanted this for you. To have to..."

"You don't get to decide."

She seemed not to have heard.

"When the voices start speaking...will you tell me what they're saying?"

Her hand retreated to her lap. "You don't want to hear those things."

"Alone they're too much to handle. But if you tell me..."

She sighed loudly and looked out the side window. "All right," I said, and started the car.

Rear wheels of vehicles threw up slush on the freeway. I made the correct turnoffs and avoided sudden stops. I turned on the heater for its noise.

"They were speaking to me years before I had you," Mom said. "I hid it from everyone at first. It was easier to control back then."

Barrie Street opened out onto campus. A stone fountain covered in a white plastic tarp. A man waiting at the bus stop looked longingly down the street. I remembered what it was like to see the bus make its final turn toward you, headlights that never doused penetrating your body, and knowing that you were found.

"The months I carried you in my belly were the only ones, the ONLY true respite from them. My head was filled with other concerns, like how I'd hold you in my arms, celebrate your birthday, how I'd make sure you were never ashamed to call me your mother." She unzipped her parka to let in some of the heat from the air vents. "I failed on that one."

"No."

A hand went to her temple. "You weren't the reason I got sick. You were my savior."

One by one, I passed the intersections that would have taken us home. When Miller House came up on the left, I turned in. Discarded flyers had become globs of papier-mâché in the front yard. The front steps were wet and stained with dirt.

"What is this?" she asked.

I unbuckled my safety belt, then hers. "Will you come with me?"

"I'm not ready to entertain."

"Just for a minute."

She made a face, but didn't resist.

We went up to the second floor to stand outside Emily's door. Sunlight came in through the stained glass windows and created dramatic shadows along the hall.

"It's dry in here, isn't it?" Mom asked, rubbing her throat.

I knocked a few times. "She's not home," I muttered.

"It's a she?"

Mom was giving me a sly, knowing look.

"Just a friend," I said.

"A friend who wants to meet me?"

"She thinks she's already met you, but..." I shook my head. "Whatever, she's not here, let's go."

"Give it a moment." And when nothing occurred she knocked, insistently.

A flickering on the other side of the peephole.

The door opened and Emily stood there in a nightgown. She looked at my mother first, then me. Her mouth opened but no words came. Her eyes filled with tears.

"Could I ask you for a glass of water, dear?" Mom asked. "I'm parched."

NOTE TO READER

A novel is a flare shot into the darkness; you don't know if someone will answer, but hope compels you. There are thousands of books out there. Taking the time to read mine and connect with Neil's story is something I am truly grateful for.

Growing up, my mother, a former English teacher, would supplement my homework with mandatory writing assignments. While the deadline was always night's end, the subject matter could be of my choosing. This unique mixture of severity and freedom served me well during the writing of *The Isolation Door*. I was 25 years old, lanky and bedeviled by insecurities, trying my best to eke out a living as an actor in Montreal. Being Indian, I'd played enough doctors on-screen to qualify for an honorary M.D. I'd grinned and capered on countless commercials, even toured across the United States as part of a Shakespeare-in-the-Park troupe. But the truth is that none of these performances succeeded in whisking me away from the sad reality of my existence, which mainly consisted of avoiding human contact and trying to feel something other than numb. The numbness was a coping mechanism which had allowed me to deal with the endless relapse and rehabilitation cycles of my mother's schizophrenia without losing my sanity in the process. But like a wild animal it now turned against me. Not a single person knew about my past; when pressed I lied, inventing elaborate back-stories. But during the course of an endless winter in 2005, I realized two things: I was rapidly descending into a serious depression, and I was sick to death of lying.

So I imagined my mother giving me one last assignment: tell the truth of what you experienced. Make others feel as you once did. First a few pages. Then a few more. Half-hours became half-days spent hunched over a laptop. The narrow confines of my apartment fell away in deference to the world inhabited by my doppelganger Neil Kapoor. I found friends in Quincy and Tim. I found love through Emily. A year and a half later, armed with a completed manuscript, my experiences in that imaginary world somehow gave me the courage to pull up stakes and move to New York City, the only place I'd ever really felt at home. And while the hardships didn't magically disappear, something inside of me had changed permanently. On a first date with Erin, the woman who'd eventually become my wife, in the fall of 2006, I did something that would have been impossible just a few short years ago. I told her the truth. Here are ways in which I am continuing to tell it:

–If you are a member of a book club, I would be glad to schedule a Phone/Skype chat to discuss *The Isolation Door*. Please send me an email at anish@dashamerican.com with the subject line, "Book Club Request".

–I am currently giving talks at high schools, colleges, and organizations about my life experiences, the importance of breaking down the wall of silence which surrounds mental illness, and related topics. The connection with a live audience is something I truly cherish. For details and booking information, please send me an email at anish@dashamerican.com with the subject line, "Talk Information".

–I love interacting with fans on Google+ (plus.google.com/+AnishMajumdar), Twitter (@dashamerican) and Facebook (facebook.com/AnishMajumdarAuthor).

Finally, a portion of the purchase price of this book will go towards supporting schizophrenia research and treatment. Your support helps to advance the conversation about mental illness and the work being done at organizations such as NAMI, and for that I cannot thank you enough.

May the light in your life overwhelm the darkness at every turn. Cheers!

Anish Majumdar
Rochester, New York
February 2014

ACKNOWLEDGMENTS

Writing is a solitary business. When I started work on this novel there was only me, but it never would have reached your hands without the support of these people:

Mom and Dad, for your ability to survive whatever life throws at you and uphold family above all else. Thank you for loving me during the difficult moments.

Jim and Norma, for helping me become the person I am today. Your warmth, generosity, and unabashed spirit is truly inspirational.

David Gee for a stroke of pure brilliance on the cover, matched by an equally impressive interior design.

Christine LaPorte for an exceptional editing job- you truly brought this story to another level. Marcia Ambramson for an expert proofreading job.

Elena, Marika, Babs and the rest of the incredible team at PR By The Book. This novel really broke through as a result of your creativity and unflagging efforts.

Jean Ring, Karen Smith, Danielle Natoli, and Christy Mraz for crucial feedback. You ladies rock!

Kirby Kim, for belief and counsel.

Kerry Walsh and Melissa Sewruk for helping to bring my story to schools and open an exciting new chapter in my life.

Ben Cummings for online marketing expertise.

And finally, Erin and Mickey, who make every moment precious. You two are the gift at journey's end, worth every hardship experienced in the getting a thousand times over.

ABOUT THE AUTHOR

As a child growing up in Montreal, Canada, Anish Majumdar's first creative writing lessons came courtesy of his mother, a former English teacher. Witnessing her struggle with schizophrenia had a profound impact and inspired *The Isolation Door*, his first novel. His non-fiction work, appearing in many publications, has garnered Independent Press Association Awards for Feature Writing and Investigative Journalism. His short fiction has been nominated for the Pushcart Prize. He lives with his wife, son, and a growing menagerie of pets in Rochester, NY.

CPSIA information can be obtained at www.ICGtesting.com
Printed in the USA
LVOW07s2159270814

401203LV00010B/1139/P

Hot rock sits deep under the crust. This rock is so hot that it melts! Hot, soft rock is called *molten* rock.

Molten rock can come out of the ground. This makes a *volcano*. Volcanoes dump molten rock onto the ground around them.

Underwater volcanoes can
make new islands.

Not all rock is the same. Some
rock is made when molten rock
cools and gets hard.

Some rock changes when the land around it pushes on it or heats it up.

Some rock is made out of sand, mud, or even seashells. Over time, they get hard and make rock.

Land covers only a small part of Earth. Land looks like it is still. But land is always moving and changing.

Challenge Words

continents (KAHN-ti-nehnts)—The seven large land areas on Earth: Asia, Africa, North America, South America, Antarctica, Europe, and Australia.

crust (krust)—The top layer of Earth.

dunes (doons)—Hills made of sand, created by wind.

earthquake (URTH-kwayk)—When pieces of the Earth's crust move.

erosion (ee-ROH-shehn)—The changing of the land by wind or water.

molten (MOHL-tehn)—Melted.

plains (planes)—Large, flat areas of land.

valleys (VAL-eez)—The low land between hills or mountains.

volcano (vahl-KAY-noh)—Molten rock coming out of the ground.

Index

Page numbers in **boldface** are illustrations.

With thanks to Nanci Vargus, Ed.D., and Beth Walker Gambro, reading consultants

Marshall Cavendish Benchmark
99 White Plains Road
Tarrytown, New York 10591-5502
www.marshallcavendish.us

Library of Congress Cataloging-in-Publication Data

Rau, Dana Meachen, 1971–
Land / by Dana Meachen Rau.
p. cm. — (Bookworms. Earth matters)
Summary: "Discusses the role of land on Earth and introduces the varied types, such as mountains, deserts, and forests"—Provided by publisher.
Includes index.
ISBN 978-0-7614-3043-8
1. Landforms—Juvenile literature. I. Title.
GB406.R34 2008
551.41—dc22
2007030279

Editor: Christina Gardeski
Publisher: Michelle Bisson
Designer: Virginia Pope
Art Director: Anahid Hamparian

Photo Research by Anne Burns Images

Cover Photo by *Peter Arnold*/Patrick Frischknect

The photographs in this book are used with permission and through the courtesy of:
Photo Researchers: pp. 1, 26 N.R. Rowan; p. 8 James Steinberg; p. 11 Dennis Flaherty; p. 14 Kenneth Murray; p. 23 Fredrik Fransson; p. 25 Kaj.R. Svensson. *Peter Arnold*: p. 2 Achim Pohl; p. 6 Galen Rowell; p. 19 David J. Cross. *Corbis*: p. 5 Images.com; p. 9 Craig Lovell; p. 10 Corbis; p. 13 Eastcott; p. 18 Mark Downey/Lucid Images; p. 22 Jim Sugar; p. 29 Paul Hardy. *NOAA*: pp. 17, 24. *SuperStock*: p. 20 Ingram Publishing.

Printed in Malaysia
1 3 5 6 4 2